FIGHT WITH THE WIND

CITY OF VIRTUE AND VICE: BOOK 4

SUSANNAH WELCH

SILKY SKY
PUBLISHING

CONTENTS

Cover Concept and Design by Art Muse (Patrisha E. Badalo)
Editing by Red Loop Editing (Victoria Basnuevo)

eISBN: 978-1-7365770-9-7
Paperback ISBN: 978-1-958568-00-2
Hardback ISBN: 978-1-958568-01-9

www.susannahwelch.com

ALSO BY SUSANNAH WELCH

For anyone who loved
Jacob, Gale, or Ducky best

THE SHINING CITY

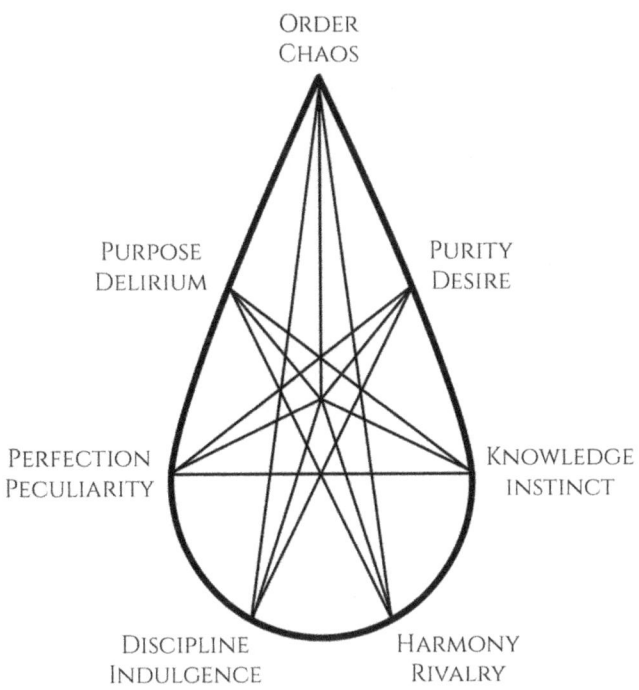

1

Rose growled and murdered another treacherous weed. She pulled her bright red hair tighter into a knot and sighed. The patch of ground she was tending seemed to have more weeds than when she started. She stood and brushed dirt off her black pants. As she swiped a loose tendril away from her face, dark soil smeared across her freckled cheek. She never realized that farming was so ... messy.

Since the Order Priests lost their Gift of magically growing food, people were scrambling to find conventional ways to plant and harvest. She tried to contribute, but she hated working so hard on a task she was terrible at. If the Goddess had returned the Gifts immediately after the battle with the Wardens, learning to farm wouldn't be necessary, but weeks had passed with no sign of the Gifts returning. Rose ground her teeth together and stomped back toward Temple Discipline.

Priests shouldn't stomp. It was undignified. But she was beyond caring about dignity. She was sweaty and tired and dirty and cranky. She didn't feel like a respectable Priest.

And since she had lost her Gift, she didn't feel like a Priest at all.

Rose stormed up the gleaming white stone steps of Temple Discipline, leaving dirty footprints in her wake. She knew she would feel guilty about the mess later and probably clean it up herself, but for now, she pretended to ignore the dirt. She crossed paths with a few other black-clad Priests in the outer courtyard, but they wisely ducked their heads and hurried off to other tasks.

She strode through the inner courtyard toward her room and avoided looking at the crystal spire in the center. Avoiding the massive crystal was an absurd idea, considering its soft, white glow filled the entire inner courtyard at all hours. The bright crystal spire was one more reminder that the Goddess saved the City during the Uprising but still hadn't returned the Gifts to her Priests.

Rose pulled open the door to her room and slammed it shut behind her. Her modest room was lit with only a single crystalline lamp above her tidy desk. After the bright light of the courtyard, the dark room felt peaceful by comparison.

After stripping off her dirty black clothes and scrubbing herself clean of all dirt, she considered her closet. Black pants, black tops, black skirts, black dresses, black jackets ... She had an abundance of clothes in a color that shouted her vocation without her saying a word. Without her Gift, was it honest to wear any of it?

She pushed the thought aside and pulled out some of her favorites. Black tights with a swirling pattern. A fitted sleeveless dress with pleats in all the right places. A structured jacket with a high stiff collar. She twisted her hair up into a slick bun and pulled on some funky boots, then stood and tugged her jacket into position. The unyielding fabric held her body firmly in place.

Held her identity firmly in place.

She pulled her shoulders back, lifted her head with the illusion of confidence, and walked out into the revealing light of the Goddess.

～

Rose headed toward the amphitheater at the center of the City, letting the glow of the crystal spire fade behind her. As her damp hair dried, she brushed the tendrils away from her face. Her Priest's circlet used to hold back her hair, but when the Wardens took over, they melted all the circlets along with the High Priests' crowns.

Messy hair was just one more way her whole life had changed.

Everywhere she looked, she found more things she had lost. She used to know most of the citizens that lived in her Diocese, but now strangers filled the streets. She felt all alone in a neighborhood that used to be her home.

It didn't help that her younger brother, Caed, had left the City with Ylena. Going on some grand adventure over the mountains sounded exciting, but Rose wasn't sure if she would ever see him again. Besides Kai, Caed was the sibling she had been closest to, and now he was gone.

Caed and Ylena might not have left at all if they'd known the Goddess wouldn't return the Gifts immediately. Despite their reassurance that the Goddess promised to return the Gifts, many people doubted the claim. Rose couldn't blame the skeptics. After all, Ylena was a strange girl from the mountains, and Caed was an atheist Priest. And after several weeks with no healers and food running low, Rose had to admit that the skeptics' concerns seemed valid.

Rose trekked up the stairs of the stone cliff that made up the seating of the amphitheater. The amphitheater had enough seating for the entire City, but today, people filled only a fraction of the rows of stone benches. As Rose took a seat next to a fellow Priest, she did a quick count of those in black compared to citizens in brightly colored clothes, and her lips drew into a hard line. How could so few Priests choose to attend when planning for the future was the most important issue to discuss?

The murmuring crowd hushed, and Rose recognized Priest Mayra from Temple Purpose gliding up the stairs and onto center stage. Her voluminous black robes gave her the weight of authority, but the silk damask fabric flowed gently as she walked. Her warm brown skin was showing signs of wrinkles, and gray strands shot through her dark hair. Without the Perfection Priests to heal and change their appearance, the people in the City were beginning to show their true age.

Mayra's deep voice resonated through the open air. "Thank you for attending this important meeting, Priests and citizens. As you know, our beloved City has struggled to find order since the Uprising."

Rose raised an eyebrow at the understatement.

Priest Mayra continued, "Order will not be restored until the Goddess blesses her Priests again with their Gifts. We cannot sustain the amount of food the City requires without the Goddess's Gift of Order. The City requires Purity Priests to keep fresh water flowing. And without Perfection Priests to heal, our people are dying from injuries and diseases we have never seen. We must convince the Goddess to bless her Priests again. It is the only way we will survive." Her ominous words echoed throughout the amphitheater.

A man in a dark suit raised a polite hand. At first glance, Rose assumed he was a Priest, until she realized his suit was such a deep midnight blue it almost appeared black. Rose's lips tightened at the impropriety of the color, but without the High Priests in charge, rules about color sacrilege had fallen away.

Priest Mayra's eyes narrowed in a similar sign of perceived slight but signaled for him to speak.

The man's voice rang out clearly through the amphitheater. "What if the Goddess never blesses her Priests with Gifts again? Maybe it's time for all to be equal."

Priest Mayra's smile froze on her face, but she managed a reply. "Have faith, child." Despite Mayra's gray hair, the man in the dark blue suit could be the same age. His golden-brown skin only showed a few wrinkles, but his dark eyes looked old. He didn't flinch at Mayra's condescending tone as she continued. "I have faith the Goddess has not forsaken us. I believe this is a test of our devotion. She will return the Gifts to us."

The man's quiet reply carried throughout the amphitheater. "You mean return the Gifts to *you*."

A slight emotional tremor ran through the crowd, and Priest Mayra drew the attention back to herself. "The Goddess has ruled this City for over a thousand years, and she will not forsake us now. We must only convince her to return."

A woman several rows back shouted, "But how do we convince her? What pleases the Goddess?"

Rose snorted and mumbled to the Priest at her side, "It's called the Pageant. Maybe she hasn't heard of it?" She rolled her eyes, then realized Priest Mayra was staring directly at her.

"What was that, Priest Rose?" Priest Mayra spoke, and the crowd turned in Rose's direction. "Did you have a suggestion to offer?"

Rose choked and looked to the Priest at her side for help, but he scooted away like he didn't know her. She cleared her throat. "Um ... I said one thing that has worked in the past was the Pageant."

Priest Mayra's eyes lit up.

Rose had the sinking suspicion that she had stepped into a trap.

A woman in a shimmery gray dress in the front row

5

groaned. "A Pageant? Isn't that what started all this? I was here the night when all the crystal spires went dark. I think the Pageant caused the Goddess to forsake us in the first place!" A murmur of agreement ran through the citizens and even among some Priests. Rose saw a look of concern pass over Priest Mayra's face before she pulled herself back together.

"You are correct," Mayra said in a halting voice. "The Pageant was exploited by those who wanted to destroy the City and the Goddess. We must reclaim the Pageant and perform it properly. I agree with Priest Rose. It's the only way the Gifts will return."

A slim Priest from the second row stood, and Priest Mayra signaled him to speak. "I think a new Pageant is exactly what we need. I propose we begin auditions immediately." His pronouncement seemed a bit practiced, and Rose wondered if he knew what Priest Mayra was planning before they arrived.

"An excellent suggestion," said Mayra smoothly. "And since Priest Rose is the one to suggest the idea, she will be the one blessed to travel throughout the City and audition new acolytes for a proper Pageant."

Rose's mouth fell open at Mayra's declaration. The Priests and citizens began discussing a timeline for auditions and the next Pageant, and Rose stared blankly ahead as they planned out her next few weeks for her. What had she stumbled into? She was completely out of control, but a part of her woke up for the first time since the Uprising.

There was a plan. A timeline. Logical steps that led to the only desire stirring in her chest: to get her Gift back.

She needed forward movement. She needed hope. This was her chance. She would convince the Goddess to return her Gift if it was the last thing she did.

2

Rose's walk back to Discipline Diocese passed in a daze. After she received her instructions for auditioning the new acolytes, her mind spun with the possibilities. She finally had a purpose again. She had missed that feeling. Her steps were light as she walked down the familiar roads, only slowing as she passed the strange tunnel to the Underneath.

During the Uprising, the Goddess reshaped the stone foundations, connecting the City above to the Underneath below. Each Diocese had a wide tunnel ending in a giant looping bridge that led to the Underneath. After the Wardens' defeat, the people swarmed up the bridges and filled the City.

Many of the people had never seen the sky before. They spent days walking beneath the open sky with tears filling their eyes before eventually moving into a cottage in the City or seeking the familiar places of the Underneath.

Rose walked down a street of matching cottages, arriving at the third house on the right. She frowned when she saw that the pansies out front looked sickly. They needed water, but all the water was being used to grow food, not flowers.

She walked in without knocking. Despite the messy world outside, inside Mims's house, everything looked perfect. Mims's living room had a couch and a few armchairs, but a long wooden table with benches took up most of the room. Rose ran her hand along the surface smoothed by age, marred only by a few scratches from scribbling toddlers and teenagers' dropped sports equipment.

Mims was in the kitchen filling up a kettle, and she tossed Rose a towel. "Will you pull that bread out of the oven?"

Rose caught the towel deftly and carefully lifted out the loaf of fresh bread, savoring the smell as she carried it out to the table along with a butter dish, small plates, and teacups. Mims brought the kettle to pour them both a cup of tea.

"Did you know I was coming?" asked Rose as she took a careful sip.

"I thought it was possible." Mims's smile revealed the new lines on her warm brown skin. "You went to the meeting at the amphitheater?"

"I did." Rose tried to judge her mother's expression. "But you didn't."

"No." Mims began slicing the bread.

"I thought you might be interested in what they are planning."

Mims met her eyes. "They?"

"Um ... we, I guess." Rose took a slice of bread and began smearing butter on it. "I'm auditioning the acolytes for another Pageant."

Mims nodded as she buttered her own bread.

Rose's butter knife stilled. "Maybe this will fix it. Maybe we can get our Gifts back and go back to the way things were."

Mims rested her hand lightly on Rose's wrist. "We might get our Gifts back someday, dear, but we will never go back to the way it was."

Rose frowned but didn't speak. Mims took a bite of the buttery bread and closed her eyes to savor the taste.

Rose had held her Gift for almost nineteen years, and without it, she felt like she'd lost a piece of herself. But Mims had been a Priest for decades before Rose was even born. Rose couldn't imagine what it must be like for her.

Mims had raised Rose and her thirteen other brothers and sisters since they were babies. Rose never knew her birth parents because they'd followed the rules and dropped her off in the temple when she'd manifested her Gift as a baby. Mims was one of the many Priests who'd raised the young child Priests as her own.

Rose took a deep breath. "So ... are all the babies ...?"

Mims sipped her tea. "They all returned to their parents. The nursery is officially empty."

During the Uprising, the Wardens had used the children with Gifts as weapons. Ylena took away the children's Gifts, along with the Gift of every Priest in the City. Without their Gift, the babies were no longer Priests. They could just go home.

"What about the older children?" Rose asked.

Mims frowned. "That's still complicated. It's not right to take them from the only family they've ever known, but there's no reason for them to continue training to be Priests."

"If this new Pageant works, then maybe—"

"Rose." Mims voice was firm but kind. "I won't ask you to give up hope for yourself, but you have to let the rest of us move on as we choose."

Rose sipped her tea to shove down the lump in her throat. She didn't want Mims to move on. She wanted her to be exactly how Rose remembered her.

The front door flew open, and Kai leaped over the bench to sit next to Rose. He ripped off a hunk of the bread and reached for the butter.

"So, you sneak in here while I am gone and eat all of Mims's bread without me?" He grabbed Rose's teacup and took a sip.

"You won't like that!" She snatched the teacup from his hand. "It's not thick with sugar!"

Kai made a fake gagging sound. "Yuck! Your tea is as bitter as you!"

Mims drew her eyebrows together. "Kai. You should not speak to your sister that way."

Kai blinked his long lashes and turned his dark brown eyes on Rose. "You know I'm just teasing you, Rosie!" He grabbed another chunk of bread and scooted closer to her. "What have you been up to? Stomping on guys' hearts? Rebuilding the temples yourself? Taking over the City?" He bit into the bread, smiling as he chewed. "You are always such an overachiever that it's hard to keep up with your projects."

She gave him a feral grin. "My projects only seem over-achieving because of your lack of ambition."

Mims stood with an exasperated huff and went back into the kitchen, ignoring their usual bickering. Kai grinned and ripped off another bite.

Rose tried to shove him, but he was so muscular he didn't budge. "Can you give me some room? You're all sweaty! Let me guess, you've been playing games with your friends."

Kai chuckled and moved to the bench across the table, facing her. "Sports, Rosie. It's called sports."

"Well, it must be nice to have enough free time for a hobby. I've got too many responsibilities to spend any time *playing* sports." She picked up her teacup and drained the last sip.

When she lowered the cup, Kai was staring at her with his penetrating dark eyes. "Do you believe restoring our Gifts is your responsibility?" She carefully set the teacup to the side as she tried to formulate an answer. He had been that way their whole lives. Playful and silly until the moment he pounced directly on her heart.

"It's not my responsibility alone, but yes, I believe I need to do something about it. This City is broken, and our lack of Gifts is the problem."

"Do you intend to force the Goddess's hand?" He raised a dark eyebrow.

She snorted. "Don't get all theological on me. These are the practical steps we have taken each year as a society for over a thousand years. We need to continue our traditions."

Kai's eyes twinkled as he bit his lips, stifling a grin. "You want to do something *traditional*?"

She narrowed her eyes at him. "I just want to do the right thing, okay? No matter how hard it is. I will do whatever it takes to get our Gifts back."

"Whatever it takes?" His dark eyes met hers again. "I believe that about you, Rosie. But I pray when it comes down to it, you find there are some costs you aren't willing to pay."

A NEW LITURGY

SHE is the Queen of Order
and the Surprise of Chaos.
SHE is the Guardian of Purity
and the Blush of Desire.
SHE is the Provider of Knowledge
and the Creativity of Instinct.
SHE is the Incarnation of Harmony
and the Heartbeat of Rivalry.
SHE is the Sustainer of Discipline
and the Delight of Indulgence.
SHE is the Essence of Perfection
and the Wonder of Peculiarity.
SHE is the Giver of Purpose
and the Peace of Delirium.
In her compassion, SHE joined us, the City above and below.
A City reunited, as the Goddess and Companion.
The mourning Goddess now weeps for joy.
AMEN.

PURPOSE

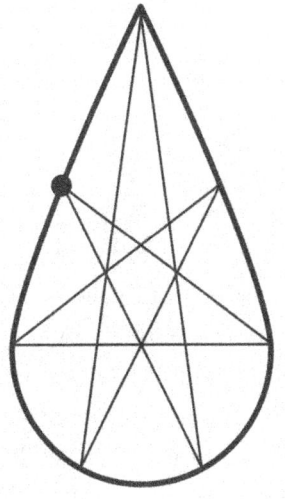

3

The walk to Temple Purpose seemed to take forever. Back when things were normal, Rose would use her Gift and let the wind speed her along wherever she wanted to go. The City was massive, but with her Gift, Rose was fast. Without her Gift, it felt like she was striding through water. The wind blew around her, but out of her control. The wind had been her friend, and now it attacked her with every step.

She adjusted her pack on her shoulders and lowered her head so the people she passed wouldn't see her scowl. It wasn't seemly for a Priest to scowl. She was supposed to be filled with the blessing of the Goddess. But on the night of the Uprising, she had seen the Goddess with her own eyes. And ever since that night, her relationship with the Goddess was ... complicated.

She didn't want to think about the Goddess right now. She wanted to think about a goal she could actually accomplish. Like the auditions.

She still wasn't exactly sure why she would be the one conducting the auditions. Priest Mayra obviously planned to suggest a Pageant from the start, so why didn't she do it herself?

Rose wondered what Priest Mayra would do all day while Rose listened to the hopefuls.

At nineteen years old, Rose was still young in the eyes of the older Priests. She was no longer lumped in with the child Priests, but she still wasn't old enough for them to consider her fully an adult. Maybe with so few Priests, her age wouldn't hold her back anymore?

Rose knew the Pageant inside and out. All Priests were required to learn the songs since it was the primary source of their theology. But beyond that, she grew up in Temple Discipline. Discipline was the home of music and dance, among other skills that relied on the wind. She knew every note and movement intimately. She wasn't the best dancer in the temple —that was Caed—but she had always found pleasure dancing while using her Gift.

But no, she wouldn't think about her Gift right now.

She looked up at crystal spire of Temple Purpose finally within view. Her walk from Temple Discipline had taken the entire morning. She used to make the run in minutes. She smoothed back her sweaty hair and walked up the temple steps.

Priest Mayra sat at a large stone table in the courtyard in a stone chair crafted to look like a magnolia in bloom. The intricate stonework was just one of the beautiful creations that Purpose Priests had created when they had access to their Gift. The unyielding stone couldn't be comfortable, but Mayra sat perfectly poised, as if the chair was a throne created just for her. Considering Mayra had spent her entire life as a Purpose Priest, it was possible she had formed the stone herself before she lost her Gift. Mayra picked up a stack of paperwork from one of the neat little piles in front of her and handed it to a young Priest.

"This is for Temple Harmony." Her voice was soft but held clear authority. "It includes the timeline for the audition in that

Diocese and the requirements for anyone planning to audition." The young Priest nodded and hurried off.

Priest Mayra smoothed back her perfectly coiffed gray hair, then turned her piercing eyes on Rose. "It's been a busy morning. I'm glad to see you are finally here to begin." Her words were sweet, but Rose could hear the bite.

Rose knew she should be deferential to the older Priest, so she hid her irritation behind a smile. "I walked all the way from Temple Discipline this morning. How blessed you are to live here in Temple Purpose already."

Priest Mayra's mouth twitched but didn't quite curve into a frown. Maybe Rose didn't hide her irritation as well as she thought.

Priest Mayra's face smoothed back into a placid expression. "Blessedly, you won't begin the auditions until tomorrow. We will spend the rest of the day working on the instructions to each Diocese." Priest Mayra waved Rose into a smaller chair at the table and handed her a stack of paper.

Rose soon became tired of the tedious work. She never sat in a chair all day doing paperwork. Above every other Virtue, Discipline was about action. Movement. She rubbed her forehead and surreptitiously peeked out from under her hand at all the lucky people who got to walk around actually *doing* something. Priests and citizens walked around the courtyard, coming in and out of the arches leading inside the temple.

There was a young woman sweeping up, although she seemed just as distracted as Rose. Her blond hair stuck out from under one of the fashionable headdresses the ladies in the City wore. The girl wore it oddly, with a twist of fabric and a curl of hair covering one eye. Her visible blue eye noticed Rose staring at her, and she turned away abruptly.

Rose recognized her. She was one of Ylena's friends from the Underneath.

Rev.

What was Rev doing at Temple Purpose? People from the Underneath could now live and work anywhere in the City, but was it just a coincidence that Rev was in the same temple where auditions began?

"Priest Rose?" Mayra's voice snapped her back to attention. "Is there something wrong? You are neglecting your work."

Rose was suspicious, but not enough that she wanted to mention anything to Mayra. "Nothing is wrong, Priest Mayra." She lowered her head and copied her pages again. When she glanced back up, Rev was gone.

After she finished her last stack of papers, she flexed her cramped fingers and leaned back in her stone chair. She was planning the means of her escape when Priest Mayra looked up. Rose expected to be handed a new stack of papers, but instead, Mayra looked over Rose's shoulder.

Then Priest Mayra smiled.

Rose froze momentarily at the unusual sight of Mayra smiling. Her brown skin had started to show wrinkles, but very few were smile lines. Once Rose's thoughts caught up, she realized the smile probably wouldn't be good news. She came out of her seat quickly, and her mouth dropped open at the cause of Mayra's delight.

Wilder.

4

Wilder stood with the same cocky posture she remembered. His deep brown skin looked warm against his cool white shirt. Unsurprisingly, the shirt was unbuttoned one button more than necessary. And his leather pants, though finely crafted, were tighter than they needed to be. A hint of a smirk touched Wilder's lips, and his lingering eyes sized Rose up slowly from head to toe.

Goddess, he was irritating.

"What are you doing here?" she asked.

"Good to see you, too, Rose." Wilder revealed his full smirk.

Priest Mayra came out of her throne and clasped Wilder's hand in both of her own.

"I'm so glad you could join us, Wilder." Mayra's eyes sparkled as she looked up at him.

Even though Rose was tall, Wilder was taller than her, forcing her to look up at him as well. The dark coils of his long hair were so full they made him seem even taller. She squared her shoulders to give herself every bit of height she could manage.

Wilder gave Mayra his most charming smile. "Priest Mayra, it is my honor to serve the Goddess in whatever way I can."

Fire bloomed in Rose's throat, and she had to speak carefully to keep from spitting. "Priest Mayra, will you please explain?"

Mayra pulled her attention from Wilder with a disappointed sigh. "Calm down, Priest Rose. Everything is arranged. Wilder will assist you with the auditions."

Her fury grew, and she hoped Mayra could see it burning in her eyes. "You arranged this without discussing it with me?"

Priest Mayra stepped closer and hissed quietly, "Rose, don't make a scene."

The words were a common refrain when High Priests ruled and punished even the slightest imperfection. Even though the High Priests were dead, the words still worked. The fire inside Rose flared white hot, then iced over.

Her voice was crisp when she replied, "Of course, Priest Mayra. I look forward to working with Wilder. I'm sure the Goddess will be pleased."

Priest Mayra frowned but couldn't complain about the perfect response. She took hold of Wilder's hand again with a hopeful smile. "I'm sure you both will get along fine."

Wilder had watched their interaction with a thoughtful expression, but at Mayra's words, he returned to his charming smile. He spoke in a conspiratorial whisper. "I will do my best to win her over."

Rose growled but didn't reply.

Priest Mayra patted his hand fondly. "I'm sure you will, dear. Why don't you both go check on the stage where you will hold auditions? I'm sure you will enjoy getting out of the temple for a while, won't you, Rose?"

Rose's nerves prickled with the condescension, but Mayra was right. Rose desperately needed to get out.

"Yes, I'll go, but there's no need for Wilder to come." She

gave Wilder a sickly sweet smile. "You can stay here with Priest Mayra. I'm sure she would love for you to entertain her."

He turned his full attention back to Rose, and his smirk returned. "No, I'm definitely going with you. You're very entertaining."

Rose huffed and stomped out of the temple, not caring if he followed.

~

Rose walked fast, hoping to lose him in the crowd, but Wilder soon caught up. He didn't speak, but she could feel his smug grin at her side.

She stomped for several blocks without speaking. His silence grated on her nerves as much as his voice.

"Do you enjoy this?" she asked.

His grin became even smugger, as if he won another victory by her speaking first. "Causing women to have a visceral reaction to my mere presence? Yes, I do enjoy it."

She rolled her eyes. "I'm glad you are having fun. Some of us are trying to do important work. I don't appreciate someone turning this into a game."

"While I enjoy watching you storm through the City, my reasons to be here are extremely serious."

She ground her teeth and slowed her pace to a calm walk. They arrived at the park and headed toward the stage. Tomorrow the park would be full of people viewing the audition, but today, few roamed across the overgrown grass. Usually, Order Priests maintained the length of the grass in all the parks, but since they lost that Gift, they hadn't found more conventional means to cut it.

They walked in silence toward the small stage at the center of the park. Stone framework supported the wooden platform, and despite the disrepair of the park, decorative fabric still billowed along the rafters.

She walked to the front of the stage and rested her hands on the smooth boards. He observed her in silence, and she cracked under his stare.

"Was it your idea to join the auditions, or were you forced into it?" She studied him with hard eyes, trying to decide if he would tell her the truth.

"If it wasn't my idea, will you stop being angry?"

She narrowed her eyes even further. "I'm not sure yet. I'll let you know."

He chuckled. "It's certainly entertaining when you're angry, but I'm not sure I've earned it yet. I think you're angry at someone else."

She released her held breath and leaned back against the stage. He was right, as much as she hated to admit it. "Mayra tricked me into the auditions, but I'm not sure why."

He nodded thoughtfully. "That's an excellent question, and I'm interested in the answer myself." A hint of his smirk returned. "Don't let me distract you from investigating."

She let that one pass. "So, are you going to tell me why you are here?"

"I'm looking for someone."

"Someone in particular? Or another silly girl like Ylena to seduce?"

She thought she detected a slight flinch. Caed had told her about Wilder's constant flirting and how Ylena had fallen for it. Could he have actually had feelings for her?

He regained his arrogant stance as if she hadn't spoken. "A woman from the Underneath named Clayr moved up here after the Uprising. She has two adult children who remained in the Underneath. Clayr would visit them every week until one day she didn't. Her children didn't know what to do, so they asked me to look around."

"Why don't you just ask someone? Getting into the middle of the auditions seems like overkill."

He backed against the stage and lifted himself to sit on the edge. It made him even taller. "I don't know if you realize this, but I'm a bit of a celebrity now."

She groaned and rubbed her forehead. "Oh, Goddess. As if you needed encouragement to be any cockier."

He straightened his shoulders proudly. "People like what they like, Rose. And right now, both the City and the Underneath like me."

"I assumed you would be notorious for your roles in the Pageant and Spectacle. Considering how those both ended, I'm surprised your fame hasn't resulted in death threats instead."

"There are those who aren't pleased at the way things went down, but overall, I think most people are glad to be out from under the rule of the High Priests and Wardens. They are grateful because we are all better off than we were."

Her mouth opened in shock. "The City is in chaos right now. We are one broken pipe away from dirty water causing an outbreak of illnesses no one can cure."

His smirk was gone. "Sounds like just another day in the Underneath. The only difference is now we can get some sunshine if we choose."

The last thing she wanted to do was defend the High Priests, but a shiver of shame went down her spine, and it made her defensive. "That might be true, but at least we had the Order Priests to grow enough food. If we don't get our Gifts back, everyone in the City and Underneath is going to starve."

Wilder hopped off the stage and stepped close to her. His voice was low and intense. "A lack of Gifts won't cause us to starve. If you want to know how we will survive, ask someone from the Underneath. We have more faith in this City than you do." He dipped his head in farewell and strode away.

5

_____

Rose took the long way back to Temple Purpose because she knew Priest Mayra would give her some sort of busy work to do the moment she walked inside. Rose was in charge of the auditions yet in control of nothing, and that fact was clear to everyone, including Wilder.

Why was he here? Who thought this would be a good idea? She couldn't deny his skill, but was he really the person they wanted associated with this Pageant? This was their chance to start over. Why would they want someone with his history of treacherous performances involved?

Rose was irritated, and when she was irritated, she looked for new clothes. Most of the time, she found her clothes in Discipline Diocese, but even in Purpose Diocese, she knew where to look.

She found the shop she wanted and stepped inside out of the warm sun. The shop was a lot louder and more crowded than she remembered. Men, women, and children roamed through the racks of bright clothing. They held up clothes to check the fit and shouted to one another when they found something they liked. This was not the relaxing experience she remembered.

A voice from the back of the shop called to her. "Priest Rose!"

Rose turned to find the shopkeeper headed her way. He was a short man with a round face and kind smile. She tried to hide her shock when she realized he appeared to be twenty years older than when she last saw him. His formerly jet-black hair was almost completely gray, and his face was deeply marked with smile lines. "Master Tae. It's good to see you."

"You know there is no need for titles. We've been just Tae and Rose for ages." He took her hand and led her to a quiet space behind a long table used for cutting fabric. "How have you been, Rose? I haven't seen you for a long time."

She squirmed in embarrassment. "I can't run across the entire City as easily as I used to. I'm a lot slower now." An almost laughable understatement, but Tae knew her well enough not to laugh.

"Ah, yes, I understand." He gripped her hand tighter in encouragement. "But you are here now. And it's so good to see you."

She smiled at his kind words. They had known each other for years, and she always enjoyed visiting his shop and discussing fashion. Everything felt so familiar and yet so strange.

Her forehead wrinkled as she surveyed the shop. "It's a lot busier in here than usual."

He took her complaint as a compliment. "It is! Thank you for noticing!" He looked around at all the people and smiled. "I wasn't sure how things would adjust after the Uprising, but I guess I'm figuring it out. All these customers are proof that you *can* teach an old dog new tricks!"

"Customers?" The word was strange to Rose. When the High Priests ruled, there was no money in the City. Everyone worked and took what they needed. If someone didn't work, they were executed. If they hoarded food or supplies, they were executed. It was brutal, but there was a cold efficiency to it. Money wasn't necessary. She knew it was different in the Underneath, but she hadn't realized how the idea had spread.

Tae seemed to sense her confusion. "It turns out that not having any currency up here put us at a disadvantage. Those from the Underneath are familiar with handling money, but I've had to learn the hard way. But now that I understand the value of clothing, I think I'm going to make it."

The new words like money, value, and cost still sounded strange, but the hope on his face gave Rose an odd, sad feeling.

"I'm glad it's going so well for you. It looks like I'm not the only one who loves your designs."

His face lit with pride. "Are you here to buy something specific?"

Her mind struggled again with the new word. "Buy?"

Tae's face fell. He looked uncomfortable for the first time since she had met him. "Um ... you know, buy with money ... You've earned money, right?"

Her face heated in shame. She had stayed hidden away in the temple for the last few weeks, avoiding all the changes in the City. She was embarrassed to admit how little she knew.

"I don't need anything today. I just stopped in to check on you." Lying was bad manners, but thankfully it wasn't a sin.

Tae sighed in relief. "Of course. You have always been a thoughtful Priest."

Her heart twinged in guilt, but she nodded graciously, which helped her avoid his eyes.

"I'd love to give you something pretty to wear because I enjoy your company so much, but I have to be careful now, you know? Every item I sell is another meal for my family or a tincture for my aching joints." He rubbed the knuckles of his right hand. "I don't have the Priests to heal my joints anymore, but the apothecaries in the Underneath have some remedies that are helpful." He looked at her with questioning eyes.

She smiled through her pain to absolve him of his unasked question. "Goddess blessing upon you, Master Tae."

He teared up in relief and replied, "And also upon you, Priest Rose."

6

She escaped Master Tae's shop as quickly as she could. She didn't feel like returning to the temple yet, but she didn't want to go into any of her other favorite shops without money and embarrass herself again. Instead, she roamed aimlessly, noting every difference she could see from the street.

There were a lot more people, and she tried to guess who was from the Underneath by looking at them. Before the High Priests had fallen, the differences would have been stark. The people of the City were all well-fed, healthy, and dressed immaculately. But now, everything was upside down. Because the people from the Underneath were the ones with the accepted form of currency, they seemed to be the most prosperous. They had money to buy clothing and food, while the people in the City struggled to figure out how to use their skills to earn money.

The sun set long before Rose arrived back at the glowing temple with unease lurking in the pit of her stomach. A few Priests wandered around inside, but most were already in bed.

She counted the closed doors until she arrived at her assigned room.

Rose jumped backward when she found someone inside. "I guess I'm in the wrong room." She fiddled with a loose tendril of hair as she recounted the doors.

"If you are Rose, then you're in the right place!" Someone had crammed an extra bed into the small room, and a young man lounged on his stomach with a book in his hands. His messy hair and thin beard were strawberry blond, and his pale green eyes lit up as he smiled. He sat up and folded the book neatly in his lap. "I'm Fitz. Your new roommate."

Rose stood blinking stupidly in the doorway. "Roommate?" Her brain struggled to comprehend yet another new word.

Fitz chuckled. "All you Upsiders seem so shocked by the idea! In the Underneath, people have roommates all the time. I guess everyone up here is used to having a lot of space for themselves."

The City always had more houses than people, and the temples had more rooms than Priests. No one ever had to share a room unless they chose to. With the addition of the people from the Underneath, everywhere was more crowded, but she had no idea she would have to share a room, too.

"Are you going to stand in the door all night?" Fitz watched her as if she were a spooked animal. It was a mixture of pity and understanding, and she straightened her spine in forced pride. She closed the door and walked the few steps to her own bed.

Priests' rooms were modest when they were for one person, and with the extra bed, the room was cramped. Her own room at Temple Discipline was filled with clothes and items she had collected over the years, but this borrowed room was empty to begin with. The clothes she'd packed were hanging neatly on one side of the closet, with Fitz's clothes on the other side. His hanging clothes were like what he currently wore: bright, mismatched, and full of rips that she wasn't sure were intentional or not.

"They thought about putting me in a room with someone else," he said tentatively.

Her head snapped around. "Oh? Were they worried I was too cranky to handle a roommate?"

"No, of course not!" His denial seemed a little too quick. "They eventually decided it would be best if we shared a room since we are traveling together."

She stared at him with a blank look. "Traveling together?"

"Yes!" His pale face brightened. "Mayra asked me to assist with the auditions."

Rose tried to stifle her growl. "Mayra." Rose knew Mayra definitely wasn't saddled with a roommate. Rose hated being young. She plopped down on the bed and removed her boots.

"I'm looking forward to it!" His eyes took on a dreamy expression. "I can't believe I get to assist with the Pageant. I never imagined that I would ever have the privilege. I've dreamed about it my whole life."

She looked up from her boots. "You dreamed about the Pageant? I didn't think anyone in the Underneath cared about the Goddess."

His smile faltered, but Rose didn't know why. He stood and carefully rested the book on the desk. He pulled back his covers and crawled into bed. "We have an early start tomorrow, so I'm going to sleep. Don't worry about keeping me awake with any noise. I'm a heavy sleeper." He rolled over to face the wall and pulled the covers up.

She watched the slow rise and fall of his form and tried to understand the strange interaction. She wasn't tired yet, so she crept quietly out of the room, seeking the exhaustion that would let her sleep.

∼

Rose woke to the sound of someone in her room. Her hand reached for the blade stashed under her bed.

"Sorry if I woke you!" Fitz's soft voice brought her awake and stilled her searching hand.

His casual apology startled her. He was clearly from the Underneath, because the people in the City never admitted fault to Priests so carelessly.

"I'm not used to finding my way around this room in the dark yet," he said. "I'll be quieter once I know where everything is."

"It's fine." Her voice was still ragged with sleep. "Just turn on a light." She pulled the blanket over her head as he switched the shutter on the crystalline lamp to its lowest setting. The light shone through the white blanket, and she squeezed her eyes shut.

"I've always been an early riser." He laughed softly. "But I promise I'll finish in the bathroom and be out of here with plenty of time for you to get ready!"

It was difficult to roll her eyes with her eyelids squeezed shut, but she tried.

She heard him gather his things and take them into the bathroom. He turned off the lamp and closed the bathroom door, plunging the room back into darkness.

She heard running water, so she pushed back her blanket and rubbed her eyes. It was bad enough talking to people before she had eaten breakfast, and now she had to talk to someone before she was out of bed? She sighed at the injustice.

She turned the lamp back on and savored the peacefulness of the room while Fitz was in the bath. She flipped through the various items of black clothing in her closet until she came up with a combination she liked. It wasn't practical to bring her entire wardrobe when she traveled from temple to temple, but she had stuffed quite a few things into her bag.

Her sleeveless cotton dress called for a bracelet, so she

moved to the desk to find one. As she sorted through the jewelry she had laid out, she picked up the book Fitz had been reading the night before.

It was a book of the Goddess's liturgies.

Fitz walked out of the bathroom. "I'm going to get some breakfast. Are you—?" He saw her holding his book and stopped.

She felt unreasonably guilty, like she had been snooping when all she had done was pick up the book. His face was unreadable, and she tried to set the book back down casually.

"Yes, I'll be there soon!" Her voice was fake and overly cheerful. She hated herself for it, but she didn't know why.

He nodded without meeting her eyes, slipped the book of liturgies into his bag, and left the room without another word.

She let her breath out in a rush. So far, she was not a fan of roommates.

7

Rose made her way down to breakfast in the Priests' dining hall, noticing again how much fuller the temples had gotten since the Uprising. Just a few months ago, a couple dozen Priests filled the handful of tables in the dining room. But now, someone had added more tables, and over a hundred people in brightly colored clothes sat mixed in with the Priests in black.

Rose grabbed food from the serving tables and looked for a seat. She couldn't see Fitz in the crowd but wasn't sure she wanted to sit by him now if she didn't have to. She didn't like the guilty feeling lingering in the pit of her stomach.

She found an open seat next to a Priest she recognized. "Good morning, Priest Frances."

His kind eyes crinkled when he smiled. "Good morning, Rose! How are you this morning?"

"Sleepy," she said with a twist of her lips. "I've got a roommate, and I'm still adjusting."

His lips twitched in amusement. "If it's any comfort, you aren't the only one with a new roommate."

She sighed. "It's all so different now. I'm not adjusting well to any of it."

Priest Frances's eyes softened into a thoughtful expression. "The Goddess has remade her City. It will take time before we can understand it all."

She looked around at the people dressed in bright colors throughout the room. "The temple is so full now. Do we really need this many temple workers?"

His dark eyebrows raised. "They aren't just temple workers, Priest Rose. Some of them have asked to train to become Priests."

Her sleepy eyes shot wide awake. "Train to become Priests? The Goddess chose us to be Priests at birth! How can someone train for that?"

He gave her a fatherly smile. "Things were different back then. Without our Gifts, being a Priest means something new. Some followers of the Goddess want to discover what that is."

She chewed on her lip as she considered Fitz and his book of liturgies. Was he here to become a Priest? She pushed the food around her plate as she replayed her words to him.

Priest Frances continued, "No one knows what the Goddess has in store for the future. Maybe these new followers are what she desires. They are all devoted to her and do her work despite their lack of Gifts. They set a good example for all of us." He smiled at the crowd of people fondly.

"You sound like Mims." She tried to keep the bitterness from her voice. "She thinks we should give up on our Gifts."

He sighed. "Sadly, we don't all agree on the best course of action, so every Priest must make their own decisions right now." His paternal smile returned. "I'm glad you are continuing your work on the Pageant, Priest Rose. We should seek the Goddess wherever we believe she can be found."

Rose picked at her breakfast in silence. She refused to consider a future where the Goddess didn't return her Gifts to the Priests. The Goddess must relent. This couldn't be the future she wanted. Wilder said the people from the Underneath had more hope than she did. She cleared her throat and pushed her unfinished breakfast away.

"Priest Frances, do you know a woman from the Underneath named Clayr?"

He turned to her with a concerned expression. "Yes, I do. I haven't seen her for several days, though. Have you spoken to her recently?"

She hadn't expected that level of concern, and she struggled with how much bad news she wanted to share. "I haven't spoken to her, but I met one of her acquaintances looking for her."

He frowned. "I had hoped she'd returned to her family in the Underneath and that's why she hadn't been here recently. Maybe she's just spending time with her friend and will be back soon."

"Her friend?" she asked.

"She told me she recognized someone in the City that she hadn't seen for a long time. I don't know who it was, but I'm sure it was a friend."

Rose recognized the sound of denial when she heard it. But since denial was how the Priests had survived so long under the High Priests' reign, she didn't convince him otherwise.

"Yes, I'm sure that's it. Thanks for the nice breakfast conversation, Priest Frances."

His gentle smile had returned. "Anytime, Priest Rose."

8

R ose sat at the table in front of the stage in the park and sorted through a stack of audition paperwork. Wilder slid into the chair at her side.

"How's the lineup? Are we in for a pleasant day?" His voice seemed neutral without his extremely flirty tone, which was a relief. She wasn't ready for a verbal sparring match yet.

"It's too early to say. We have a lot more sign-ups than in previous years. I'm not sure what to expect." She handed him a matching stack of papers. "You can see for yourself."

Wilder licked his thumb as he flipped through the pages. "I wonder how many of these people are from the Underneath."

Rose's mouth dropped open. She hadn't considered that could cause the higher numbers. Wilder had pretended to be from the City to audition for the last Pageant, but now that the bridges were open, there was no way to keep someone from the Underneath from auditioning.

"Do you think many people from the Underneath would care about auditioning?" she asked.

He looked at her over his stack of papers. His eyes weighed

her question, then weighed her. "I think the number would surprise you."

Before meeting Fitz and the others who wanted to train to become Priests, even one person would have surprised her. But now, she kept that thought to herself.

Fitz walked out from behind the stage and joined them at the table. "I lined everyone up, and they're ready to go. Are both of you ready?"

"As ready as we can be," she said. "Fitz, have you met Wilder? He's also assisting with the auditions."

Wilder and Fitz exchanged looks, and Wilder struggled to hide his smile. "Fitz and I go way back. We've auditioned together quite a few times."

"Let's hope there are a lot fewer weapons involved this time." Fitz grinned, then ran back to where the auditioners stood.

Rose looked at Wilder to see if this was a joke, but his face remained perfectly calm. She didn't have time to ask, because the crowd began murmuring.

A girl walked to center stage and stared in amazement at the crowd spread out on the grass. She kept looking around with wide, blinking eyes until Wilder said, "What will you be singing today?"

The girl said, "I'd like to sing a lullaby my mother sang to me as a baby." Then she began singing the Goddess's Aria.

Everyone in the City knew the story about how Ylena had wandered into the Pageant auditions and said those exact words. People told the story in a reverential tone formerly reserved for the Goddess. Ylena's audition was becoming a new legend.

Rose groaned but listened to the performance as objectively as she could. When the girl finished, she stood at center stage, waiting for the announcement that she would be the Goddess. Rose ground her teeth and spoke with a forced smile.

"Thank you for your audition. We will let you know if you are chosen."

The girl frowned and shuffled off stage. Only to be replaced by another girl who looked around in the same starry-eyed wonder. When she gave the same lullaby line, Rose closed her eyes and sighed. She suddenly realized why someone as young as herself had been given this job.

No one else wanted it.

Beyond the strategy of copying Ylena's audition, the other startling change from past auditions was the quality of the performers. When the High Priests ruled, they had strict standards of perfection. It hadn't happened for decades, but there were stories of people executed by the High Priests for a bad audition. Rose didn't approve of their methods, but she had to give them credit for scaring off weak performers. And this year, every person in the Diocese thought it was now their chance to audition.

She turned to find Wilder staring at each performer with rapt attention. Each girl walked off stage believing Wilder truly loved her performance. She couldn't imagine how he could fake his interest for so long.

Rose couldn't pretend anymore, so she signaled to Fitz that they would take a quick break. She stood and stretched her neck and shoulders. "Sitting here all day is going to kill me. How are you still so focused?"

His lips curled in a slow smile. "I'm known for my stamina."

Rose groaned. "Oh, Goddess. I'm getting water."

As she left, a group of girls swarmed the table around Wilder. They were full of sweet smiles, giggles, and lowered lashes. Rose rolled her eyes. Did girls actually fall for his lines? She could admit that Wilder was attractive, but she found his flirting exhausting.

She couldn't find the Priest with the water in the crowd, but she noticed a man who had spoken at the convocation. He again wore midnight blue, this time a suit with a long asymmetrical jacket. He saw her looking at him and stepped closer to talk.

"Has it been this interesting all day?" His short black hair and goatee were neatly trimmed, and his warm brown skin was mostly unlined, except for a few wrinkles at the creases of his eyes. It gave him the appearance of a perpetual grin. It was difficult to determine ages in the City, but she guessed he was at least twice her age. He smiled, and a single dimple appeared on his cheek.

It was precisely the kind of smug smile that set her on edge.

"An audition doesn't need to be interesting. It needs to be productive." She gave him a disinterested smile and turned back to look for the Priest with the water.

"Ah, that's true. I guess I shouldn't expect the full Pageant when this is just the audition."

She didn't think his statement warranted a response, so she didn't give one.

He kept talking, seemingly unaware of her disinterest. "The Pageant is going to be very different this time, isn't it? Usually, Priests wield their Gifts to add to the performance. I guess that won't happen this year."

Rose turned to face him with a calm expression she certainly didn't feel. She studied his face to see if he was purposely trying to bait her into getting angry or if he was a socially inept idiot. She couldn't detect anything malicious on his friendly face.

So ... idiot.

"Yes. It will be different." She spoke the words in a clipped tone, then turned back to search the crowd again.

He hovered casually at her side. "It makes you wonder, doesn't it?" He paused, as if waiting for an answer.

She continued studying the crowd, only grunting in response.

He answered her grunt with a smooth attack. "If the Goddess truly cares for her people, why is it so difficult to receive her blessing?"

Her breath caught in her throat at the question she had never voiced aloud. He still lingered at her side, but she couldn't face him without revealing how his verbal attack had struck true.

The flock of girls giggled as Wilder bowed dramatically to the Priest with the jug of water. Her flare of irritation distracted her enough to pull herself together. When Rose turned to challenge the man in the navy suit, he was gone.

Rose walked slowly back to the table, but her mind kept replaying the man's question. It was the question that woke her up in the dark of night. She would lie in bed, staring at the ceiling, sick with the shame of the question. She felt exposed, like the man had plucked the question straight out of her heart.

The Goddess created the Gifts. She chose who received them. She could have made it easy for her people to receive her blessing.

She had appeared in the flesh, then left the City in even more chaos than before.

Burning heat crawled up Rose's chest and neck. She pulled her neckline higher because she didn't want Wilder to see her flush and assume he'd caused it. She needed to appear calm, but her body betrayed her.

Rose needed to be in control.

Her head snapped to the giggling girls. "Time to go back to your seats, ladies. Let's remember the Goddess requires Purity." She wielded her sweet smile like a knife and saw it strike home.

The girls bowed their heads and mumbled the Goddess's blessing to her. She watched them slink off as she clung to the soothing relief of control.

Then she turned to see Wilder's face, and the control slid from her fingers.

He looked at her with a mixture of confusion and disgust. She felt the hot shame threatening to rise, but she pushed it below the surface and reached for control again.

"Are you ready to begin?" she asked. "Or are you planning to use your stamina for something other than the Goddess's work?"

She saw anger flash behind his eyes, but he smoothly covered it. "You are a Priest of the Goddess. You obviously know her will."

She nodded her head stiffly as Wilder waved for Fitz to send up the next performer. She flipped through the paperwork without seeing it, keeping her attention focused on anything but Wilder's silent presence at her side. Rose had regained control, but she felt even more ashamed than before.

9

As she walked back to Temple Purpose, Rose focused on relaxing her hands. They kept forming fists.

Once the final auditioner sang her final flat note, Rose had sighed with relief. She felt the anger rolling off Wilder in waves, and it stoked her own flames. She knew she had spoken harshly to the girls, but who was he to judge her? She was the Priest. Judging was her job.

He had thanked the last girl on stage, then walked away without a word to Rose. She didn't care if he was angry. If he didn't like it, he shouldn't have signed up to spend all day in the company of a Priest. And he shouldn't have been wasting so much time flirting with those girls.

She relaxed her clenched fists again.

Things wouldn't have spiraled out of control if that strange man hadn't riled her up. How dare he ask theological questions while she was trying to focus on the audition? While she looked for a glass of water, he ambushed her with a question she hadn't dared speak aloud.

She shoved her fists in her pockets.

When she entered Temple Purpose, Priests scattered before

her. She was glad they had things to do, because she didn't feel like talking to anyone.

As she opened her bedroom door, she found a slip of paper on the floor.

Meet us in the statue garden tonight.

- Rev

She stared at the note and tried to understand the few simple words. Rose knew where the statue garden was, but why would Rev want her to meet there? And who was included in "us"? Wilder was part of their crew. Was he going to be there? Maybe Rev didn't know Wilder was furious with her.

However, their crew seemed tough. Maybe Wilder was trying to lead her into an ambush?

She shrugged off that idea as a little unrealistic. She was angry at Wilder for being an ungoddessly flirt, but she honestly didn't think he would plan an ambush at night.

He seemed more likely to attack in broad daylight.

However, Rose didn't like the commanding tone. Rev didn't invite her. She didn't ask. She *told* Rose to meet them. Did Rev think she could just leave a demanding note and Rose would follow? She wouldn't be ruled by anyone. Not anymore. That's exactly what she would tell Rev when she found her. She stalked to her closet to pick out the perfect outfit for the occasion.

Like most people in the City, Rose believed fashion to be one of the highest forms of art. Some people believed that only wearing black clothing limited the Priests' fashion choices, but Rose savored the challenge. Instead of using color as the means to create interest, she had to use texture, sheen, and shape to build her style. She tilted her head as she looked in her closet, considering what sort of effect she wanted to create tonight.

After a few tries, she finally settled on something suitable. A black silk tank with sleek black pants and knee-high boots with shining silver buckles. She grabbed her cropped black jacket with the high collar and shook her hair from its knot to fall in shining red waves down her back. Since she wasn't sure what to expect, she strapped a blade to the holster at her thigh and hid another blade in the sheath inside her jacket. She looked pulled together and confident on the outside, despite how she felt on the inside.

She passed through the common room and saw Priest Mayra seated in an armchair talking quietly to another Priest. Mayra's eyes followed Rose as she walked to the door, but she didn't call out. Rose was a Priest in her own right and not under anyone's authority, especially after the overthrow of the High Priests. But that didn't stop Priest Mayra's eyes from narrowing as she considered Rose's late-night destination.

The people from the City rarely went out after dark. It was a habit from when the High Priests ruled. Most of the activities that happened at night were execution-worthy under their regime. Now that more people from the Underneath lived in the City, going out after dark was dangerous in a new way. Even though she and Caed had done plenty of spying at night while avoiding the Sentinels, she still felt anxious being out after dark.

Which didn't bode well for whatever she was doing.

Rose arrived at the ornate front gate of the statue garden. She heard laughing through the garden's surrounding walls and realized other people besides the crew were spending time inside. She passed beyond the high walls and found it a struggle not to smile. It had been a long time since she had visited the statue garden, and she found it enchanting every time.

She walked down a curving white stone path surrounded by delicate flowering plants created from stone. Priests from Purpose had crafted the stone garden over centuries, reshaping entire portions of the garden until it was a perfect scene frozen in time. They used their Gift to make the stone flow like water into whatever shape they imagined, and based on the result, they could imagine a lot.

White tree branches arched gracefully over the pathway. If she looked closely, she could see birds perched among the limbs, each wing and feather tenderly crafted. Stone lamp posts topped with crystalline lined the path, casting a soft glow. The crystal spire in the temple was close enough to add to the glow and created patterned shadows as the light fell through the branches and leaves.

A loud group of laughing girls came into view, and she ducked behind a stone tree. She saw no reason to reveal her presence to strangers if it wasn't necessary. She shifted from one tree to another until the girls walked out of sight.

The path split in multiple directions, and she picked one randomly. The statue garden was a large maze, and she wondered if she had made a mistake thinking she could find them without specific directions. She avoided more people: three people who walked close together, talking in sharp whispers, and a couple that wouldn't have noticed her if she stood right in front of them.

At the end of another tree-lined path, she saw Quinn sitting on the ground, running his hand along a patch of stone clover. He leaned down to look closer and rubbed his hand through his adorably messy hair to get it away from his face. He wore a light blue shirt that brought out the color of his blue eyes behind his dark-rimmed glasses.

Tayeh stood with her hands on her hips, looking down at him with a hint of a smile. Her structured leather vest and armored wrist guards stood in contrast to her thick hair floating like a soft cloud around her face.

Rev was stretched out on a stone bench, staring up at the night sky. As Rose approached, she heard Rev singing. Her quiet voice filled the space between the trees, and Rose could almost feel the notes as they vibrated through the air.

Wilder stepped out from behind a tree into the path.

Rev's song halted.

He stood only a few feet away, and Rose lifted her eyes to meet his. She refused to tilt her neck to look up at him. He had changed out of what he had worn to the audition and was now wearing a new fashion from the Underneath. His sleeveless dark gray tunic looked like a simple work shirt, except she knew that most workers didn't try so hard to show off their biceps, and his tight pants weren't suitable for honest work.

"Good evening, Wilder."

His dark eyes analyzed her. It wasn't his usual sensual gaze as he looked her up and down. She felt him boring into her soul.

Based on his expression, she wasn't sure she measured up.

"Wilder! Stop monopolizing the new girl! It's my turn!" Rev ran forward and grabbed Rose in a hug that was way more familiar than she expected. "You're looking good, honey!" Rev still wore the headdress covering part of her face, and her single blue eye roved across Rose's body in a very intimate way.

"Come sit by me!" Rev sat back down on her stone bench and patted the spot beside her. Her voice was so friendly it pulled Rose away from her irritation with Wilder. Rev's lips curled in a grin. "Don't let yourself get distracted by him. He's a hopeless flirt."

Wilder leaned back on the stone bench beside Quinn and Tayeh with a smug look on his face, daring Rose to speak.

Rev shook her head at him like she was reprimanding a child. "He leaves most girls either furious or blushing or both."

Quinn looked up from examining the clover and grinned. "He leaves plenty of guys that way, too."

Tayeh chuckled softly. Wilder smiled and smacked Quinn good-naturedly on the back.

Rose thought she missed a backstory in their exchange.

They had a long history together, and she felt left out of their circle.

Rev looped her arm through Rose's and pulled her close. "Thanks for showing up! I thought you might be like most City folk. Afraid of the dark."

Rose refused to admit any of the unease she felt. "I'm not scared easily."

Two wolves leaped into their midst, their white fur gleaming brighter than the stone. Rose flinched despite her previous statement. The wolves stared at her with pale blue eyes like ice.

"Don't worry about them," said Quinn. "They rarely attack unless Wilder asks them to."

She held perfectly still as the wolves sniffed her. "Rarely?" Her voice came out in a whisper.

"She's with us, ladies." At Wilder's calm voice, the wolves moved to his side on the stone bench and took up a regal position at his feet. "Sorry about that. They can be over-protective." Wilder wouldn't meet Rose's eyes. He seemed almost embarrassed.

Rose cleared her throat and tried to regain her dignity. "I saw them during the Uprising, but I didn't realize they belonged to you."

The wolves growled softly, and Tayeh chuckled. "The wolves don't belong to him. It's more accurate to say that Wilder belongs to them."

Wilder scowled at Tayeh, and the wolves stopped growling and settled down to rest on their front paws. Rose's eyes widened, and she opened her mouth to ask how Wilder came to belong to two wolves, but Rev pulled her closer.

"Wilder told you we are looking for Clayr. Did you learn anything about her?" Rev clung to Rose's arm with a hopeful look on her face.

Rose squirmed away from her touch. "Priest Frances said he

hasn't seen her in several days. The last thing she said to him was that she had recognized someone from her past. He's hoping it was a friend, but he doesn't know for sure." They looked at her like she might know more, but she shrugged. "That's all I know."

Wilder shrugged. "We understand. You aren't as skilled at finding out information as we are."

Rose spit her words out between clenched teeth. "And just what have you discovered?"

Wilder's eyes flared, but Quinn responded in his cheerful voice. "There's a Sentinel in the City."

Rose snapped her head in his direction. "A Sentinel? They were all killed when the Wardens defeated the High Priests."

"Apparently not," said Tayeh. "No one knew the identities of the masked Sentinels. Even if this person wasn't formerly a Sentinel, they found the uniform and became one."

"Whoever told you this must be mistaken," said Rose. "The Sentinels wore all black. The person probably saw a Priest and had an active imagination."

Wilder leaned forward on the stone bench. "Do you think we are idiots, Rose?" The wolves didn't move from their relaxed position, but they narrowed their eyes at her. "It's our job to collect reliable information. When we say there is at least one Sentinel roaming around the City, there is one."

Rose bit her cheeks to keep from snapping out a harsh reply. She didn't believe they were idiots, but it couldn't be true.

Rev sighed. "I know you don't want to believe it, hon. But this is why we need people inside the temples. The Sentinels were the High Priests' creatures. What does it mean that they are back? Did some fool find a pile of their uniforms and decide to scare people? Or is something dangerous stirring to life?"

Rose struggled to breathe as she considered the implications. "It has to be a stupid kid. Why would someone resurrect the High Priests' symbol of authority and death?"

Wilder held her with his calm, dark eyes. "That's exactly what we intend to find out."

She didn't break his stare as she replied, "The Sentinels belonged to the High Priests. They are my problem. I'll figure out who is wearing their armor."

Rev smothered her in a hug. "I knew you would say that. This is why I liked you from the first night we met."

"Considering we met in a standoff between your crew and my fellow Priests, that's saying something," said Rose.

Quinn laughed. "You and Wilder had knives to each other's throats! It will be fun to see if that happens again!" Tayeh chuckled darkly, and Rev swatted Quinn's arm playfully.

Wilder's eyes sparkled in challenge.

She took mental inventory of the blades she carried and decided to pick up a few more.

10

As Rose walked back to Temple Purpose, she imagined Sentinels lurking in every shadow. The Sentinels couldn't be back. They had belonged to the High Priests with no authority on their own. Rose never knew how the High Priests found people to accomplish their will. If someone's child grew up to become a Sentinel, no one admitted it.

It was her job as a Priest to discover who found a Sentinel's uniform. But she couldn't stop wondering what Wilder and the others believed about the Sentinels. Did they think there were Priests who wanted the Sentinels back? The Sentinels had killed a lot of Priests, including her oldest sister and two brothers. Sentinels could kill anyone. Anyone except a High Priest.

Was someone trying to raise up new High Priests? She hadn't heard the faintest rumor about that. No one would choose to give anyone the authority of the High Priests again. The Priests would never go back to the way it was.

Except Rose and her fellow Priests were recreating a perfect Pageant to win the Goddess's blessing. She herself wanted some things back the way they were. Could someone actually believe they would be better off with High Priests again?

Her feet struggled the last few steps up to the temple court-yard. Her legs shook with exhaustion, and her eyes felt gritty from the long day. A part of her wanted nothing more to head to her room and fall asleep, but she knew she wouldn't be able to sleep yet. She turned to a rehearsal room instead.

The room was open to the night air, with only sheer curtains floating in the night wind. The polished floor and wall-to-wall mirrors bounced the dim light from the crystal spires. Compared to the bright crystalline light and all the people in the rest of the temple, the rehearsal studio was a peaceful escape.

Her boots clicked softly against the maple floorboards as she walked to the front of the studio. She sank down against the mirror, unbuckled her boots, and removed her hidden weapons. She pulled off her jacket, stacking it neatly on her boots and weapons, until all she wore were her pants and black silk tank. She twisted her hair up into a tight knot and walked to the center of the dance floor.

Rose swept her arms overhead, then bent forward to rest her hands on the floor as her head relaxed. The blood rushed to her head, and she imagined her stress pouring out. She pulled herself up slowly, stacking each vertebra into its proper place, then rolled her shoulders up and back. She took a deep breath and opened her eyes to study herself in the mirror.

Her body was strong and healthy, her mind filled with knowledge and skills, but it was not enough.

She was not enough. Not anymore.

Rose raised her arms again, and the wind remained limp at her sides. She spun away from the mirror, and the wind pressed against her, holding her back. Her leap barely skimmed the floor. She reached forward, and her fingers grasped nothing. The storm, the breeze, the breath ... each type of wind slipped out of her fingers. She could hold nothing.

She was nothing.

Her movements became more frantic. Dance combinations bled into fighting katas, which slid back into dance. She reached and grasped and kicked and slid, and at each step, the wind fought back. The wind slowed her. It pressed down on her. The air was thick, and each movement was a battle. The wind had been her closest friend.

Now it was gone.

She couldn't remember the first time she summoned the wind. It would have been before her first birthday, and soon after, her birth parents had dutifully dropped her off at the temple to be raised as a Priest. Her first hazy memory of the wind was when she was four years old. In the middle of a race with Kai and Caed, she'd fallen and skinned her knee. As she looked down at the little droplets of blood forming on her knee, tears slid out of her eyes. She was sad and angry that she would lose the race. As she stood, the wind grabbed her hand. Currents flowed around her little ankles, and she ran faster than she had ever run in her life. Kai and Caed had claimed she'd cheated because they weren't supposed to be racing with the wind this time. But she didn't stop smiling all day.

The wind was her friend.

And together, they were fast.

From that day on, Rose had devoted herself to Discipline. She'd learned how to fight and how to dance and how to run. She called the wind, and it always listened. The wind made sense. Air flow, currents, trajectory, patterns, lift. The wind followed rules, and Rose liked rules.

But now, the wind flowed where it wished. She called, and it didn't listen.

Rose danced alone.

She danced until her muscles shook with exhaustion. Her breath came in gasps, but still, she battled the absent wind. On and on she danced until tears and sweat soaked her face. She glimpsed her devastated eyes in the mirror and had to look away. Her weakness was shameful to her.

She stumbled toward the mirror and picked up her jacket and boots. She didn't have enough energy to put them back on, so she padded back to her room barefoot. Fitz was snoring quietly when she opened the door and stumbled into bed. She fell asleep the moment her tear-stained cheeks hit the pillow.

11

Rose cracked her eyes open and groaned in disgust. Her face was stiff with dried sweat and tears, and her sheets clung to her damp skin. Every muscle groaned as she sat up and rubbed her eyes. Fitz's bed was tidily made, with his few belongings packed in a bag ready to go. They were moving to Temple Perfection today, and she was already behind schedule.

She rushed through a desperately needed bath, dressed, and packed her bag as quickly as she could without help from the wind. Her clothes from the night before smelled awful. She didn't want to put them in the bag with the clothes the temple attendants had washed, but most of her clothing was still back at Temple Discipline, and she didn't want to give up the few items she had. Especially now that she knew she didn't have money to buy more.

She hurried downstairs to grab a quick breakfast before they made the trek to Temple Perfection. Eating breakfast was her gift to her companions. They definitely didn't want to travel with her on an empty stomach.

She shoved an apple into her pocket and finished her last

bite of a blueberry muffin as she stepped into the laundry. A woman lifted her head from a sloshing tub of sudsy water and brushed her thick hair away from her face.

"Rose! How are you? Or, the more important question, how are your clothes?" Her eyes twinkled as she dried her hands on a towel.

"My clothes are perfect, as you well know, Kita. You got the stain out of my charmeuse blouse, and I'm still not sure how you did it."

Kita's lips curled into a satisfied smile. "I have three messy children and a love of fashion, so I've had to learn a few skills." She studied Rose's empty hands. "You aren't dropping off any clothes today, so what can I do for you?"

"I have a delicate question for you."

Kita raised an eyebrow. "Well, you have trusted me to wash your delicates ..."

Rose rolled her eyes. "Yes, this is more delicate than that." She looked around to make sure they were alone. "Do you know if any Sentinel uniforms remain?"

Kita's eyes opened wide. "Why do you want to know?"

Rose debated how much she should share. "There are rumors of a Sentinel roaming through the City. I need to know how easy it would be for someone to steal an old uniform and use it to scare people."

Kita bit her lip, then took Rose's hand. "I'll show you."

Rose stumbled before catching herself. She had expected the answer to be a firm *no*.

Kita led her deeper into the laundry, watching for observers. She walked through a room with racks of black clothes. They were a variety of black fabrics and textures and shapes, but Kita pulled her to the last rack.

Sentinel black matte armor and hooded masks stood at attention in a neat line. Rose looked around the open room of Priests' clothing.

"So, anyone can come in here?"

"Of course," said Kita. "I wouldn't stop anyone from getting the clothes they need." She shied away from the rack of armor. "But this has been here since the High Priests were overthrown. No one would want to take this."

Rose ran her fingers down the matte armor. It was light enough to be comfortable but strong enough for protection. Not that anyone ever fought back against a Sentinel. If a Sentinel wanted you dead, you were dead.

"I think someone wants to take this. I know it isn't in your nature to ruin fine clothing, but will you destroy these?" She touched the hooded mask and shivered. "I think it's dangerous to hold on to this armor."

Kita's eyes locked on the mask, and she nodded. "Yes, I think you are right."

Rose left the laundry with a sour taste in her mouth. She had held on to the hope that the rumor wasn't true until the moment she saw the armor. There weren't any locks on the temple. A lot of rooms didn't even have doors, just archways. The symbol of the High Priests' power was laid out in neat formation for anyone to come and take. If someone said they saw a Sentinel roaming the City, then they did.

Kita didn't notice any of the uniforms missing, so someone must have stolen them from another temple. Rose made plans to check the armor in the laundry at the next temple. She found it beneficial to make friends with the people caring for her clothes, so she knew the people who worked in the laundry in each temple. She would find out who had taken the uniform and get an answer to the disturbing question ...

Why?

PERFECTION

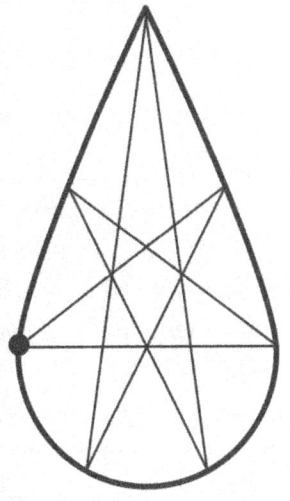

12

Rose stifled her surprised expression when she found Wilder and Fitz waiting for her in the courtyard. Their bags rested on the stone benches shaped like flowers. They stopped their quiet conversation when she approached.

"Good morning, Priest Rose," said Fitz. His strawberry blond beard was so pale it was almost transparent in the bright sunlight. After their awkward interaction regarding the book of liturgies, she wasn't sure if Fitz liked her or not, but his smile looked genuine.

"Good morning, gentlemen," she said politely. "Are we walking to Temple Perfection together?"

"Fitz thought it might be a good idea." Wilder's face implied he wasn't so sure.

Rose wouldn't give him the satisfaction of a reaction, either positive or negative. "That's acceptable."

Fitz's green eyes sparkled. "That's the level of excitement I expected, so let's get going!"

Wilder wore his standard City clothes again: a barely

buttoned white shirt and black boots over his dark gray pants. She wondered if he hid his blades in his boots, because his pants were so tight he definitely couldn't hide them there.

Fitz dressed much differently than Wilder. His soft cotton shirt was a pale green that matched his eyes, but his oversized jacket was a faded orange that clashed with his strawberry blond hair. Even if Rose wore colors other than black, she wouldn't be caught dead in orange. His baggy pants were long enough to drag along the ground. His ill-fitting clothes signaled to everyone he was from the Underneath. The people in the City loved to wear bright and sometimes mismatched clothes as a statement; however, they could always find a good tailor.

Fitz walked between her and Wilder, and Rose thought they must make an interesting trio. She tried to judge the reactions of the people in the streets, and she realized something she hadn't noticed before. Wilder drew the attention of everyone they passed. He wasn't exaggerating. He really was a celebrity.

Her eyes shot to his face. He was basking in their attention. His face practically glowed with pride. And with each step, his swagger grew.

The people weren't brave enough to approach, but Rose saw their smiles and waves and ducked heads. Couples whispered to one another, and a mother stilled her son to watch them pass. She saw several people touch the corner of their eye making the sign of the Goddess, and she realized they weren't making it for her, but for Wilder. She was glad no one approached them, because she wasn't sure she could control her response.

"That's exactly why we brought you." Fitz stared ahead as he walked, but a smile curled his lips.

She had almost forgotten Fitz was there. "What are you talking about?"

"Last time I walked through the City with Wilder, he kept

getting swarmed by fans, and it really slowed down the walk. I wasn't enough to hold them off, but your glare works perfectly."

Wilder bit his bottom lip, struggling to hide a grin. She wanted to explode in anger, but she knew that would only contribute to their joke.

"Funny," she said stiffly. "It must be such a burden to be so loved."

Wilder glanced at her out of the corner of his eye. "We all sacrifice for the Goddess, Priest."

She forced her scowl to become a smile. She didn't know if she succeeded.

"That's not the only reason I wanted us to walk together," said Fitz. "We're roommates, and I barely know you. I know you aren't used to having a roommate, so maybe you don't know that it's customary to spend some time getting to know each other. It makes it a little easier to sleep at night."

"That's how it works? You have a little chat, and then it's suddenly easier to share a room with a stranger?" she asked.

Wilder didn't look at her when he spoke. "I don't know if anything could make it easier to share a room with you. But Fitz is trying, so maybe you could offer him some courtesy, Priest?"

She had never in her life had someone speak her title with such disdain. She wouldn't let Wilder get under her skin.

"What should we talk about, Fitz?" She decided it might be easiest to just ignore Wilder.

"Family, hobbies, favorite restaurants ... Take your pick!"

She sighed. "I have thirteen brothers and sisters... Well, only ten are still alive, but we were all raised by Mims in Temple Discipline. I'm the second youngest and am closest to my older brother, Kai, and my baby brother, Caed."

Wilder snorted. "Baby brother?"

"He's only a few months younger, but that's enough. Especially when we all discovered how irritated it made him when we called him that." She saw her own wicked grin echoed on Wilder's lips. It annoyed her how much his smile pleased her.

Fitz rubbed his soft beard as he regarded her. "I never considered how Priests would raise the babies with Gifts. They divided you up into families?"

"Once a baby manifests a Gift, their parents drop them off at the temple. After the babies officially bond with the City, they join a family in the temple of their respective Gift. My entire family possesses the Gift of Discipline and can summon the wind. Well, we could …" She cleared her throat. "I'm sure we will again."

Her voice faltered, but Fitz was too kind to draw attention to it. "I bet it was interesting growing up in a family that could all summon the wind. The storms in my house were metaphorical, not literal."

Rose smiled, but she didn't trust herself to speak without a tremble in her voice.

Fitz took over. "My family is much smaller. I have a younger sister. Our mother died when my sister was small, so I raised her. My dad was a fighter in one of the fight clubs in Rivalry. He made enough money for us to get by, but he wasn't home much. My sister has very strong opinions, and we got into some serious fights, but for the most part, we learned to have each other's back. There are a lot of awful things out there, so it's good to know you have someone you trust on your side."

An image flashed in her mind of fighting back-to-back with Caed in a training session. They both controlled the wind, passing currents of air between them as they fought. She could defeat anyone in front of her because she held the wind in her hands and Caed was at her back.

Now the wind and Caed were both gone. If someone attacked her, she would fall. She was weak and alone.

Fitz's voice brought her back to the present. "What about you, Wilder? Have you told Rose where we met?"

Wilder frowned, but he couldn't refuse after their stories. "I met Fitz in a performing arts school in Rivalry. We grew up together."

She stared at them both with wide eyes. "There are performing arts schools in the Underneath?"

Fitz laughed. "I'm sure it's a lot different from anything you have up here."

Rose raised an eyebrow at Wilder. "That's where you learned to sing so well?"

"No. I was born good at that." A hint of his smirk returned.

Fitz slapped him on the back. "That is the Goddess-honest truth! He could charm anyone with his voice, even as a child. That's why the headmaster was so quick to take him in."

Rose looked at him with a question in her eyes, but she didn't feel brave enough to ask. Wilder's jaw flexed, and she could see he was trying to decide if he would explain.

He spoke, but the words came grudgingly. "I was five when my father did a favor for the Warden of Chaos and earned his way Upstairs. He left my mother and me without a backward glance. My mother ... she wasn't a good person. She should never have had a child. I was eight when I left. I made it to Rivalry, and the headmaster found me. The rest is history."

So few words, and yet Rose heard a lifetime in them. She tried to imagine the tall, swaggering man beside her as a young, frightened child traveling alone through the Underneath. She couldn't imagine how he survived.

Rose wanted to respond but didn't know what to say. If she tried to compare his life to anything in her childhood, she would sound like a fool. But she couldn't let the silence stretch any further.

"Thank you," she said.

He turned to her with a confused expression, and she

fought down her embarrassment as she explained, "You didn't have to share that with me. I'm grateful you did." She was careful the words held none of their usual bite.

He stared at her a moment, then nodded his head once. The three of them continued their walk toward Perfection.

13

Priest Mayra sat in the courtyard at Temple Perfection at a small desk that fit neatly between newly planted rows of lavender and echinacea. Without a word of greeting, she handed Rose a stack of papers and motioned for her to take a seat.

Rose ground her teeth together, clutching the audition forms in her hand. Fitz startled her from her thoughts by taking Rose's bag and offering to put it in their room, causing Mayra to give him a maternal nod of appreciation.

As Rose sat down at her own desk next to a thick patch of aloe, Priest Mayra gave Wilder a pleasant smile. "Enjoy the rest of your day, Wilder. We are so grateful for all your hard work on the Pageant."

Mayra was focused on Wilder, so she couldn't see Rose's eye roll, but Wilder did. He spoke to Mayra, but Rose felt him aiming the words right at her.

"Thank you, Priest. I will spend this afternoon in quiet contemplation, and this evening, I will discover what Perfection Diocese can teach me about the Goddess."

Priest Mayra almost swooned in religious fervor. "You are such a devoted young man. Goddess blessing upon you."

Rose watched him bow, and his eyes met hers. "And also upon you, Priest."

Rose watched him go and wondered where in Perfection Diocese he would head tonight. She wasn't sure if that was a subtle invitation or if she would find a note in her room again. She hadn't mentioned the Sentinel uniforms in front of Fitz because Wilder hadn't brought it up. Maybe he would meet with the others tonight and she could share what she learned. He didn't seem to be as angry with her, so maybe he would speak to her more than he had last time.

"Priest Rose?" Mayra was staring at Rose from across her stack of paperwork. "You aren't letting yourself get distracted, are you? I know Wilder is an attractive young man, but you must focus on the auditions."

It took a minute before Priest Mayra's words registered. Rose's eyes opened wide. "What? No! I'm not distracted by ... that. Goddess, why would you say that?"

Mayra's lips pinched into a straight line. "You shouldn't speak her name in vain, Priest Rose."

Rose was so flustered she hadn't even realized she had. She couldn't meet Mayra's eyes as she answered, "Yes, Priest Mayra. Of course. I ... I promise to focus and not get distracted."

Mayra narrowed her eyes at Rose, then turned her attention to the stack of papers. Rose threw herself whole-heartedly into her own paperwork. She didn't want to give Mayra the slightest hint that she might be distracted by ... that sort of thing.

Rose was not some silly girl to lose her head over a boy. She had too much to do, and a relationship was an unnecessary complication. How dare Priest Mayra question her dedication to her goals?

In fact, her family usually accused her of being too focused on her work. Mims's hints that Rose should find a nice boy became less subtle as time passed. Rose had even come home a few times to find "nice boys" that Mims had invited to dinner. After Rose made one of them so furious he stormed out, Mims stopped inviting them.

Rose had proven her dedication to the Goddess and her Gift, and she proved her devotion again by taking the auditions seriously. Being a Priest was her entire life. She was nothing apart from the priesthood. She was the pinnacle of an ideal Priest.

And Mayra thought she would let herself get distracted ... by a boy.

Rose clenched her pen so tightly her knuckles turned white. She wanted to glare her displeasure at Mayra but didn't dare let her eyes leave the paper. She wouldn't give Mayra even the illusion of being right.

She went through every page until the words bled together and her hand wouldn't straighten from a permanent cramp. She turned over the final page and returned the stack of papers to Mayra.

"If there is nothing else I can assist you with, Priest Mayra, I will attend to the Goddess's work." Rose's bow was stiff but polite.

Mayra gave her a barely disguised look of irritation but gave her the sign of the Goddess in return.

Rose was careful to walk slowly out of the room. Once she turned the corner, she allowed the anger to shake through her body. She took several deep breaths before continuing down the hall.

Priest Mayra wouldn't ruin the rest of her night. Rose was free until the audition the next morning, and she planned to spend her time doing what she pleased. She grabbed a sand-wich from the kitchen and made her way to the laundry.

She found Saya stitching a ripped seam in a jacket. She

removed the pins from her mouth and hugged Rose with one arm without dropping the needle in her hand.

"It's nice to see you back, Rose. Did you rip something while fighting? Or were you dancing this time?"

"No rips, I promise." She pulled up a seat next to the young woman. "I have a serious question, though. Have any of the Sentinel uniforms gone missing recently?"

Saya set down the needle and jacket as she leaned across the table. "As a matter of fact, yes. Have you found Remy?"

Rose tried to follow the train of thought. "Who is Remy?"

"Remy used to work here. He disappeared at the same time the Sentinel uniforms did."

"I haven't heard anything about him. Had he worked here long?"

"Since the Uprising. He seemed like a nice guy. He talked a lot about his family and how he wanted to provide for them. One day, he was here, working as hard as usual, then the next day, he was gone, along with the uniforms."

"Do you think he took them?" This isn't the way Rose thought the conversation would go, but she needed to follow it to the end.

"I don't know. I wouldn't have expected it from him. But honestly, just thinking about those uniforms is enough to give me the chills."

Rose agreed with her on that. "So, one night, with no warning, he just walked out with a couple uniforms?"

"Twenty-seven," said Saya.

"Excuse me?"

"There are twenty-seven Sentinel uniforms missing."

Rose leaned back in her chair with a thump.

"That was how many we had left," said Saya. "No one had taken the time to repair any of the damaged uniforms, but we had twenty-seven sets in good condition lined up in the back. I wonder now if we should have disposed of them, but we were hesitant to even touch them." She looked ashamed to admit it. "The Sentinels were terrifying," she whispered.

"It's not your fault, Saya." Rose grasped the young woman's hand. "The Sentinels terrified us all. Everyone lost someone to them."

Saya gave the sign of the Goddess.

"Is there anything else you can remember about him? Maybe the two things are unrelated. I'd like to find him to make sure he's okay."

Saya's eyes lit up at the hopeful thought. Rose didn't want to tell her it was highly unlikely that was the case.

"Remy said he shared an apartment with roommates." Saya seemed as unfamiliar with the word as Rose had been. "He said it was across from the healing center. Above a new shop where someone is selling tattoos."

"What are tattoos?" asked Rose.

Saya shrugged.

"Thank you for the helpful information, Saya." Rose tried to fill her voice with hope she didn't feel. "I'm sure it will all work out. Goddess blessing upon you."

"And also upon you, Priest Rose."

Saya picked up the jacket and began stitching again. She seemed a little brighter than when Rose had first entered, but Rose felt foreboding settle along her shoulders.

14

Rose wasn't sure where Fitz spent his time, but she was glad to have the room to herself for a while. She took time to hang all her clothes in their closet. They were only staying a few days in each place, but she felt better when her clothes hung in neat black lines in the closet instead of cramped in her bag.

She pulled on a thin long-sleeve sweater and black shorts. Wearing pants would let her attach a sheath for her dagger on her thigh, but her high-waisted shorts had a hidden sheath along the back of her waist. She couldn't draw it as fast as the one on her hip, but it was nice if she wanted to keep a weapon hidden until necessary.

She never had to consider where to hide weapons until the Wardens took over. Before that, all her fighting had been theoretical training sessions. It wasn't until the Wardens and their soldiers had hunted the Priests that she had to worry about how to incorporate weapons into her wardrobe.

She wasn't sure exactly where she was going tonight, so she pulled on her jacket with the extra sheath for one more blade and put her hair up into a knot with a few sharp pins, just in case.

Rose left the temple and walked into Perfection Diocese. Each part of the City had changed drastically since the High Priests fell, and Perfection was no different. During the Wardens' reign, they had boarded up and walled off parts of the City, but after the Uprising, the City flowed from one Diocese to the other again. The differences became clearer the closer to the center you walked.

Perfection Diocese had always been marked by its high regard for fashion and beauty. The Priests could bring everyone to complete physical health and change their appearance. Smooth skin, colorful hair, and extravagant fashion appeared everywhere in the City, but in Perfection, it was the ultimate art form. But since the Priests had lost the Gift, the people had to find new ways to adapt.

The unique clothing choices seemed to have increased with the addition of people from the Underneath. Rose studied fashion more than the most people, and she thought she knew the trends, but looking at the people walking down the street in Perfection, she knew nothing.

Besides the feathers and ruffles and sequins traditional in the City, she saw ripped silk and shredded ribbons and strange textures, like the woven nets previously used to carry produce. She couldn't identify who was from the City or the Underneath, because everyone was draped in such a strange combination of textiles.

The hair trends seemed to be the same, but several small shops in the Diocese now poured dye on their clients' hair. It appeared the Underneath had discovered methods to perfect the body without using a Gift.

She walked through the busy streets as a stranger. She found it odd to hear so many people laughing. Her entire world had been turned upside down, and some people had already found enough normalcy to spend a night walking around town laughing.

Rose continued through the Diocese until she arrived at the closest healing center. This was where Saya said Remy lived— near the place where they sold tattoos. Whatever tattoos were.

She walked past several shops with hair dye when she spotted something unusual. Inside a shop, a woman appeared to be painting a twisted vine around a man's bicep. From the grimace on his face, Rose didn't think the woman used paint.

A looming figure appeared at her back, and she imagined a Sentinel hovering over her. Her elbow reflexively whipped back to strike him in the stomach. The imagined Sentinel exhaled sharply, and Rose turned around, ready to drive her fist into his jaw, when she realized it was Wilder.

She sighed in relief. "Thank the Goddess it's just you."

"I guess I should remember not to sneak up behind you." He rubbed his stomach gingerly. "Who did you think I was?"

She considered lying, but that seemed even more embarrassing than telling the truth. "I thought you were a Sentinel."

He crossed his arms over his chest with a smug smile. "So, you believe us now? What convinced you we aren't stupid?"

She bit back a saucy comment and again went with the truth. "I spoke to friends in the temple's laundry and discovered that someone stole Sentinel uniforms."

He gave her an odd look. "You are friends with laundry workers?"

She pulled herself up straighter. "Yes, I am. Do you have a problem with that?"

"No, I just didn't expect it."

Rose crossed her arms to match his. "I do have friends, you know."

He laughed. "Okay, fine. You have friends. Did these friends tell you anything else besides the fact that someone stole the armor?"

"She said twenty-seven sets of armor were taken." Wilder's eyes widened, but she continued. "And she said the armor disappeared at the same time as another laundry worker named Remy." She looked around at the surrounding buildings. "He lives here somewhere."

"I'm impressed." He tilted his head, nodding slowly as he studied her. "I didn't expect you to find anything so quickly."

She didn't want him to know how much his praise affected her. "I'm glad I could prove you wrong."

"Fair enough. So, where do you think this Remy lives?"

"Saya said that he lives above a shop with someone selling tattoos. Is that what this is?" She looked inside to see the man moving into another position so the woman could continue painting.

"Yes, it is. I guess you haven't seen a tattoo before?"

"No, I haven't. Is it paint?"

"It's ink applied with a needle."

Rose studied the man's grimace. "That explains his expression. What's the reasoning?"

"People in the Underneath like to mark their skin for either fashion or meaning or both. It's a permanent type of art."

"Permanent?" Her eyes widened in shock. "What in the Abyss would you want to wear on your skin forever? I can't imagine any art I love that much."

He stared at her in that considering way that made her feel weighed and found lacking. He shook his head and changed the subject.

"I think the stairs to the apartment are probably in back. Maybe we should look around?" he asked.

They walked through the alley and found several staircases leading up to apartments above the shops. They walked up the narrow stone stairs to the landing outside the door.

Wilder knocked, and the door opened under his hand. He met Rose's eyes in silence. She nodded and followed him in.

The room was a disaster. She sometimes used that word to describe Kai's messy room since he didn't hold her standards for being tidy. However, this time, "disaster" was not an exaggeration.

A crystalline lamp flickered on the wall. The smashed metal shade blew in the wind coming through the open door. Someone had ripped apart the sofa, splitting its wood frame and shredding the cushions with a knife. A table lay on its side with papers scattered across the floor. The cabinets in the kitchen area were open, with a few doors ripped off the hinges.

Rose looked around for any sign of the man named Remy or the twenty-seven sets of armor, but she found nothing that made sense. Did someone break in and steal the armor from Remy? Or did he trash his own apartment to cover his trail?

Rose bent down to pick up one of the scattered pages and walked toward the lamp to read it. Her back was to the door, so she didn't notice the three men walk in until one pulled her roughly to his chest; the other two held Wilder between them.

"Who are you?" asked the stout man who held a blade to her side. "What are you doing here?"

Rose couldn't speak. Her mind moved slowly, as if through molasses.

Wilder was as quick as ever. "We are looking for a man named Remy. Have you heard of him?"

The men holding Wilder reacted slightly to the name, but she wasn't sure what that meant. Were they protecting him? Or had they attacked him, too?

Wilder slid his eyes over her body. She couldn't believe he would ogle her at a time like this! Then she realized his eyes weren't roaming across her body, but over her jacket. Or more accurately, his eyes slid over the place where she had a hidden sheath.

Despite being rough handled by a smelly criminal, she was

irritated that Wilder knew where she held a hidden knife. She scowled at him, but nodded in understanding.

Wilder slammed his head back into the nose of the attacker on his left. As the man let go, Wilder elbowed the other man in the neck.

Rose pulled her knife out of the sheath and called the wind to slide the blade into place.

The blade dropped to the ground.

She stared stupidly at the blade as her attacker laughed. The man gripped her arm tighter and pulled her into his chest, wrapping her arms around her body. She knew dozens of maneuvers to get out of his unsophisticated hold, but her mind couldn't grasp even one.

She finally remembered Wilder fighting two men. When she pried her eyes away from her fallen blade, Wilder stood panting with both men on the ground. His sleeve had been sliced open, and blood poured down his arm.

He took a step toward her, but her attacker waved his knife. "Stay back!"

Wilder had taken down two men, while she trembled like a child in the arms of an unskilled brute. Wilder stared at her, assessing her for damage, but he couldn't see the gaping wound in her mind.

One man at Wilder's feet stirred, and Rose's captor yelled at him, "Get up, you idiot! We need to grab them and get out before the others arrive."

Her thoughts snapped to icy clarity. Others. Others could be good. Maybe someone coming to help her. Or others could be much, much worse. And Wilder was losing blood while there were no more healers in the City. She would deal with the shame of what happened later. For now, it was time to leave.

Rose looked Wilder in the eyes again and hoped he could read the intention there. She took a deep breath and stretched behind her for the knife sheathed in her shorts' waistband. She slashed the blade across the man's arm, and he released her in surprise.

Wilder used the man's shock to attack. He leaped across the room, and his fist connected directly with the man's jaw, dropping him to the ground.

"Time to go." Wilder pushed her ahead of him out the door.

15

They ran down the alley, across a street, and down another alley. Rose stopped when she realized Wilder was stumbling. She pulled him into a recessed doorway, away from the bright white light of the crystal spire. He slid to the ground, and his eyes unfocused. She dropped to her knees beside him.

"I'm fine," he said. "I just need to catch my breath."

"You aren't fine," she said. She still gripped the blade in her hand and used it to cut away the sleeve of his shirt. Blood poured down his arm, but it wasn't from an artery. She breathed in relief when she realized he wouldn't die from the wound.

Wilder closed his eyes as he rolled his head around in circles. "It's not the blood loss. One of those guys knocked me hard on the temple. I'm a little dizzy, but I'll be fine."

"The blood loss might not kill you, but it's definitely not good." She lifted the ripped sleeve and wrapped it tightly around his arm. She needed to get him back to the temple to get it cleaned and properly wrapped.

"What happened back there?" Wilder stared at her with

dark eyes intently focused on her. She could have pretended his question was about the trashed apartment or their attackers, but she knew exactly what he meant. She looked away from him, unable to answer.

"I've seen you fight before," he said. "You pulled a knife on me the first night we met. That guy wasn't even close to your skill level. Not only did you drop your blade, you froze when I know you could have knocked him out in several creative ways. What happened?"

If his voice had been judgmental, she wouldn't have responded. If his voice had been angry, she would have walked away to let him bleed alone. But his voice held honest concern, and it cracked a tiny sliver of the ice in her heart.

"I can't fight anymore," she confessed, unable to look at him. "I only knew how to fight with the wind on my side. Now it's only me, and I'm not enough." The words hung in the quiet night air. She couldn't believe she had voiced them out loud. And to Wilder, who would surely use the words against her.

His voice was barely a whisper. "I'm so sorry, Rose."

She flinched, and her eyes widened. "Why are you apologizing?"

His voice was still quiet. "I'm sorry I didn't realize how that loss would affect you."

"Well ... yes. Thank you for saying that." She cleared her throat. "It's fine. It's why I have to work so hard to make this Pageant successful. Getting my Gift back is the only way I can be myself again."

He raised his eyebrows. "So, you won't be able to fight unless you get your Gift back?" She nodded sadly, but he shook his head. "No, Rose. Losing your Gift didn't make you weak or tame. You will always be fierce." His eyes captured hers and didn't let go. "Even when all seems lost, you will still fight."

Rose's breath caught in her chest. She felt his words settle over her, more powerful than any blessing she had ever received. He called her fierce. A fighter. He named something deep within her soul, and it rattled through her bones.

She looked at his face, truly seeing him for the first time. His long lashes blinked slowly, and crystalline reflected in his dark, serious eyes. No hint of a smile lingered on his full lips. A few drops of blood glittered on his temple. Her hand floated without conscious thought to the side of his face, and she brushed his temple with soft fingers.

He sat perfectly still but hissed in quiet pain, and she flinched. Her breath returned to her lungs in a rush, and she pulled her hand to her chest.

"Oh, Goddess, I'm sorry," she said. "I shouldn't have touched you ... You're injured."

A small smile played across his lips. "I'm okay. There's no need to apologize."

Her mouth dropped open in surprise. She couldn't believe she had apologized to him. And yet, she wanted to apologize again.

Everything was strange. The night air felt warmer than usual. Invisible sparks danced across her skin. She felt light-headed. Maybe she was the one who had lost blood.

"We should go," she said. She stood slowly so she wouldn't topple over with dizziness. She turned to face him, and he reached his uninjured arm to her.

"If you can help me stand, I think I can walk." His voice was light, but she studied him again, judging his injuries.

She took his hand and braced herself to lift him. He pulled himself up directly in front of her, and they stood with their hands clasped together between them. She looked up into his eyes and felt something she had not felt the entire night.

Danger.

This was dangerous.

The thought was not rational, and she couldn't explain it.

But as they stood together on the dark doorstep, panic shot through her system.

Something had shifted tonight.

Shifted between the two of them.

Shifted inside of herself.

This was something different. Something new. And the world was already too different. She couldn't handle something new.

Rose dropped his hand and stepped back. She tried to put herself back together the way she was before but couldn't figure out how to make it all fit. She gathered up all her mismatched pieces and shoved them beneath the surface until she could figure it out.

"Can you walk? I'm not sure I can carry you." Her voice sounded hollow in her ears.

Wilder studied her with the same intense stare. "I can walk. We aren't far."

She nodded but didn't open her mouth to let out any more hollow words. They walked to the temple together in silence as the loud strangeness of the world echoed in her ears.

16

The next morning, Rose woke even earlier than Fitz. She couldn't really call it "waking up" since she hadn't slept. Her mind was scattered, her thoughts moving both too fast and too slow. Her room was scorching hot, and the sheets prickled against her skin. She lay flat on her back, dragging her fingers through her sweaty hair, praying for a cool breeze.

The wind offered no relief, so she eventually gave up on sleep and hopped out of bed. She struggled to get dressed in the dark. Her clothes felt too tight against her feverish skin. She tried on every item of clothing she brought and then discarded it all in a pile at the bottom of the closet. She finally settled on a short, black linen dress that felt cool against her skin. But the thin dress offered little protection, so she pulled on her boots and jacket with the sheath. She slid a couple blades into place and went outside to search for some fresh air.

The City was already awake. People roamed the streets at all times of day and night now. She guessed there were so many people packed into the City that they needed to move at different times of day or else they wouldn't all fit.

A man rolled a cart to a stop in front of her. "Breakfast, Priest?"

He lifted a piece of wrapped flatbread, and she could smell the sausage and egg.

"It's only two copper." He smiled encouragingly.

She thought through his words. Money. Of course. And she had none.

"Um ... No, thank you. I'm not hungry."

"Oh, okay." His face fell. "Goddess blessing upon you, Priest."

Her stomach growled as she passed more food vendors on her way to the park. It was her own fault for leaving the temple so quickly and not eating breakfast while she was there.

She suddenly wondered where the temple was getting the food for everyone who lived inside. Without the Priests' Gifts, she believed the City would starve but didn't know how long that would take. The Priests' meager attempts at farming wouldn't be enough to sustain them all, but maybe there was a larger stockpile of food than she imagined. She could have asked one of the other Priests, but she had spent the last few weeks in a daze of anger and sadness and let some of those practical questions go unasked.

Someone had already set up a table for her near the front of the stage. A table for her and Wilder. The two chairs seemed to be closer together than last time. She set the stack of audition forms on the table and pushed the chairs a little further apart.

The audition wouldn't start for a couple hours yet, so she wandered onto the stage to look around. The wooden floor wasn't as polished as the ones in the temple studios, but it was finely made. When there were night performances, Purpose Priests used to build stone structures that allowed the crystalline to flow to light the stage, but for now, simple wooden rafters stretched overhead. Vines grew behind the stage, forming a woven backdrop of leaves and flowers. She ran her fingers across a smooth leaf. The vines were more ragged than they used to be, but they were resilient and appeared to still thrive.

She sat down in the wings, behind a fluttering curtain, and leaned against the soft leaves to savor the cool breeze. The wind brushed across her tingling skin, bringing a peace she had not felt all night. Her eyes grew heavier as she watched the wind caress the sky blue curtain until it trembled.

Her mind floated on a current of air. She soared high above the City, held tenderly by fluffy clouds. Her black silk slip flowed against her thighs as the wind wound around her. A breeze curled through her hair, pulling out the pins until the red locks floated around her face. A breath of air curled down her neck and brushed against her collarbone. She turned to face the breeze.

Wilder soared beside her. The wind pressed his white shirt against his chest, and his thick spirals of hair floated as if weightless. She could see each current of air as it flowed over him, until it intensified into a furious windstorm, and the tempest surrounding her answered in kind. The air between them fled before their respective storms, pulling them closer together.

Wilder was close enough to touch, but she didn't know what would happen when their storms collided. She didn't know, but she wanted to find out. She reached out a hand, and he spoke.

"Rose."

Her eyes shot open. Wilder was kneeling beside her on stage floor.

"Rose? Are you awake? I'm sorry if I startled you."

He was kneeling so close, and her dream still drifted on the surface of her thoughts. Her groggy mind imagined he was close enough to pluck her dream out of the air. Fire bloomed across her freckled cheeks.

A twinkle lit his eyes, and she panicked that her crazy notion was correct.

"You're blushing." His smile was gentle, but his eyes were knowing.

Too knowing.

She clapped her hands on her treasonous cheeks. "I don't blush."

He chuckled. "Blushing isn't a sin, Rose. It means you are alive. It means you're human."

She lowered her hands and let the breeze cool her cheeks. She might be human, but she didn't have to like it.

He stood and reached out his hand to help her to her feet. She remembered how that maneuver had ended the night before, and she choose to stand on her own. He dropped his arm, and she noticed the difference in the size of his arms beneath his sleeves.

"How is your arm?" she asked.

He patted the bulky place on his left bicep. "Overly cared for. A few of the Perfection Priests were happy to use me for training. Apparently, since they previously only healed everyone using their Gift, they aren't the best at wrapping bandages. I tried to talk them through it, but they need some more training. I'm sure they will track me down later to practice rewrapping it."

He seemed pleased at their determination, but the thought of healers learning to wrap wounds instead of healing them disturbed her.

It felt like giving up.

His dark eyes studied her. "They are adapting, Rose. It doesn't mean they are giving up."

She ground her teeth together, but tried to keep her face neutral. How could he read her thoughts so plainly on her face?

"We should get out there," he said. "It's time to begin."

Rose looked out from behind the curtain at the audience lined up on the grass. "I can't believe I fell asleep backstage."

"Did you not sleep well last night?"

His voice was casual, but her shoulders stiffened as she imagined him invading her thoughts from the night before. She kept her expression neutral as she turned slowly to face him. His expression was innocent.

A little too innocent.

She stood up tall. "If you are ready, it's time to begin."

"Of course, Priest. I was ready before you were," he said smoothly.

She narrowed her eyes at him, then strode out to start the audition.

17

Rose sat through the entire audition acutely aware of Wilder's presence at her side. She tried to stay as far away as possible because she didn't want to touch his wounded arm. No matter how far away she scooted her chair, she could still feel the heat radiating off him.

It was distracting. Just like Priest Mayra had warned.

Rose raged silently at the woman. How dare she plant the thought in Rose's head? Before that conversation, Rose had never had such a vivid dream. Sure, she had often dreamed of flying, but she had always been alone. Her thoughts had always been her own, and now her thoughts had been invaded.

"Rose? Did you hear me?"

She jumped when she realized Wilder had spoken.

"Sorry ... I was ... distracted." She growled the word.

A slow smile spread across his lips, and she realized she had apologized to him. Again.

"I said I'm going to check on Fitz and confirm how many people we have left. Try not to miss me too much while I'm gone."

"I think I'll live," she said drily.

As she stood to stretch her legs, the man with the midnight blue suit walked up. "Looks like today's audition was as interesting as the last one."

His dimple was as irritating as last time.

She considered which to give: a polite response or an honest one. She decided on both. "Can I help you with something? Or will you be at every audition, passive-aggressively commenting on the performers?" She focused on stacking her papers as a sign that she wasn't interested in the conversation.

He chuckled and ran a hand over his close-cropped black hair. "You're Priest Rose, correct?" She narrowed her eyes but nodded. "It's nice to meet you. I'm Vaylan. I guess I'm like many people in the City—interested in the Pageant and yet concerned about its consequences."

She shifted the papers to her side to face him squarely. "The consequences of the Pageant will be that the Goddess returns her Gifts to her Priests and we can return to normal."

He raised an eyebrow. "Maybe you've forgotten, but it was 'normal' for people to be executed for the slightest infraction. Those are exactly the consequences people are concerned about."

Her hands crushed the paperwork she held, but she tried to hold her smile in place. "Obviously, execution is not high on the list of things to bring back."

Vaylan's serene smile disguised his harsh words. "Murder by Priests is a recurring theme in our City's history. There is no reason to believe it will stop."

Rose couldn't hold her forced smile anymore. "It wasn't the Priests doing the killing. It was the High Priests."

"The High Priests kept their authority because of Priests who did nothing to stop them."

Rose's cheeks burned with both shame and anger. "You don't know the cost we paid trying to stop them. I lost a sister and two brothers trying to take out just one of them. It didn't work, and they paid the price."

"I don't blame you, child. You were too young during their reign." Vaylan's voice was fatherly, which only fueled her rage. "But now you are grown and must decide what kind of City you want to live in. A City where the powerful few rule everyone else, or a City based on equality and freedom."

Rage and confusion froze the words on her tongue. She wanted to yell at him for his condescending use of the word "child" but was taken aback at the type of City he proposed.

"And how do you propose we create a City like that?" she snapped.

He smiled in that infuriatingly paternal way. "There are so many places we could go from here without going backward. We need to find the way forward, but we can't do that if we stay divided between Priests and everyone else." He bent down and picked up a few of the crumpled pages Rose had dropped. "I'm sorry if I angered you. Thanks for listening." He handed her the pages, and the dimple returned as he walked away.

She dropped the papers she was clutching on the table. Why were there so many irritating people in the City? Why couldn't they leave her to do her job in peace?

She turned back to the stage in time to see Wilder jump off the front edge. His hair bounced as he landed, and he smiled as he headed her way.

Her heart skipped a beat.

She clutched her hands into fists. Her body continued to betray her. She had to pull herself back together. She sat down and smoothed the crumpled pages as Wilder approached.

"Only five more left, and then we are free!"

She didn't look up from her task. "Wonderful. I can't wait to finish this."

She felt his eyes watching her, but she continued smoothing out the papers against the table.

Out of the corner of her eye, she saw him wave for Fitz to send on the next person.

A girl wandered onto the stage. Rose groaned as the girl gave the same Ylena-like intro: looking around in amazement, saying she would sing a lullaby her mother sang to her, then launching into the Goddess's Aria.

The difference was, this girl was terrible.

Despite Ylena's powers, Rose still thought she was a silly girl. But at least she was a silly girl who could sing. This girl clearly could not.

Rose tried to imagine a Pageant with performers as terrible as this girl. A stage full of bumbling fools who could not stay on pitch to save their life. During previous auditions, a performance that terrible would literally cost someone them their life. But now, every person who had ever sung in their bathtub thought they deserved the right to come out here and waste her time. Was she the only one who took this seriously? Was this a joke to the rest of the City?

The girl hit her final terrible note, and Rose picked up the sheet of paper with the girl's information. Anna, seventeen, Perfection Diocese. This was the part where Rose was supposed to say they would either contact her later or immediately pronounce the girl had a role. It was the same routine over and over. Silly girls who thought they deserved a place in the Goddess's most sacred ceremony. Rose's entire future depended on this Pageant, and yet, Rose was the only one who cared. Cold fury settled inside her.

"Have you watched the Pageant before, Anna?" asked Rose.

The girl brightened. That was not a question that Rose had asked anyone else that day.

"Yes, Priest. I've seen four Pageants, including the last one." She gave Wilder a shy look.

"Would you say your performance is up to the same standard as the performers in those previous Pageants?" Rose's voice was as flat as cold steel.

The girl squirmed and cast her eyes between Rose and Wilder, unsure where to look.

Rose felt Wilder's attention turn to her, but she continued staring at the girl. "I think if you are honest with yourself, you will realize it is not."

The girl's throat bobbed, and she blinked her eyes furiously.

Rose leaned forward and clasped her hands before her on the table. "This Pageant is the highest form of devotion we can offer to the Goddess. You love the Goddess, don't you?"

The girl nodded, and a tear slid down her cheek.

"Good." Rose sat up tall in her seat. Wilder's eyes were boring into the side of her head, but she wouldn't let him distract her from this. "Then please honor her by taking this Pageant seriously and walking off the stage."

The girl breathed in one shaking sob. She straightened her shoulders and walked slowly off stage. Rose was impressed the girl didn't run off. The girl was a terrible singer, but at least she had enough backbone to walk off proudly.

Rose picked up the next slightly crumpled paper. "Who's next?"

She became slowly aware of the hushed crowd behind her and the unnaturally calm Wilder at her side.

"Why, Rose?" His voice was soft, but in the dead silence, it felt like a shout. "Why did you say that to her?"

"This is a joke to them, Wilder," she hissed. "No one is taking this Pageant seriously except me. The entire City acts like we can survive without the Goddess's Gifts. But we can't. This Pageant is our only chance! And these people want to ruin it."

Wilder closed his eyes and rubbed his hands across his face.

He took a deep breath and turned in his chair to face her straight on.

"You can't return the City to the way it was, Rose. That City is dead. Even if the Goddess returns her Gifts to the Priests, everything will still be different. You can't fix your problems with a Pageant."

His quiet words did the opposite of calm her. "Of course you don't care about this Pageant, Wilder. You already ruined the last one. Why not do it again?"

She saw a spark light behind his eyes and was glad to see she struck him.

His jaw flexed as if he was holding back a stream of words. He leaned forward and whispered so only she could hear. "You have no idea what you want, Rose." He was so close she could count the tiny flecks of gold in his dark eyes. "But if you want to be a follower of the Goddess, then act like one."

18

Rose made it back to Temple Perfection sooner than expected. After her "conversation" with the last girl, the four remaining auditioners left. Rose was relieved. She assumed they left because they were as terrible as the girl.

She felt a twinge of guilt at the rude thought but was accustomed to pushing down her guilt. Priests shouldn't feel guilty. They should be above mistakes. They should be perfect. Even if they felt like a failure.

She didn't want to risk running into Fitz in their room, so she found a seat near one of the relaxation pools in the courtyard. If Fitz looked at her with the same disappointed expression as Wilder, she wouldn't be able to sleep in the same room as him tonight. Wilder's accusatory eyes had followed her as she left the park. It wasn't seemly for a Priest to hurry, but she walked quicker than usual to escape his glare at her back.

The relaxation pool wasn't as relaxing as she hoped. Without the Purity Priests to move the water, keeping clean water flowing through the pipes was a complicated job. Priests abandoned the decorative pools to focus on providing clean drinking water. As she looked around the courtyard, she saw a Priest working on a set of pipes alongside a rough-looking older man. The man from the Underneath was teaching the Priest how to work on pipes without the help of a Gift.

The Priest was learning to become a plumber.

Everywhere she turned, there was more proof. Wilder was right. The City would never go back the way it was. She didn't want to think about everything Wilder said, so she got her papers out and sorted through them.

Despite the abundance of terrible to mediocre singers, they had seen several outstanding performances. She had taken plenty of notes so she would remember who was who. She'd thought she would go over the list of possibilities with Wilder later, but that idea seemed unlikely now.

She turned a page and found something different in the stack. It wasn't performance notes. It was a flyer.

Celebrate equality and freedom at the circus tonight!
Gymnasts, trained horses, freaks, and fun!
Bring coin for the food and drink vendors,
but enjoy the show for free!

She recognized Vaylan's words on the page. He mixed this invitation into her stack of papers when he handed them back to her. She found the backhanded method of invitation irritating. She obviously was not going.

However, if this was where people like Vaylan gathered, maybe she should go. He clearly wasn't a fan of Priests, and by association, she assumed whoever created this circus wasn't either. She owed it to her fellow Priests to discover who might set themselves up as their opposition.

She looked closer at the hand-drawn designs around the edges and realized where she had seen more of these flyers.

Scattered on the floor in Remy's trashed apartment.

Was this group associated with whoever took the Sentinel armor? Maybe the people who stole it weren't trying to set themselves up as new High Priests, but as something else?

Rose made her way to her room and was pleased to see that Fitz was out. Her clothes were piled in the bottom of her closet, and she frowned at her unusually sloppy behavior. She hung up each item carefully in its proper order and then considered her options.

What did one wear to the circus?

The sun had already set when Rose left for the circus. She hadn't seen Fitz all afternoon. Was it normal to have a roommate but never see them? She didn't mind because it gave her plenty of time to get ready alone. She had changed out of her flowy dress and wore her leather pants with the knife holster along with her high collar jacket with the secret sheath. And because she didn't want to look too serious, she wore her crop top underneath the short jacket. She got the feeling she would still be showing less skin than anyone there.

The only experience she had with a circus was when she had broken into Temple Perfection when the Warden of Peculiarity occupied it. The Warden had set up a circus in the center of the temple courtyard, and Rose and Ylena had walked into the middle of it. They'd ended the night in sequined leotards, riding a horse through the City.

Highly undignified, but Rose had to admit she'd quite enjoyed it.

She heard the circus before she saw it. Laughter and music rang through the dark streets. She couldn't imagine what the High Priests would do if they were still alive. They'd likely execute everyone within a five-block radius and go from there.

She approached the edge of the park and looked around. She was correct about the limited clothing. Bare skin was the fabric of choice. It wasn't until she studied the bright colors of their minimal clothing that she realized what she should have considered earlier.

She was the only Priest here.

Besides the fact that most respectable Priests didn't venture out into the City at night to do questionable activities, she received the invite from someone who obviously wasn't a fan of Priests. Rose should have realized that she would be the only Priest in attendance. She hadn't disguised the fact that she was a Priest since before the Wardens were defeated. She wondered if she needed to pick up a few items of clothing that weren't black.

If she could find some money to pay for it.

The street leading to the giant stone bridges was ringed with stone pillars topped in glowing crystalline, so she clung to the dark shadows in between. People filled the streets— laughing and eating and drinking—but she couldn't detect any signs of a circus. She considered giving up and heading back to the temple.

Galloping hoofbeats sounded on the stone a moment before a horse leaped from behind her.

Rose jumped out of the way and tried to catch her breath. A woman sat bareback on a horse that shone a pale gray in the crystalline's light. She wore a glittery leotard, and ribbons flowed through her unbound hair. She laughed in glee as she rode the horse through the crowd of people. Rose thought that if she wasn't successful with the Pageant returning the Gifts, maybe she would train for that woman's job.

Then she felt guilty for the sacrilege.

Rose moved closer to the stage and stood in the shadows within a cluster of trees. The woman bounded up to the front of the crowd, and the horse turned in circles under her careful hand.

"Ladies and gentlemen!" The woman's loud voice rang through the park. "Welcome to the circus above!" The people cheered and moved closer to the stage. The woman raised her arms, and the crowd quieted under her touch. "Tonight, we celebrate our freedom! The High Priests and Wardens were defeated, and now we live as we choose. The Virtues of the Goddess and the rules of the Priests constrain us no longer. We are all equal, whether we are from above or below. So we celebrate! Eat, drink, and play as a people united!"

The crowd cheered as contortionists and gymnasts and flame eaters flowed out from the stage. Rose was in the middle of a crowd of people who had cheered at the downfall of her religion, then devolved into a dance party frenzy. She didn't know how to get back to the temple without walking through a crowd of people.

She looked into the crowd, trying to find the shortest path, when a man stepped in front of her, blocking her view. She gasped, fumbling for her knife as she pressed herself further back against the wall.

Vaylan smoothed his hand over his goatee to hide his smile. "I didn't expect you to wear all black."

Relief and irritation washed through her at the familiar voice. "You could have warned me there was a dress code. And perhaps a warning on the heresy as well?"

He chuckled. "Maybe they will write it on the flyer next time." He lifted a bright orange cloak he held at his side. "This is all I could find on short notice."

She grabbed the cloak out of his hand and stepped out of the shadows as she slipped it on. Anonymity slid over her shoulders, and she sighed in relief.

"Thank you," she said. "I'll return this to you at the next

audition. I assume you will be there. Enjoy your night." She strode purposefully through the crowd, but her shoulders slumped as she considered her normally proud Priest attire hidden under the ugly orange cloak.

19

Rose didn't want Vaylan to see her run away, so she kept her pace quick but steady. She had to weave through groups of dancing people with the orange cloak pulled tight around her shoulders. She hopped out of the way of a careening set of dancers and ran straight into Tayeh.

Their collision knocked the breath out of Rose, but Tayeh was unfazed. She crossed her arms over her chest. "I didn't expect to find you in a place like this." She grunted. "Nice cloak."

Rose adjusted the cloak self-consciously. "I didn't have much choice. No one told me there was a dress code."

The corner of Tayeh's mouth twitched. "I think there is probably only one clothing rule here, and everything you own breaks it."

Rose rolled her eyes. "Yeah, that information would have been helpful a couple of hours ago, thanks."

Tayeh raised an eyebrow but didn't respond.

The two white wolves sprinted out of the bushes and stopped at Rose's feet. The ruff of their necks fluffed, and she heard their low growl, despite the noise of the busy street.

"You!" Rose pointed at them. "Where were you last night?" They sat down, but their necks still twitched. "You realize that Wilder could have been knocked out and dragged off to Goddess knows where, and then what would you do?" She crossed her arms as she glared at them. "I assume you smelled the blood on him? That failure is on you, girls. If he belongs to you, then do your job, you hear me?"

The wolves lowered onto their front paws and let out a brief whine. Rose nodded her head. "Don't let it happen again. You can go now." They leaped up and ran into the night.

Tayeh stared at her with wide eyes.

Rose straightened her cloak. "Well, I must be going."

Tayeh shook her head as if waking up. "Would you like me to walk you back to the temple?" She stared off in the direction the wolves had run. "Not that I don't think you can defend yourself, but there are a lot of weirdos out tonight and um ... you are dressed wrong."

Rose sighed. "You're right. Sure, I'd appreciate the escort."

Tayeh fell into step beside her, and they walked in silence for a while. It surprised Rose when Tayeh spoke.

"I saw Wilder earlier. He told me what you found at the apartment last night."

"Did he tell you how I was an idiot and dropped my blade when I tried to fight?"

Tayeh's head turned sharply. "What? No ... That happened?"

"Yes. It was embarrassing." Rose sighed. "And I'm not sure why I revealed it to you when Wilder didn't." Maybe it was a good sign Wilder hadn't been telling his friends every stupid thing she had done over the last few days.

"Fumbling a blade might be embarrassing, but you're alive, so you obviously recovered. That's the important part."

Rose studied Tayeh out of the corner of her eye. Tayeh walked confidently with her head held high. Her full textured hair added to her height, making her appear taller. Her eyes scanned the crowd, looking for threats and finding no one to challenge her. She was strong, despite never calling the wind.

"I didn't just fumble the blade. I tried calling the wind. I forgot it was gone." She realized she once again had confessed to this stupid mistake. But Tayeh was calm and always appeared unruffled. Rose instinctively felt safe with her.

Tayeh shrugged. "You relied on your training. That's nothing to be ashamed of. But you should have trained without the wind, too."

Rose prickled. "It's not like anyone expected this. I wasn't supposed to lose my Gift."

"Maybe," said Tayeh. "But there's a tea out there that can smother your Gift. Even if your Gift returns, you should be prepared."

Rose furrowed her brow in thought. She hadn't considered that. She had heard about the tea, but no one had ever used it on her. Tayeh made a good point, though. Rose had been short-sighted to never train without the wind.

"You're right," said Rose.

Tayeh raised an eyebrow but continued walking straight ahead.

"I need to train as if my Gift won't return. And when it does, I'll be ready for anything."

They arrived at Temple Perfection. Rose thanked Tayeh for the protection, then headed up the stairs.

Tayeh cleared her throat. "If you are serious about training, I'd be happy to help when I'm free. But until then, maybe you should ask Wilder. He's an excellent teacher."

Rose wasn't sure if Wilder would want to teach her anything since he was so disappointed in her. But she said, "Thanks, Tayeh. Maybe I'll ask him."

"I think training together will be good for you both." Tayeh's lips curled in a sly grin as she headed off into the night.

DISCIPLINE

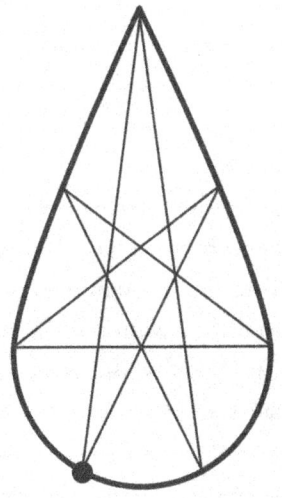

20

Rose walked into the temple courtyard the next morning and found Fitz, Wilder, and the two wolves waiting. She had prepared to make the walk on her own and was surprised they waited for her again. The last time they traveled through the City, the conversation was pleasant, but their presence caused a stir. And now they had wolves.

"Good morning, gentlemen," she said to Wilder and Fitz. "Ladies," she nodded to the wolves. They ducked their heads as if in a bow.

Wilder gave the wolves an odd look. "They didn't leave my side all night. Usually, they roam at night and find me in the morning." He looked back up at Rose and shrugged. "Maybe I've been gone too much and they missed me?"

Rose snorted. Maybe they were finally taking their job seriously. If only everyone in the City would do the same.

Fitz lifted his bag onto his shoulder and smiled at Rose. "Are you ready to head home?"

She sucked in a small breath. The question felt very personal. "Um ... actually, yes." She started walking down the temple stairs so she could avoid their eyes. "It will be good to be back for a few days."

Wilder looked at the temple in the distance with a thoughtful expression. "The temples all seem so similar to me. I never considered that only one would be your home."

She sniffed. "Well, I guess Fitz is more considerate than you."

Wilder slapped him on the back as they walked. "That's true. Fitz has always been one of the kindest people in the Underneath. I don't know where I would be today without him."

Fitz ducked his head, but his face lit up. "Thanks, Wilder. That means a lot to me."

His hair shone pale pink in the morning sunlight. He was in his orange jacket again, though it looked like he had found some better-fitting pants. Or maybe he had just made friends with a tailor.

"I rarely see you in our room, Fitz. What do you do when you aren't assisting with the auditions?"

Fitz didn't want to meet her eyes and bit his lips as he considered his answer. "I spend a lot of time studying." He gulped, then said quickly, "And praying." He locked his eyes firmly on the ground.

She caught Wilder staring at her with those intense eyes. It was important to him how she responded. She didn't want to see the disappointment in his eyes again, so she decided to respond well.

"That's ... good." Her response was not as brilliant as she hoped.

It was enough encouragement that Fitz raised his head a little. "I never had access to so many books in the Underneath. I had to save up for months to buy a book. Or hope a good friend would steal one for me." He gave a sideways grin to Wilder.

Wilder grinned back, then locked his eyes on Rose, waiting for her response. She gave an honest one.

"You had to steal books? You should have had access to them. The Goddess says, 'Knowledge is available to all.'"

Fitz gave her an eager look. "I rarely had books, but I always had access to Knowledge. You can always gain Knowledge, if you know where to look."

She pulled back in surprise. "That's a very progressive idea, Fitz. I know theologians who could debate that idea for hours."

His eager look became tentative. Wilder's eyes grew even more intense.

She took a breath and weighed her words. "I find most debates tedious, but I respect those with the skill. I always appreciate a worthy fight. Sounds like you would fit in."

His face beamed, and his shoulders straightened under his orange jacket.

Wilder's dark eyes settled into a comfortable warmth.

Rose thought through Fitz's words and remembered his book of liturgies she discovered on the day they met. "Have you found enough books to read? Even if they aren't the only path to Knowledge."

He smiled at her with honest delight. "You are kind to ask. Up here, people leave books casually lying about. The temples have books in forgotten cabinets or stacked on shelves as decoration. It's so strange to me that no one cares if I pick up a book to read. I try to put them back where I found them since I don't know if the Library will change their mind about free books lying around."

Her eyebrows drew together at his strange statement. "What do you mean?"

"The Library in Knowledge charges a fee for people to read the books inside. I don't know—"

Rose stopped in the center of the road. "What did you say?" she growled.

Fitz leaned back in surprise. "Um ... I heard you need money to read the books, and ..." His words trailed off as he saw the look in Rose's eyes.

Her voice was fiery as she breathed out a single word.

"Blasphemy."

Her body shook with rage. How could anyone think this was acceptable? Who was responsible for sacrilege so heinous?

There was only one answer.

Priests.

She couldn't blame this on the High Priests. This was the work of the surviving Priests. Shame burned in her at the blasphemy committed by Priests like her.

Not like her.

She looked Fitz in the eyes. "I won't let this stand. I will fix it."

He took her hand and gave her a warm smile. "You are a good Priest, Rose. The City is blessed to have you."

The gentle blessing caught her off guard. Her fury at the Priests warred with her feelings of gratitude for his kind words.

She choked down the warm feelings and fueled the fire again. "I'm going to the Library right now. I don't know how long it will take, but I hope to be there and back before the audition. If I had my Gift, I could run to Knowledge so much faster ..." She straightened her bag on her shoulder and started running.

Wilder left Fitz behind and ran to catch her by the arm. "Rose, wait." He pulled her to a stop. His dark eyes glittered in the sunlight, and his hand on her arm was warm. He spoke quietly and for her alone. "Thank you."

"For what?" she asked. "I haven't done anything yet. And if you don't let go, I'll be late." She needed to leave now to get all the way across the City, but a part of her didn't want him to let go.

"For the way you spoke to Fitz. I was worried you might

speak like ..." His voice trailed off.

She saw the lingering disappointment in his eyes. "Like I spoke to the girl yesterday?"

He nodded.

She tried to retain her dignity, despite her desire to remove that look from his eyes. "Occasionally, I can be a little ... harsh."

He raised an eyebrow at the understatement.

She stood up taller. "And you might not like to hear this, but I plan on walking into that Library today and being *very* harsh." She refused to back down from her intensity.

She thought the disappointment would return to his eyes, but instead, she saw something very different.

A fire to match her own.

She imagined bursting into the Library with him at her side. They would call out the blasphemy of those Priests and reopen the Library as it should be. She could picture herself doing it.

With Wilder.

She swayed under the realization, but his warm hand held her firm. She wanted her vision to be true, but it terrified her.

"You can't go now, Rose." His voice was still quiet, and Fitz had remained a few steps behind, pretending to look at something else. "We have a responsibility to the people counting on us for these auditions. But we will arrive in Knowledge soon enough. You will make it right. I believe in you."

There wasn't enough air flowing through the wide street. Her skin heated under the bright sun with no breeze to cool her. She dragged a breath into her lungs.

"I will wait," she said.

Wilder's fierce eyes settled into a simmer, and he released her arm. "Good," he said. "But don't wait too long." His smile shot through her.

He summoned Fitz and the wolves with a nod of his head, and they continued the walk to Discipline.

21

Rose's body relaxed as she neared home. The streets were still busy with new shops and vendors and people she had never seen, but she knew the shape of the buildings well. She had only been gone a few days, but the familiar pattern of the streets was enough to calm her.

She transferred her fury about the Library to a back shelf in her mind. She would deal with it. There was no doubt about that. But for now, she would enjoy her time in Discipline and continue to do her job.

Wilder, Fitz, and the wolves followed her up the steps into the temple. She passed the familiar training equipment: balance beams, rings, and climbing walls. They walked around the circular courtyard until she found the training room she wanted. She came to a sharp stop when she looked inside.

Dozens of kids were running in a loop around the large gym. Windows along the tall ceiling let in the bright sunlight, and the arched doorways let in a breeze. The kids all wore matching uniforms of bright blue shirts and shorts with gleaming white shoes. And at the center of the running children stood her brother, Kai.

His black uniform was the traditional wrapped jacket with loose-fitting pants they often wore to train in Discipline. She could tell he had been running along with the kids by the glimmer of sweat on his forehead. He pushed his glossy black hair away from his face and whistled loudly.

The kids stopped in their tracks before lining up in neat lines before him. He nodded and walked around them while he talked.

"Good work today. You all have made a lot of progress with your weight training. As usual, we need to keep working on our agility. Learning how to be quick is a skill that will help us, no matter what job we are doing. See you tomorrow." The kids ran toward the doors. He called after them, "Get some water before you leave!"

Wilder, Rose, and Fitz held still as the kids swarmed past them. A few kids squealed in delight at the sight of the wolves, and the wolves hopped out into the courtyard and submitted themselves to what Rose thought were some very undignified belly rubs. Kai looked up and waved the three humans inside.

"Rosie! I thought you would arrive soon." Kai pointed at the children as they left. "What do you think of my kids? Do you think I can whip them into shape?"

"I didn't know you were training students now." She knew she would find him in their usual training room, but the kids were unexpected.

He shrugged. "It's a new day. Everybody has to find new ways to be useful. It turns out I'm a decent teacher. People actually pay me to train their kids to be more like me."

"They pay you?" she asked.

He laughed. "It shocked me, too! But like I said, it's a new day." He looked up at Wilder and Fitz. "So, are you going to introduce me or be as rude as usual?"

She slapped him on the arm. "Kai, this is Wilder and Fitz.

We are working on the auditions together. Wilder, Fitz, this is my brother, Kai. He is exactly as obnoxious as he seems."

Kai studied Wilder. "Wilder ... I've heard about you."

Rose smacked Kai's arm again. "He already knows he's famous. Don't encourage him."

Wilder grinned at her.

"No," said Kai. "I heard about him from Caed."

Wilder's face went slack.

Rose looked between them, unsure how she could recover the situation.

"If I may say so,"—Fitz rested a supportive arm on Wilder's shoulder—"rumors don't always tell the full story. I think it's best to make your own decisions about someone, preferably over a good meal."

Rose and Kai both stared at Fitz with wide eyes. Wilder remained silent.

Kai looked at Rose. "Did you actually make friends with a smart person for a change, Rosie?"

She smacked him again.

"I like the way you think, Fitz," said Kai, with a crooked grin. "I guess we should go get some dinner."

"Not until you shower, Kai." Rose scrunched her nose. "You smell worse than the kids."

Rose and Fitz took their bags to her old room. Someone had moved an extra bed in, and it seemed even more cramped than at the other temples because all of Rose's possessions were still inside. She sighed upon seeing her full closet of clothes and planned to swap out what she took to the remaining temples so she wouldn't have to suffer the indignity of continuing to wear the same things repeatedly.

Since Kai was taking time to shower and change, she took

some time for herself as well. She chose a fitted long-sleeve top with a frilly tulle skirt. She loved the fluffy skirt, and since it wouldn't pack well, she wanted to wear it while she could.

They met in the courtyard, and Kai led them to a new restaurant near the temple. There had been restaurants in the City before, but it seemed like they were everywhere now. She wasn't sure how Kai knew which one to pick unless he went out to eat a lot more than she ever had.

The restaurant's interior glowed with welcoming light. The owners had covered the crystalline lamps with red and gold glass covers, and they cast the individual tables in soft light. Kai led the four of them to a booth, and she sat beside him. Wilder sat across from her and gave her an encouraging smile.

Kai ordered four plates of the curry special, then turned back to the table. "How are the auditions going?"

Fitz laughed. "Fine, as long as Rose doesn't scare off anyone else."

Kai clutched his chest in mock alarm. "Rosie is terrifying the young people auditioning? That is so shocking! Who would have guessed?"

She smacked his arm. "It's not my fault that some of them are awful, Kai. It's embarrassing." She met Wilder's eyes across the table. "Although, I think I might try to traumatize them a little less. It will be quicker without all the crying."

Wilder's eyes held hers, but he hid his smile behind his water glass. His disappointed look was gone, and she hoped to keep it that way.

Kai said, "Interesting ..." She turned to find him studying her.

"What?" she said defensively. "I'm not mean all the time! Only when someone deserves it."

He gave a sardonic grin. "We often disagree on who deserves it. But yes, sometimes you can be surprisingly nice."

He turned to Wilder. "So, Wilder, you are assisting with the Pageant. Are you a follower of the Goddess?"

He asked the question in a warm and casual tone, but Rose's mouth still dropped open. It was just like Kai to drop a serious question into what was supposed to be a fun dinner.

Wilder's usual smile was gone, his face serious but not angry. "Yes. I'm a follower of the Goddess."

At his words, she realized she had never asked him the question herself. Even after her stupid assumption about Fitz, she still never considered Wilder might be a follower of the Goddess. She thought back to their last conversation with Mayra when Wilder mentioned spending time in quiet contemplation of the Goddess. Rose had assumed he was lying. She lowered her head, fidgeting with her napkin.

Kai smiled at Wilder and appeared to be genuinely interested. "I've met a few of the new followers who want to become Priests, and I'm fascinated by their stories. I've heard that most people from the Underneath don't believe in her but that there has always been a very devout group of her followers. Did you learn about the Goddess from them?"

Rose stared at Kai in shock. How had he learned all that? Then she realized that *this* was how he learned it. By asking questions of people he had just met, even if those questions were personal.

Wilder didn't appear to be embarrassed sharing with Kai, but he looked at Rose with apprehension. Did he not want to tell this story in front of her? Why would he trust Kai but not her?

Wilder cleared his throat and continued, "Yes, I met some of those followers. Fitz here was one of them. He is a brilliant theologian, despite his lack of formal training in a temple. And as for how I learned about the Goddess ... Knowledge of her is available to all. You just have to know where to look."

Rose stared at him like she had never seen him. Wilder ...

playful, flirty, swaggering Wilder. Devoted follower of the Goddess Wilder. How had she missed seeing this? She was a Priest. She should have seen this.

He ducked his head, more self-conscious than she had ever seen him. This was personal. Even though she hadn't been the one brave enough to ask, this was a deep and honest piece of him, and he shared it with her.

She took a deep breath and caught his eyes. He shared something intimate with her, and she wanted to be vulnerable with him in return.

"Would you train me to fight?" She cleared her throat, trying to hide her nervousness. "To fight without the wind." His eyes widened, but she continued. "Not that I don't think my Gift will return, but there is that tea, you know, so it is really quite practical."

He asked in a low voice, "You would trust me to train you?"

"Yes," she said. "Tayeh suggested I ask you."

"She did?"

Rose shrugged. "She said it would be good for both of us." Now it was her turn to feel timid. She bit her lips, then asked again. "Will you train me?"

He nodded with serious eyes. "Of course, Rose. I will train you."

"I like this," said Kai.

Rose jumped in her seat. She had forgotten he and Fitz were still there.

"This curry, of course." He pointed at his plate of food that had arrived. "I like this curry." He gave Fitz a meaningful look, which Fitz returned with a thoughtful nod.

22

Rose left the restaurant with the warm feeling of curry in her stomach. She'd enjoyed the meal, but there was one awkward moment at the end when it was time to pay. Because she ate all of her meals at the temple, she forgot that everywhere else in the City charged for meals. She felt a moment of panic at being unprepared.

When the waitress came to take their money, Fitz and Kai handed over their coins, as expected. Rose just stared at the woman, trying to decide on the spot how she would earn money for the meal.

"Oh, Rosie." Kai shook his head. "I guess you haven't found a paying job since you are working on the auditions." He reached into his pocket with a sigh.

"I've got her covered," said Wilder as he handed the coins to the waitress.

"I can't let you do that," said Rose. "You shouldn't have to pay for me."

Kai smacked her on the arm. "Don't be a brat, Rosie. Just say thank you."

She glared at Kai but said to Wilder, "Thank you. That was nice of you."

Kai nodded in approval, then leaned in for a conspiratorial whisper. "Besides, he's from the Underneath. They're the ones with all the money. He's probably loaded."

Her eyes shot to Wilder, who only gave her a sly smile.

When they arrived at the temple, Kai wished her good night, and Fitz said he had some reading to do. Rose and Wilder stood looking at each other in the courtyard.

"I guess we could start training now?" she asked.

He pointed at her frilly tulle skirt. "I don't know if you're dressed for training."

She laughed. "I've got shorts on under this. Besides, I should train in the clothes I might have to fight in."

"Good point." He motioned her to lead the way.

She led him to the dance studio. It was smaller and felt less intimidating than the full gymnasium. The room was dark with only the dim light filtering through the arches.

"Are there lights in here?" he asked.

She felt along the wall for a switch. "I usually dance in the dark, so I forget where the switch is."

"You dance in the dark?" he asked.

She hesitated but answered in the privacy of the dark room. "I don't like to see how bad I've become at it."

She thought he might respond, but she found a switch and turned it on. A metal shield dropped to reveal a slim line of crystalline hugging the stone pipes along the top of the room. She saw more switches but didn't flip them. It was going to be rough enough viewing herself in the mirror, much less if it was under bright crystalline light.

She sighed and joined him in the center of the dance floor.

He studied her face. "It doesn't seem like you really want to be here. Are you sure you want this?"

"I do!" She tried to respond confidently, but her voice still seemed weak. "They hurt you because I wasn't strong enough to do my part. I can't afford to make the same mistake again." She couldn't look at him. "It's ... embarrassing to know how much skill I've lost."

He gripped her forearms gently to get her attention. "Rose, you haven't lost your skill. You lost what gave you an edge, but your former training still applies. Now you only have to learn how to fight like the rest of us mortals."

She looked up to see the smirk she heard in his words. "I'm mortal," she said with a non-committal eye roll.

"Good," he said. "Then you won't have any problems relearning your skills. How about we start with some stretches?"

They flowed through a common warm-up pattern in time with one another. She kept glancing at Wilder's body in the mirror.

But only to check his form, of course. To make sure he was doing it properly. She needed to keep a *very* close eye on him to be sure.

By the end of the warm-up, she was extremely warm. Night air circulated in through the billowing curtains, but not enough to cool her down. The tulle on her frilly skirt was sticking to her sweaty arms and legs, so she took the skirt off and kicked it to the front of the room near her shoes.

When she turned back to face Wilder, he was staring at her with wide eyes. She still wore her long-sleeve top along with the tight shorts that had been under the skirt, so it wasn't like she was naked. She frequently danced or trained in less. But she had surprised him, and he seemed off-kilter.

She found it invigorating.

Wilder liked to tease and flirt and throw women off balance, and here he was, avoiding looking at her in the mirror. And yet, something inside her knew he desperately wanted to look.

She savored the feeling for one more breath, then rescued him.

"I learned all the katas from Priests in the temple. Are they the same ones as in the Underneath?"

He turned to face her, and he blinked several times, apparently getting his brain to catch up to her questions. "For the most part. Different fighting styles adapt them for their practice, but the basic katas are the foundation."

"Should we start with the basics?" she asked.

He took a breath in and seemed to be back to normal. "Great idea. Let's begin."

They stood side by side, facing the mirror, and ran through the basic katas. Their smooth movements blurred the line between fighting and dancing. Slow, deliberate motions alternated with sharp, simulated attacks. Since they both knew every step, they moved from form to form with few words. Their bodies flowed smoothly through the intricate combinations—each step meticulous and each finger a precise work of art. They looked in the mirror, timing the exact positions of their bodies with one another.

She watched his body closely to make sure all her movements were as precise as his.

He watched her body closely to give corrections to her form.

They watched each other so closely that their moves were perfectly in sync. Their breathing echoed through the room in matched harmony.

They studied each other's movements until they were both sweating and breathless, then Wilder held up a hand to pause.

They had never touched during the katas, but when he raised his hand, she felt like she had won a battle. She smiled and looked in the mirror to twist her sweaty hair into a better knot.

He squinted in pain. "I probably should have tightened this

bandage before we started." In the mirror, she saw him study the sleeve of his white shirt where a spot of blood was blooming.

She ran to him and swatted his hand away so she could roll up his sleeve.

"I can't believe I forgot you were injured," she said.

"I'm sure you are used to only training with people who are in perfect condition." He stood still, allowing her to rewrap his bandage.

"Yes, of course," she said. "There are Perfection Priests who live close by for that specific reason. There's no reason to train while injured."

"Except that sometimes you have to fight while injured," he said.

Her hands stilled on his arm. "I guess I should learn to fight without the wind and also while injured." She tucked the last bit of the bandage into place. He lowered his arm, but she couldn't remove her hand from where she held him.

"When the time comes, you will do what needs to be done, Rose. The other night, when it really mattered, you did what was necessary. You just have to believe in yourself again."

She couldn't bring herself to look into his eyes. He believed she could do whatever it took. But she had lost that faith in herself.

"It will take time." His voice was quiet. "I'm not going anywhere."

She finally looked up to meet his eyes. His face glistened in the faint light of the crystalline, and his hair shimmered in perfectly shaped little spirals. He studied her with an intensity that threatened to buckle her knees. She tried to take a breath but couldn't move her lungs.

It was too powerful. It was too much.

It was too dangerous.

The warning bells in her mind went off again. She tried to

play this moment forward in her brain and couldn't imagine where it would end. Her plans and dreams didn't have this moment factored into it. She couldn't make it fit.

She let go of his arm and stepped back.

"Thank you for the training." She bit her lip and tried to figure out where to go from there.

Wilder took a deep breath in, as if the air had suddenly returned to the room. "Of course, Rose." His voice was polite.

"I should go," she said. She gathered her skirt and shoes and backed toward an arch. She felt herself filling the room with words. "And thanks again for dinner. I guess I need to find a job if I'm going to go out anymore."

He stood in the middle of the floor and watched her go.

23

Rose spent the morning enjoying the familiar courtyard of Temple Discipline. She took her breakfast outside and watched the people, both Priests and not, walking in and out of the temple. The breakfast choices were limited since the Uprising, but she was grateful to have food she didn't have to pay for.

She leaned back against the warm stone of the temple when Priest Mayra stepped out flanked by two Priests of Temple Discipline. Rose wouldn't have thought about them at all, except that as they walked down the temple steps, Mayra looked around to see if anyone was watching them. She couldn't see Rose in her spot against the temple wall, so she smoothed back her neat gray hair and continued on her way without stopping.

Priest Mayra's glance might have been innocent, but Rose's senses perked up because of the two Priests that followed her.

Rose despised them both.

Rose hated when people lumped all Priests together with the High Priests. She knew there were a lot of good Priests like Priest Frances and her brothers and sisters. But she wasn't under the illusion that all Priests were good. She wanted to defend them just because they were Priests, but there were several she didn't trust at all.

Dalton and Travers were two Priests in that category. They were older Priests in Temple Discipline, and she had known them her entire life. Dalton enjoyed berating the students in his training sessions, and Travers seemed to always have his hands on his young dancers. They both made Rose's skin crawl, but with no blatant sins, they'd always escaped the notice of the High Priests. Or they were politically clever enough to negotiate with the High Priests to overlook their sins.

And Priest Mayra was traveling to every temple and meeting with people like them.

She stood to follow them when Wilder walked out of the temple.

He smiled at her. "One night of training, and now you are heading out to a fight."

"What? How do you know where I'm heading?"

"I've seen that look in your eyes before. You look ready to fight."

"Maybe I am." She looked in the direction they had gone. "And I've got to go now before I lose them." She headed down the stairs, and Wilder fell into step at her side.

"So, what's the plan here?" he asked.

She looked at him in confusion. "Plan? Mayra is meeting with two Priests I don't trust. It looks suspicious. I'm going to find out what they are doing."

Wilder nodded. "Okay, that's the start of a plan. Any idea how you will overhear them without being seen?"

She lost her focus on Mayra for a minute to look at Wilder. "Without being seen? Of course they will see me. I'm going to demand they tell me what is going on here."

Wilder bit his lip but couldn't hide his grin. "That is one strategy."

She narrowed her eyes at him but continued following Mayra. "You have a problem with my plan?"

"No," he said. "It sounds perfect. If you want them to be on their guard and hide whatever they are doing."

"And you have a better plan?"

His lips twitched with a restrained smile. "I have a bit of experience in this line of work."

"Work? Following suspicious people is a job people pay for?"

"If you are good at it. But honestly, Rose, I'm not sure you will be good at it."

She rounded on him with a glare, but his eyes followed Mayra and the other two about a block ahead of them. If she hadn't seen the hint of a teasing grin, she would have smacked him on his injured arm.

"I'm good at a lot of things," she said. "I'll be good at this."

Mayra opened the door to a flower shop and ushered the other two Priests inside. Wilder headed to the back of the building and nodded for Rose to follow.

She scrambled to his side as he pressed his ear against the door. He turned the doorknob, and when he found it unlocked, he shook his head with a quiet laugh.

"There are only two rules if you want to be good at this." He held up two fingers. "Don't be seen, and don't be heard."

She rolled her eyes. "I can do that."

He gave her a look that said, "We'll see about that."

He cracked the door open slowly, then slid inside. She followed on his heels, stepping as quietly as possible. She would prove to him she was good at this.

They tiptoed through the cool storage room. The lingering scent of flowers hung in the air, but the shop was no longer in use. She guessed people weren't wasting their money on decorative flowers right now.

Wilder pressed his ear against the door leading to the front of the shop, and she copied the movement.

"... the other temples. We must find Priests who are thinking about the long term." Mayra's voice was clear. "We have to make decisions that will ensure the best future for the City."

"Of course we want that," said Travers. "But these ideas are controversial. How do you propose we convince the others?"

"There's one way to convince people," said Dalton. "We need more money."

Rose's eyes widened, but she didn't move. Wilder faced her with his ear still against the door, and she refused to move first.

"I'll get you money," said Mayra. "But you have to work for it. You must guarantee that we have the support we need. We need all the Priests in agreement when we select the new High Priests."

Rose's mind caught fire. They were planning on selecting High Priests by paying Priests to ensure their support. She would put an end to this right now.

Wilder pressed a finger against her lips.

Her mind skidded to a halt.

Then he held up two fingers in his other hand. Two rules. Don't be seen. Don't be heard.

Wilder's callused finger rested lightly on her lips, delicately holding her in place by her own choice.

"We will get the support," said Travers from the other room.

Wilder's finger dropped, leaving warmth in its wake.

"If you keep the money flowing, we can do miracles, Mayra," said Dalton.

Rose shook with anger, but she stilled at Wilder's raised eyebrow. She would follow the rules.

"Leave the miracles to the Goddess," said Mayra with disgust. "Just help me bring this City back under control. Understood?"

Rose didn't know if they understood, but she heard the door close as they left. Before she had time to put her anger into words, Wilder led the way to the back door and into the alley.

He didn't speak until they were a few blocks away. "I have to admit, you did better than I thought."

"Exactly what did you think I would do?" she asked.

"I thought you would storm into the room at the first thing you didn't approve of."

"It's not about my approval, Wilder. They are talking about setting up new High Priests. How can anyone think that is a good idea?"

He cleared his throat. "A third rule to spying is that you shouldn't walk down the street, yelling about what you heard."

She lowered her voice and looked around. "I can't just pretend I didn't hear that. So, what are we going to do?"

A small smile crept across his lips. "You think *we* should do something about it?"

"Yes. You care about this too, right?"

"I do care," he said. "But I won't force you to work with me if you don't want to."

She dropped her voice even lower. "I never said I didn't want to work with you." She straightened her shoulders. "Besides, it's actually you working with me, not me working with you."

He grinned. "Of course, Priest Rose."

24

After spying on Mayra, Rose and Wilder headed straight to the park for the audition. Fitz paced near their table with the paperwork in his hands.

"You're here!" Fitz sagged in relief. "I had no idea what to do if you were late. I thought I'd have dozens of angry Goddess hopefuls to deal with."

"Sorry to worry you," said Wilder. "I was assisting Rose with some very important Priest business. I learned a lot by watching her handle the situation."

Fitz gave him a look that said he didn't know what that meant and didn't want to find out.

Rose huffed and took her seat at the table. "I'm ready to begin whenever the two of you are."

Wilder and Fitz exchanged grins, then took their places.

The audition went smoother than last time. Rose wondered if word about what she had said to the terrible singer had moved to this location. If so, she was glad it helped filter out some of the worst singers, but she wouldn't tell Wilder that.

No matter how good or bad the singer was, Rose reacted

with calm coolness. She was proud of her restraint. She hoped Wilder noticed how nice she was.

A young man took the stage. He looked out at Wilder and gave him a slight nod, which Wilder returned. She looked at him with a question in her eyes.

"I know him. He was one of Tayeh's roommates." At her raised eyebrows, he added, "Don't worry. I can be impartial."

Wilder had misinterpreted her look. Her reaction was because she had forgotten that some performers might be from the Underneath. They weren't required to say where they were from on their paperwork, but she always assumed the performers were from the Diocese they were auditioning in.

If Wilder hadn't told her that this young man was from the Underneath, she wouldn't have guessed it. He sang one of the Companion's songs with the same passion as the other auditioners, and his voice was better than most. She asked herself if she expected the performers from the Underneath to be less skilled than those from the City and didn't like her honest answer.

The audience gave his performance the same polite applause as the others.

Wilder turned to her. "Do you mind if we take a break now? I haven't talked to him for a while, and I'd like to see if he has any helpful news from the Underneath."

"Sure. Of course," she said. It felt strange for her to consider Wilder's life in the Underneath. He had an entire network of friends that she would probably never meet.

He smiled and jogged up to the stage. She watched him talk to the young man and tried to imagine their conversation.

Vaylan slid smoothly into Wilder's chair. "Looks like you forgot to bring my cloak with you."

Irritation flared at herself for forgetting and at him for bringing it up.

He chuckled. "I'm joking. I would never wear an orange cloak. You can keep it."

Vaylan was wearing another well-tailored dark blue suit, and she had to admit his style was on point.

"Are you here to invite me to another one of your heresy parties?" she asked.

"Would you attend if I did?"

"Unlikely. I think the last one was educational enough."

"I think you understand the ideas more than you'd like to admit." He looked at Wilder and the young man from the Underneath. "If things had remained as they were, the people from the Underneath would still be trapped below under the rule of the Priests."

She growled. "It was the High Priests' doing. Not the Priests."

"If the Priests had defeated the High Priests on their own, would they have thrown open the doors to the Underneath?"

She opened her mouth to retort but then closed it again. Would Priests like Mayra and her cronies have opened the doors to the Underneath and let the people stream up the staircases inside the temples?

Would she?

His low voice crawled into her mind. "I think you know the answer to that question, if you're honest. But maybe circumstances have caused you to reconsider." He looked at Wilder again. "Maybe you are questioning if some things you believed are actually true."

She didn't want to admit to him the doubts she had. She pushed those dark fears into the icy part of her soul and turned to face Vaylan.

"I know what I believe, and no one will change that." She put on her coldest Priest stare. "I'd appreciate it if you leave now. I have the Goddess's work to do."

"Of course, Priest Rose." Vaylan stood. "But you can't

unhear what I've said. And you won't get rid of your doubts by getting rid of me. I'm not the only person causing you to reconsider what you believe." He bowed to her before walking away.

Rose was quiet during the rest of the auditions and relied on Wilder to thank each person and send them on their way. She took her notes on each performer, but her mind was replaying her conversation with Vaylan. Were her beliefs changing? Considering that her whole world had changed, it made sense that her beliefs might follow. But something about that rubbed her the wrong way. Even if the world changed, she didn't want to.

Vaylan said that he wasn't the only one causing her beliefs to change. She was intensely aware of Wilder's presence at her side. Was Wilder affecting what she believed? What did it say about her if she changed her beliefs because of a boy? She found the idea distasteful.

The auditions wrapped for the day with no drama. Rose gathered her papers and started the walk back to the temple. Wilder waved goodbye to Fitz and fell into step beside her.

"You've been quiet this afternoon. Is everything okay?" he asked.

She didn't want to discuss the shameful doubt in her heart, so instead she asked, "Do you believe the Priests were chosen by the Goddess?"

Wilder stiffened like an animal sensing a trap. "I wasn't sure if you were interested in my opinions about religion."

She pulled herself up taller. "It's not that your opinion will change my mind, of course. I'm just curious about what you believe."

Out of the corner of her eye, she could see him consider his response. "I believe there are a lot of ways to be chosen by the Goddess."

She narrowed her eyes as she thought through his answer,

but she didn't discuss it further. They walked on in silence until they approached the temple.

And found Mayra waiting in the courtyard.

Rose's fury returned in a rush, and she hurried her steps.

Wilder pulled her to a stop before they were close enough for Mayra to overhear.

"Rose, if you go up there with that look in your eyes, she will know something is going on."

Rose ground her teeth together. "Maybe I want her to know that I know."

Wilder frowned. "If she knows you are suspicious, she will be more secretive about her meetings and make it harder for us to follow her. The more information we can gather about this in secret, the better."

Rose breathed in deeply and nodded. Wilder removed his hand from her arm and walked up the stairs to the courtyard by her side.

"Good afternoon, Priest Rose. Wilder." Mayra nodded to them properly. "I pray the auditions are going well."

"Yes, Priest Mayra," Wilder's voice was smooth as usual. "We will have no problems choosing skilled acolytes."

Priest Mayra gave Wilder her usual fond smile, then turned her hard eyes on Rose. "And how is it going with you, Priest Rose? Are you avoiding distractions?"

Mayra had watched her conversation with Wilder before they approached. From Mayra's place, it appeared the two of them had a private conversation with his hand on her arm. Even though that is exactly what happened, Rose was not pleased that Mayra noticed.

"With all due respect, Priest Mayra." Rose could sense Wilder holding his breath, but she continued. "I am an adult Priest, and I will manage my own distractions." Rose gave her a piercing glare. "Unless you've become High Priest recently?"

Wilder closed his eyes and shook his head slowly.

Priest Mayra's hard eyes turned shrewd. Rose could feel Mayra studying her to determine exactly what she knew.

"Of course not, Priest Rose," said Mayra slowly. "I think it is a kindness to warn fellow Priests before they walk into dangerous territory."

"Thank you for your kindness." Rose held Mayra's brown eyes without blinking. "I offer the same kindness to you."

Mayra gave her a brittle smile. "Goddess blessing upon you, Priest Rose."

"And also upon you, Priest Mayra." She bowed shortly, then turned on her heel and walked away.

Wilder followed Rose with a sigh. "That didn't turn out the way I hoped."

She continued storming through the temple. "Sorry, I can't fake my emotions as easily as you."

"It's not about being fake, Rose. It's about being strategic. It's about believing in the big picture."

She stopped walking abruptly. "Maybe we don't believe in the same big picture."

A flash sparked behind his dark eyes. "I thought we both believed that choosing new High Priests is a bad idea."

"I do believe that." She pulled herself taller. "But maybe I also believe it is a problem for Priests to solve."

His eyes simmered as he said in a low voice. "Just a few hours ago, you asked me, 'What are *we* going to do about this?' Have you already changed your mind?"

Her blood was still boiling from her conversation with Vaylan and then with Mayra. She could feel it bubbling over, and she didn't want to stop it. "I don't change my mind. Not for you. Not for anyone."

She could feel the anger rolling beneath his skin as he struggled to keep his expression calm. She was pleased to see that he couldn't always fake his emotions.

When his voice came, it was calm and cold. "I'm not asking

you to change, Rose. I'm asking you to be honest about what you want. But if you are too scared to be honest, there's nothing I can do to change that."

He strode away, anger clearly written across his shoulders. Rose watched him go and let her own anger smother her fear.

25

Rose didn't want to spend the evening in her room under the disapproving glare of Fitz. Either Wilder told him what had happened, or Fitz guessed enough from Wilder's attitude. Wilder's bad mood wasn't her fault. Besides, he was good at hiding what he was feeling. He should try a little harder.

She wandered around the streets of Discipline with no exact destination in mind. She heard music and laughter coming from inside a shop. Colorful lights spilled out of the windows, and she went to take a closer look.

Rev grabbed hold of her arm. "Rose! It's so good to see you!"

Rose tried to disguise her flinch, but Rev was determined to not let her go. Rev's blond ponytail was pulled up high on her head, and her eye patch sparkled with silver sequins. She wore a matching short silver sequin dress that rustled faintly when she moved.

"I'm so glad you stopped by! I've been dying to have a girl talk!"

Rose blinked. "A girl talk?"

"You know, so we can get to know one another better. We

haven't spent a lot of time together, and I think that should change. I think we have a lot in common."

"We do?" Rose couldn't imagine what she had in common with this petite sparkly young woman from the Underneath.

"Of course!" She pulled Rose inside. "They have some nice private seating in the bar. It'll be fun!"

Rose examined the room as Rev led her further inside. There was loud music in the larger room, but Rev led her into a smaller room off to the left. It appeared to have been part of the shop next door and someone had knocked down walls to expand.

Rev pulled Rose down beside her on a burgundy velvet couch. She pulled her pale pink legs under her sequined skirt and patted Rose's hand fondly. "So, tell me ... how are the auditions going?"

"Um ... fine?" said Rose with a shrug.

"Good!" said Rev cheerfully. "Have you had a lot of skilled performers audition?"

"Skilled enough, I guess." Rose wasn't sure what to do with the strange conversation.

"That's great!" Rev's voice stayed sweet but turned sharp as a blade. "What's the situation with you and Wilder?"

Rose coughed. "Situation? There is no *situation* with us."

"Hmm ... You sure about that? He seemed a bit cranky when I saw him earlier."

"Oh. Well, sure, we've had some disagreements. Is that what you meant by *situation*?"

"It's unusual to see Wilder's feathers so ruffled, so I'm curious to talk to the one doing the ruffling." She rested her chin on her hand and leaned against the back of the couch. "So, do you have any other sweethearts I should know about?"

"Sweethearts? What are you talking about?"

"Just curious if you have any pre-existing relationships we should discuss."

Rose blinked in confusion. She barely knew Rev. What kind of conversation was this? "Uh … no relationships, but thanks for asking, I guess? I don't have time for relationships."

"Ah, I see," said Rev. "That's what the situation is. I guess that's better than the alternative. I just thought I'd give you the chance to confess up front."

Rose straightened in her seat. "Confess? Why would I confess to you? What is this all about?"

Rev's lips still curled in a soft smile, but her voice held a clear threat. "Wilder is a good man, and I won't allow anyone to hurt him again."

Rose stopped breathing and leaned back under the stare of Rev's piercing blue eye.

"There is something about you I like." Rev's voice was matter of fact, but her glare was deadly serious. "But if you hurt him, I will rip you apart with my bare hands. Do you understand?"

Rose was so shocked at her words that she just nodded numbly.

"Fantastic!" Rev's cheerful smile returned. "To answer your other question, people confess to me all the time. It's one of the services I offer."

"Receiving confessions is a service you offer?" Rose was still off balance from the threat, and Rev continued to confuse her.

"It's a very lucrative business. Most people have a lot they need to get off their chest. I'm skilled at listening and helping them move on."

The concept was so foreign to Rose that she didn't know how to respond.

"If you ever have anything you need to confess, let me know. I'll give you the rate for friends." She squeezed Rose's hand affectionately. "Is this your first time in a bar?"

Rose blinked at the change of topic. "A bar? Is that what that is?"

Rev practically bounced on her seat in excitement. "Yes! I heard that there weren't any bars in the City before the Uprising. Do you even know what alcohol is?"

"Of course I know what alcohol is!" said Rose defensively. "I'm not an idiot. Just because I never drank alcohol before doesn't mean I don't understand the concept."

"Well, that's good to know. I'd hate to get you into the same predicament I got Ylena into. Do you want to order something?" Rev signaled to call a waitress over.

"Um ... I'm assuming that probably takes money?"

"Don't worry about it," said Rev. "Your first drink is on me!"

The waitress returned with two drinks with sugar-coated rims. Rose took hers with a skeptical expression. She sipped it and decided the sour drink with sugar was a nice combo; plus, it felt pleasantly warm as it slid down her throat. But other than that, the experience seemed less thrilling than she expected.

Rev stood and pulled Rose to her feet. "Let's go find the others!"

Rose held her glass carefully to keep from spilling the drink as Rev pulled her into the larger room. The music was louder in this room, and people stood in front of a long counter with rows of bottles lined up along the back wall. A smiling young woman poured drinks one after another in an unending stream. Rev pulled Rose up to the bar and leaned back to study the room.

"What are you doing here?" Wilder appeared out of the crowd and stepped between Rose and Rev. His eyes were moving between Rose's face and the drink in her hand.

Rev grabbed his arm and pulled him close. "Isn't it fabulous, Wilder? I found her wandering around outside, so I invited her in."

"Fabulous," he said dryly. "Do you know what you are getting yourself into, Rose?"

"That's not your concern, thank you very much," said Rose with a glare.

Wilder scowled. He signaled to the waitress, and she poured him a small glass of clear liquid with a lingering smile. He caught the woman's eyes with a smile, and she blushed.

Rose rolled her eyes.

As Wilder turned back, he caught her eye roll, and his scowl returned. He picked up his small glass and threw it back in one gulp.

Rose tilted her head as she considered his small glass and the sugary drink in her own hand.

Rev laughed at Rose's side. "I should have considered the fact that you might not be a fruity drink kind of girl." She waved at the waitress again. "I'll buy you one of those, too. You might as well get the full experience."

Wilder gave Rev a disapproving glare. "Do you remember the last time we were in this situation, Rev? Things got out of hand."

Rev patted him on the arm. "Yes, but Ylena and Rose are two very different people."

His face went expressionless. He signaled the waitress to pour another for him as well.

Rev picked up her small glass and clinked it against the one in Rose's hand. "To new beginnings!" She tossed her drink back, and Rose followed.

It burned like pure fire. She wanted to cough out the flames, but she held it in and let it burn her to the core. Her eyes lit up as the heat simmered through her.

Rev laughed. "See, Wilder? Very different."

Wilder gave her a flat look, then threw back his own drink.

A man stepped up to the bar, followed by a giggling young woman. He waved the waitress over. "Tonight is her first night out drinking. Bring her some shots!"

The waitress nodded and started pouring a drink.

The man set a coin down on the bar and smiled at the girl. "I bet you can't drink that shot without coughing."

The girl looked hungrily at the coin. Then she smiled at the man and nodded in challenge. She grabbed the little glass and drank it all down.

Her golden curls shook as she coughed uncontrollably.

The man chuckled and pushed the coin toward the waitress. "Let's try it again!"

Wilder glared at the man, then looked at the young woman with concern. Something in his expression caused the warm liquid sitting in Rose's gut to churn.

The man noticed Rose staring at the shots. He leaned toward her across the bar. "You want in on the game, sweetheart?" He put a stack of coins on the bar. "I'll give this to whichever one of you can drink the most shots tonight. I'm curious how well a Priest can hold her liquor." His eyes glittered in a way that reminded Rose of a circling hawk.

She was about to give the man a piece of her mind when Wilder spoke.

"Rose, don't do this. When I took Ylena to her first bar, she drank too much because I didn't warn her. I won't let you get that drunk, too."

The fiery liquid sprang to life again. "You won't *let me*?"

Rev groaned. "Good Goddess, Wilder." She rolled her eye dramatically. "You might as well pour the drinks yourself now."

Rose clicked her hard nail against the bar to emphasize her words. "You don't *let* me do anything, Wilder. I am my own woman, not a silly child like Ylena or this girl." The golden-curled young woman narrowed her eyes, but Rose purposefully ignored it. "I am stronger than they are and stronger than anything the bartender has back there."

Wilder sighed and rubbed his forehead.

The man clapped his hands in excitement. "This is going to be more fun than I expected!"

26

"Good morning, sunshine!" Kai's soft voice slammed into Rose's skull like a mallet.

She reached for her blade so she could stab him.

"I already hid all your blades." His unreasonably pleasant voice was too bright for her dark bedroom. "It's time to wake up and deal with your extremely poor life choices, Rosie."

She blinked open her gummy eyes to see his smiling face staring back at her. She rolled onto her back, and the room spun. Her voice sounded like gravel and tasted like bile. "Why are you so Goddess-damn cheerful this morning?"

He clicked his tongue. "Now, Rosie, good Priests don't curse. Although after last night, your good Priest status is in question."

"I'm not a good Priest anymore because I drank too much?" She wanted to look at him with indignation, but that expression hurt her brain.

"The drinking isn't the issue. Your status is in question because of all the terrible things you said and did."

She rubbed her eyes as she filtered through the events she

could remember. She remembered the creepy guy who had offered coin for drinking the shots. Rose knew she would crush the girl, and she did. It didn't take long before the girl was vomiting, and Rose had collected her coins.

Rose patted the pocket of her pants where she put the coins but then realized she was in her pajamas. She didn't remember getting home, much less stripping out of her clothes into pajamas. The break in her memory was disorienting. She tried to sit up quickly, but the room spun again. She had to cling to Kai seated on the edge of her bed to keep from falling.

"How did I get here?" she asked.

"Existential questions this early?"

She tightened her grip on him with a glare.

"I brought you home. Wilder sent one of his friends to find me. Dragging you home like a spitting wildcat is not the way I planned to spend my night."

Wilder. She felt shame bubble up at his name but couldn't identify the exact memory to say why. She pushed it away to consider later.

"I should get ready. The others will want to leave soon." She pushed herself to standing, using Kai's shoulder as a crutch.

"Wilder and Fitz already left."

"Oh. I guess I'll just meet them in Harmony." She wasn't sure why them walking on without her made her sad.

Kai stood and walked to the door. "Pack your stuff, and I'll walk with you." She opened her mouth to protest, but he continued. "I know you don't need an escort. We didn't get to spend enough time together, and I don't have any classes today." His eyes twinkled with a hidden joke. "And I want to take note of every time you stumble or vomit on your walk to Harmony so I can make fun of you for years to come."

He slid out the door before her shoe could hit him in the head.

She felt closer to human after her bath, but only barely. Her head was throbbing in tempo to her pulse as she scooped up clothes to shove in her bag. She had planned on being strategic with what clothes she packed for the rest of the trip, but her thoughts weren't clear enough for strategy. She shoved as many items of black clothing as possible into her bag. And as an afterthought, she threw in Vaylan's orange cloak as well.

She looked in the pockets of last night's pants, trying to find the coins she'd won. After a moment's thought, she vaguely remembered spending the coins to buy more drinks for herself. And for a random guy? That memory was fuzzy, so she pushed it away.

She earned coins and then spent them all within a single night. That seemed pointless. Why even have coins if she could spend them so quickly?

Her bag weighed more than it did the last time she packed it. She hoisted it onto her shoulder and went to find Kai.

On her way, she stopped by the laundry. She knew every one of the laundry workers in Temple Discipline personally, and she begged a few of the girls to please not squeal so loud. It did not surprise her to learn that the Sentinels' armor had turned up missing about a week ago.

Kai waited for her in the courtyard with breakfast.

"There is no way I am eating," said Rose. Her gut churned with acid and fire.

He shoved the food into her hand. "Eat it. The Underneath brought their alcohol Upstairs, but they were also kind enough to bring their remedies."

She narrowed her eyes but ate the food before they walked.

"Ugh. I still feel terrible." The sun stabbed rays into her eyeballs, and her stomach threatened to heave at any moment.

Kai chuckled as he walked by her side. "The food won't stop

you from feeling terrible. I'm just hoping it gives you the strength to handle the walk all the way to Harmony today. And if you are lucky, you'll still have the strength to handle Mayra when she sees you."

Rose groaned. "Oh, Goddess. I don't have the energy for her." She imagined the judgmental look on Mayra's face. Then she imagined vomiting on Mayra's shoes. She couldn't decide if the thought was embarrassing or pleasing.

"You're going to have to find the energy to see her. And to see Wilder."

Shame welled up again at his name, and she swallowed down bile. "I honestly don't remember everything that happened."

"I can tell you the part I saw. After Wilder's friend led me into the bar, I found you challenging someone to a drinking contest, which involved throwing knives. I suggested perhaps that wasn't a good idea. You grabbed my shirt in your fist and swore you would win." He shook his head. "You've always been a confident girl, Rosie, but while drinking, you were invincible."

His words stirred a hazy memory. Had she claimed she could throw her knife through an apple balanced on someone's head? She couldn't remember if she had realized the wind could no longer guide her. It was a wonder she hadn't killed someone.

"You weren't happy with me or Wilder when I tried to take you home. Apparently, there was some girl you had challenged earlier in the evening that he was taking home. You had quite a few nasty things to say to him about that."

She remembered the giggling golden-haired girl hanging on Wilder's arm. The girl had looked at him with an adoring gaze, and the man who had offered the coins had stared at Wilder with cold fury. Rose couldn't remember what she had said, but the memory still rankled.

"I dragged you out of there, dodging your knives and fists,

and finally got you put to bed. You owe me an apology for last night. I'm bruised." He rubbed his arm.

She slapped him on the same arm. "Don't be a baby, Kai."

"I'm not the only one you owe an apology." He crossed his arms and gave her a serious look.

She straightened her back at the implication. "Priests have no need to apologize."

He snorted. "Really brilliant theology, Rosie. You should examine that belief."

"Are you trying to get me to change my beliefs, too?" Her eyebrows drew together as she scowled at him. "I thought you believed in the Goddess?"

He raised an eyebrow. "And was it the Goddess who said Priests should never apologize?"

She wanted to retort with the Goddess's words but couldn't remember anything about apologizing in any of the liturgies.

"Exactly," Kai said smugly.

She smacked him on the arm again.

"I'm just saying, if the Goddess isn't the one who said it, you should consider where that idea came from. And then apologize to a few people."

She didn't reply but finally dug up the memories she had been avoiding.

After she won the coins from the man with the predatory eyes, he'd tried to get her to drink more. She'd agreed to allow him to buy her another drink if he could beat her at arm wrestling.

He lost interest in Rose after she won.

Another man, almost as tall as Wilder, wasn't intimidated by her arm-wrestling prowess. With every drink he bought her, he took a step closer. She could feel Wilder staring at her from across the bar. His eyes felt both possessive and pitying, and it fueled her fire. She didn't need Wilder's pity. Rose could take care of herself. She let the man get closer and closer, and when his hand finally reached to embrace her, she made sure Wilder saw her knife at the man's throat.

The man lost interest in Rose after that.

When another man offered to buy Rose a drink, Wilder stepped in.

"You should find someone else, buddy." Wilder's unsmiling face was enough to send the guy off to easier prey.

"I don't need you to protect me, Wilder."

He stared down at her with serious dark eyes. "I'm not protecting you. I'm protecting him."

She growled and considered what type of fight to challenge him to. Her blood was still singing with battle, and she wanted to best Wilder more than anyone.

"Rose, please, I'm begging you. Just go home. You are out of control and need to stop."

She tapped her finger against his hard chest. "I am in complete control. I don't need you telling me how to act."

"You don't want to act this way. You will regret it tomorrow." He placed a gentle hand on her arm. "Please let me take you back to the temple so you can sleep this off."

She shook off his hand. "You want to walk me home and get me in bed? I'm not surprised you'd suggest that after I've had a few drinks."

"Goddess-dammit, Rose!" Fury flowed off him, and she drank it in. "If you truly believe that about me, you're even more willfully ignorant than I thought."

His flames stoked her own, and she was determined to win. "You shouldn't swear by the Goddess, Wilder." Her voice was sweet and pious enough to wound. "I thought you were one of her followers? Or is the Goddess just another woman for you to toy with?"

She saw her verbal blade strike home, but it wasn't the winning stroke she hoped. His face lost its fury and fell into hurt and disgust.

He leaned closer, and his voice was a deep rumble laced with pain. "I expected to be mocked for my beliefs in the Underneath, but I didn't expect it from you."

He walked away into the crowd. Her alcohol-riddled mind hadn't known what to do with her rampaging emotions. She'd had a few more drinks in the attempt to settle her mind, but they hadn't helped. After that, she'd started looking for challengers in the knife-throwing contest.

Rose looked at Kai walking silently by her side, wondering how much he had heard about her behavior last night besides what he had seen.

"If Wilder ended up taking that girl home, at least he enjoyed the rest of his evening." She wanted the statement to have her usual haughtiness, but it carried an embarrassing hint of pouting.

Kai rolled his eyes. "Rosie, you really are an idiot sometimes. Wilder made sure that girl got home safely because that creepy guy was still hovering around her. You had a brother to take you home. She didn't have anyone."

Shame prickled along her spine. Had she honestly believed Wilder would take advantage of the girl?

Kai didn't let her off the hook. "Wilder protected her by taking her home. He protected you by finding me. There's no telling how many guys he protected from knife wounds from you. And you treated him like he was garbage. So, if the Goddess ever requires a good apology, I think this is one of those times."

HARMONY

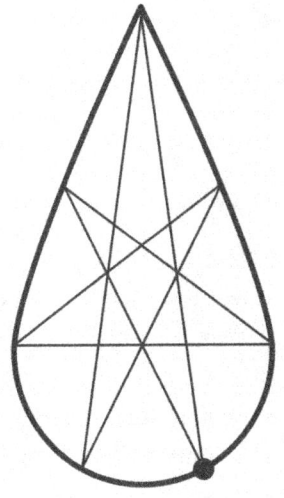

27

Priest Mayra glared as Rose finally stumbled up the steps of Temple Harmony.

"Hello, Priest Rose. You look unwell. I didn't realize you were so delicate that the walk between temples strained you."

Rose used all her effort to focus on not puking, so she didn't have a witty response available. She stuck with a classic glare.

Kai bowed with perfect grace. "Greetings, Priest Mayra. My sister is unwell, but I am here to assist with whatever administrative work she was supposed to do today. She should spend some time in her room recovering so she is well for the audition tomorrow."

Rose stared at him with wide eyes. While she hated anyone telling her what to do, the relief at not having to sit through hours of paperwork was enough to keep her mouth shut.

Priest Mayra glared at Rose, but other than accusing her of impropriety, she couldn't refuse the offer. "I welcome your assistance, Priest Kai. I will see you inside." She bowed stiffly before leaving.

"Why are you being so nice to me?" Rose looked at Kai with suspicious eyes.

"I know this might be hard to believe, but some of us know how to be a nice person."

She glared and started to hit him but reconsidered.

His eyes lit up. "There's hope for you yet!"

She did smack him then.

He laughed, then looked at her with serious eyes. "I only ask one thing in return for this. Please consider apologizing. Not to me. To Wilder."

She ground her teeth and didn't respond.

"I'm serious, Rosie. He didn't deserve the way you treated him. And despite the way Caed described him, I think he's a good guy. He's one of the few people I've met that's strong enough to stand toe to toe with you." He gave her a small smile. "I think he's a good match for you."

She groaned. "Kai! I'm not looking for a match right now! I just want to make it through the auditions, get my Gift back, and start my life over. A relationship isn't on my mind at all!"

He smirked. "Of course it isn't."

She smacked him one last time before heading to her room.

She awoke several hours later, fully dressed on top of the covers with her shoes still on. The second she had entered her calm room, she'd lain on the bed and fell asleep. Now her stomach rumbled with hunger, which she hoped was a good sign.

She took a bath to wash off the alcohol that was seeping out of every pore. The books she had read about the consequences of alcohol had severely underplayed the aftereffects. She dressed in fresh clothes, then carried her alcohol-sweat-soaked clothes to the laundry personally.

She asked about the Sentinels' armor, only to find they

were already gone. She gave up on finding any remaining armor in the other temples. Whoever wanted the armor was way ahead of her. The thought of Sentinels roaming around the City again filled her with terror. She couldn't imagine who would want that.

The only people who were safe from Sentinels were High Priests, so then again, maybe she could imagine it. If Mayra and her cronies were trying to set themselves up as the new High Priests, they would look for ways to enforce their authority. What better way than with the Sentinels?

She stomped into the dining hall, hoping to run into Mayra. She didn't care if Wilder thought she should hide her suspicions. Mayra deserved an earful from Rose, and she would get it the next time she saw her. But instead of Mayra, she found Fitz.

He was sitting at a table alone, with a sandwich in one hand and a book in the other. She thought he was so engrossed in the book that he might not notice her, but no such luck. He waved to her with his book and used the sandwich to point her into the seat across from him.

"How are you feeling?" His eyes looked sincerely concerned.

"Better," she said. "How much did you hear about what happened last night?"

"Enough to know that you probably feel terrible today. For multiple reasons." He raised his eyebrows and took a bite of his sandwich.

"Well, smart guy, you're correct. I do feel terrible." She scowled and took a bite.

"Don't feel too bad, Rose. You aren't the first person to have a terrible experience with alcohol. What really matters is where you go from here."

They ate in silence for a while until Rose jumped into the

topic simmering in her mind. "Wilder said you are a theologian."

Fitz's eyes perked up. "Yes! Maybe it's presumptuous to call myself that, considering the lack of books available in the Underneath, but I have studied everything I could find." His pale cheeks colored a soft pink.

"In your studies, did you find anything regarding apologizing? I've always heard that there is no reason for a Priest to apologize, but until today, I never realized that I don't know where that comes from."

His eyes practically glowed. "That's a good question! There are a lot of discrepancies between how apologizing and forgiveness occur Upstairs and in the Underneath. While the liturgies of the Goddess never speak specifically on the topic, there are multiple authors who write about it. Most believe the split in theology is because of the High Priests enacting such strict control Upstairs. They viewed apologies as admitting sin, and if every sin is worthy of execution, it makes sense that a culture around avoiding apologies would thrive."

Her eyes widened in disbelief. She was the Priest, and yet this guy from the Underneath spouted more theology in moments than she had spoken in months.

She shook her head. "I can't believe I'm so far behind on this topic."

"I have plenty of books to recommend if you want to study more. There is one theologian from three centuries ago who ..." His voice trailed off as he considered her dazed expression. He rubbed an awkward hand across his blond beard. "Sometimes I get caught up in the theoretical and lose sight of the actual issue. Are you trying to decide if you should ask someone for forgiveness?"

She opened her mouth to deny it but sighed instead. "Yes." She rubbed her eyes to block out her vision of Wilder's hurt expression. "I said some truly awful things to a good person. I questioned his character and mocked his faith. I was an idiot. He shouldn't forgive me, but I desperately hope he will."

Fitz nodded. "That's a good start! Being specific about what you did wrong is helpful. Not offering excuses. You are on the right track." His smile was encouraging.

She was ashamed of the sound of her small voice. "But what if he doesn't … forgive me?"

He patted her hand. "That's the scary part. You have to ask for forgiveness and understand you might not receive it. You can't demand it."

"But I'm great at demanding." She offered a weak smile.

His soft green eyes held hers. "Being vulnerable is hard. But if you can manage it, your relationship ends up stronger than before."

She wasn't sure she wanted to consider what kind of relationship she had with Wilder, but she wanted to apologize for what she did.

"Thanks, Fitz," she said. "You are a brilliant theologian. And a good friend." As she said the words, she realized it was true.

He glowed with pride. "Thanks, Rose." He stood and gathered his book under his arm. "It might not make it any easier to apologize, but I believe Wilder will forgive you." He patted her hand before walking away.

28

The sandwich and discussion with Fitz revived her, so Rose took a walk around Harmony Diocese to see what had changed since her last visit. Animals of every kind had always filled the Diocese, perfectly trained by Harmony Priests. She could see the ways the Diocese had tried to adapt without their Gifts. Hastily constructed fences now kept livestock contained, and they had converted shops into care centers for the animals injured during the chaos of the Uprising.

The other noticeable change was the number of shops now advertising various types of fight clubs. She didn't mind seeing all the boxing or grappling gyms, other than they seemed out of place. The fighting arts used to be studied only in Discipline, but now Harmony was gaining its own type of fighting from Rivalry below.

The two white wolves shocked her out of her melancholy when they ran up. They tugged on her pants and pulled her forward by her jacket sleeve.

"What's the matter, ladies?" Their paws scrabbled on the hard stone as they tried to pull Rose even harder. What could make them so upset? "Is Wilder okay? Is he hurt?" They pulled her forward until her fear kicked in, and she ran behind them.

She followed them as they leaped over bushes and spun around corners. She prayed for her Gift to return so she could speed through the streets on a gust of wind, but not even a breeze stirred.

Her breath burned in her lungs, but she refused to slow. The wolves ran inside a building, with Rose close behind. She drew her blades, prepared to fight whoever was hurting Wilder enough to scare the wolves.

She skidded to a halt to find Rev and Quinn seated calmly on a bench, watching Wilder and Tayeh preparing to spar inside of a ring.

"Look who it is!" Rev's voice was as friendly as yesterday, but the edge running below had sharpened. "I think we've all been curious to see what you would do next. I didn't expect you to barge in here with weapons bared, but I guess you continue to amaze us."

Rose stared stupidly around the dim boxing club as she tried to understand what had happened. Her blood was still pounding in her ears, looking for the danger. She turned to find the wolves sitting on their haunches, with heads bowed and unwilling to meet her eyes.

She growled at them under her breath. "You little dogs."

Rose sheathed her weapons, then turned to the crew. "I thought you were in danger." Her voice still held a growl, and she heard the wolves whimper an apology.

Wilder hadn't turned to face her, but both Rev and Tayeh stared at her with hard eyes. Quinn was the only one who looked pleased to see her.

"The wolves are very clever," he said. "They must have been convincing to get you to barge in here ready to fight."

Tayeh leaned against the rope at the edge of the ring, and her dark bronze eyes blazed. "Rose is always ready to fight."

"I think you're right, Tayeh," said Rev. "Why don't you come sit with me, Rose? Let's finish our girl talk." She patted the bench at her side, and Quinn scooted out of the way.

Rose didn't want any more of Rev's supposed "girl talk," but fleeing the room would look weak. And she desperately wanted Wilder to turn around and meet her eyes.

She sat down next to Rev, taking mental inventory of her knives just in case she needed them.

"How are you feeling, honey?" Rev's voice still held a deceptive calm.

"Better," she said. Wilder started sparring with Tayeh, and Rose glanced at him out of the corner of her eye. "But also terrible."

Rev snorted. "Good. If you had answered otherwise, you would limp out of here."

The sharp blue of Rev's eye made the statement believable.

"So, you feel terrible," Rev said. "What are you planning to do about it?"

"I'm going to ..." Rose's voice dropped to an embarrassed whisper. "... apologize."

Rev nodded once. "I would hope so. And have you figured out how you can avoid this situation in the future?"

"Believe me. I don't plan on drinking again soon."

Rev narrowed her eye. "Drinking wasn't the problem, Rose. It's the hurtful words you said. They were there below the surface the whole time, or else the alcohol wouldn't have brought them out. Plenty of people drank too much last night, but you were one of the few who was mean to someone you care about."

Her breath stilled. That was why she felt so awful. She said a lot of nasty things to other people at the bar, but the words eating away at her were the words she spoke to Wilder.

Because she cared about him.

"You're right," said Rose. "What I said to Wilder is the problem. I was wrong. I'm sorry."

Rev settled back on the bench, and her face softened slightly. She considered Rose's words, then nodded. "You don't owe me an apology. You will have to offer that to Wilder and see what happens. However, I accept your confession. You can pay me later."

Rev stood and called in a loud voice, "Tayeh, I'm tired of girl talk with Rose. It's your turn." Rev pushed Rose forward. "It's time for Rose to have some time in the ring. I'd like to see if she can be in a fight without burning the whole place down." Tayeh shrugged and stepped out between the ropes.

Rose walked slowly to the ring. Wilder hadn't moved after he stopped sparring, and his back was still facing Rose. She wasn't sure if he would consent to be in the same ring as her. She took a deep breath and stepped through the ropes.

29

She crossed the ring to stand in front of him. His eyes were unreadable. She bit her lips, unsure where to start. The silence stretched so long it became painful. Her body itched to move.

"Are we going to spar?" she asked.

He snorted. "You like to take cheap shots. I'm not sure I trust you in an honest round of sparring."

His words stung, but they were fair. "This will give you the chance to get some payback. You have permission to take as many cheap shots as you want."

He frowned. "I don't want to hurt you, Rose."

"I don't think you can," she whispered.

His eyes narrowed, and she realized he misunderstood. She meant she didn't think he *would*.

"Fine," he said. "No blades, though." He started pulling knives out from hidden sheaths and depositing them at the side of the ring.

She pulled out her own knives and removed her jacket before turning to find Wilder pulling his shirt over his head.

She suddenly understood the look on his face when she

had kicked her skirt off during their last training. The professional part of her training tried to kick in, considering him as an opponent and examining him for weaknesses, but she just couldn't stop *examining* him.

His clearly defined muscles told the story of years spent training, but the scars on his dark skin revealed the high stakes of conflict in the Underneath. On his bicep, a thin bandage covered his almost healed wound. He would be weaker on that side, and she considered ways to exploit that weakness, but her plans evaporated when he clasped his wrist and stretched his arms slowly above his head. He luxuriated in the motion like a cat who knows they are pretty.

As he stepped closer, her eyes dropped to his chest again, almost against her will. Right above his heart was a tattoo of a seven-pointed star inside a teardrop.

"The sign of the Goddess," she whispered. Her hand floated up unconsciously as she reached to touch the symbol. Her mind caught up to her hand, and she dropped it abruptly to her side. "When we were at the tattoo shop, I said that I couldn't imagine a symbol I'd want tattooed on my body." She looked up into his serious eyes. "You already had this?"

He snorted. "Yes, Rose. I've known about the Goddess for a long time. Not that I expect you to care what I believe."

She bit her lips. His words again were fair, even though they stung.

"Goddess blessing upon you." Wilder bowed in the traditional manner of sparring in Discipline.

Her response and bow were automatic. "And also upon you."

She couldn't bring herself to strike first, so she watched him for the slightest twitch of movement. Even though she never looked away, when he finally lunged for her, she barely stumbled away from his grasp.

Her limbs were slow, not only because of her lost Gift but also because she was still sluggish from lingering alcohol.

She feinted a lunge, and when he twisted away from her, she dropped to the ground while sweeping her leg, trying to trip him. He leaped out of her way as she hopped back to standing, slower than she wanted.

He seemed to hold himself back, matching the speed of her movements, but going no further. The thought of him holding back for her sake sent the sharp pain of shame through her. She tried to move faster.

Her punches failed to land because he dodged them easily. She tried to grapple with him, but her hands against his warm chest caused conflicting feelings that ruined her tactics. She was flexible enough to aim a few kicks at his head, but he easily ducked away.

This is what she had been afraid of. She couldn't fight anymore. With the wind on her side, she could have defeated him in moments. Now every movement was a struggle, and he could end the fight at any time.

But he didn't end it. He kept fighting. His punches weren't full strength, and she blocked most. He caught her in a hold with her arm twisted behind her back, but instead of leaning into it, he allowed her to escape with a simple trick. Each step he took taught her something new. He was out of breath and sweating, but it was because he worked so hard to hit her without hitting her and to kick her without kicking her.

She was furious.

She was in awe.

Her body slowed, and she couldn't kick as high anymore. She tried a few more punches, but they struck his hard muscles with less force than planned. Her breath came in gasps, and she was a step away from surrendering.

He grabbed her by the arm and flipped her onto her back. She hit the floor of the ring with a bounce, and the breath escaped her lungs in a rush. He pinned her down with the full length of his body on hers and his forearm on her neck. As she stared up at him, she struggled to pull in more air. His dark eyes were quiet but intense. He hadn't flipped her in anger.

It was the last lesson of the class.

He fought passionately, but he never harmed her. Even now, she could feel him holding the full weight of his body off her with just enough pressure to pin her. His forearm was warm against her neck but so gentle she could feel her pulse beating against his skin.

He knew how to fight without hurting those he cared about.

"Wilder," she breathed. "I'm sorry." His eyes widened, but he didn't move. Rose couldn't see the crew, but she heard the shuffling sound of them leaving the room. Until that moment, she had forgotten they were still there.

"I slandered your character with no reason to do so. I have never seen you take advantage of a woman. In fact, you always rush to protect those who need help. And ridiculing your faith was awful. I would take back the words if I could. But I know I can't."

Wilder hovered perfectly still above her. His forearm never changed pressure against her throat, but his eyes studied her as if trying to understand.

"I ask for your forgiveness," she said. "I know you don't have to give it to me. In fact, if it were me, I'm not sure I could." She swallowed down the fear that he might be as stubborn as she was. "But ... I'm asking you for forgiveness anyway."

She counted out her heartbeats against his arm as she waited for his reply. She could feel his warm chest pressed against hers. His tattoo was a brand searing into her own heart.

He narrowed his eyes, and when he spoke, his voice was low but lacking any sign of anger. "For someone who has never apologized before, you are suddenly very good at it."

A cool breath of relief entered her lungs. "Um ... I took a class?"

He chuckled quietly, and the movement of his body against hers sent sparks through her.

Before she had time to savor the feeling, he stood, offered her a hand, and pulled her to standing. She stood unmoving against him in the center of the ring. She didn't even dare to risk breathing.

He reached a soft hand under her chin and tilted her head to look him in the eyes.

"I forgive you, Rose."

She wanted to sag in relief, but worried movement might break the fragile moment.

He dropped his hand from her chin. "But I can't say I trust you not to do the same thing again."

She wanted to protest, except she didn't trust herself, either.

"Maybe I'm a fool, setting myself up for another fall." He sighed as he picked up his shirt and sheathed his knives. "But I guess I'm back in the game." He hopped out of the ring and bowed to her. "The next move is yours." He pulled his shirt on as he left.

30

R ose woke the next morning better rested than she had been for weeks. Apparently, apologizing was helpful for getting a good night's sleep. As she walked to the park for the auditions, her muscles were tender from sparring, but she didn't have any bruises. She marveled at Wilder's level of control. The way he'd pinned her at the end of the fight, so firm, yet so gentle ...

She sped up her walk. That's why her pulse was racing.

Wilder lounged in his usual spot at their table. She wasn't sure how he could look so relaxed in a wooden chair, but he seemed completely at ease. He spoke to a guy and two girls gathered close to him. As she approached, he finished his story, and they laughed. They saw Rose approach and hurried away.

She frowned as she watched them go. "You didn't have to stop your conversation for my sake."

Wilder grinned. "I'm afraid you have a bit of a reputation for being terrifying." She scowled at him, but he laughed. "Yes, that face contributes to your reputation."

It was an effort to smooth her face into a placid expression.

His eyes twinkled in the bright morning sunlight. "I appreciate the effort, but you don't have to pretend for me. I'm not afraid of you."

Her faced eased into its more natural position; however, she wasn't sure whether that was any less terrifying. "That's comforting," she said. "So, who were they?"

"Rivalry is where I spent most of my life. I know a lot of the performers. I think we will see quite a few people I know today."

She raised an eyebrow. "Were they over here trying to earn extra points to get them the role?"

She thought he would protest, but he nodded. "One rule of Rivalry is to gain the upper hand by whatever means necessary."

"And laughing at your stories is one of those means?"

"Those three don't know me as well as some of the others, so they gave it a shot. The others who know me better probably have other tactics in mind."

"Tactics?" she asked. "Is this audition a sport or a battle?"

"Yes." His face was serious. "If there was any advantage to taking me out, it wouldn't surprise me if one of them tried."

"Wow." She shook her head. "You take your auditions seriously in the Underneath."

He gave her a wry grin. "I knew a few performers Upstairs who were just as cutthroat." He sighed, then whispered. "Goddess rest their souls."

She stilled for a moment, then took her seat at his side.

Rose was pleased to see that the overall quality of auditions was significantly higher than some of the other Dioceses. After a particularly skilled young man finished his song, she turned to Wilder.

"He was great. I know we still have a few more Dioceses to go, but I think he should play the Companion."

Wilder sighed and slumped back in his chair. "I was afraid you would say that."

"You disagree?"

"No, I don't. He's skilled enough that he was the Warden's second choice after me to play the Companion last year. If he'd won our audition for the Wardens, he might have been the one sitting by your side today."

She tried to imagine a reality that didn't include Wilder sitting by her side. The thought was uncomfortable, so she pushed it away.

"Then you agree he's good. What's the issue?" she asked.

Wilder seemed embarrassed to answer, but he dropped his voice and said, "Kieran is mean."

She laughed, then cut off abruptly when he looked away. "Oh, you're serious." She spoke gently to soften her words. "Okay, he's mean. But I'm mean, and you've learned to work with me."

"You aren't always mean." His low voice reminded her of their conversation on the floor of the ring, and her heartbeat fluttered. "But you are right. I've learned to adapt." He took a deep breath, then circled Kieran's name on the paperwork. "If I'm strong enough to handle you, I can definitely handle Kieran."

She arched an eyebrow. "So, you think you can *handle* me?" He opened his mouth to backtrack, but she laughed. "See? You've learned."

During their break, Wilder went backstage to talk to the performers he knew and to offer Kieran the role of the Companion. She was curious how that conversation would go, but Wilder asked to give him the news on his own. She wasn't sure if he was trying to protect Rose from Kieran or vice versa. After a moment's thought, she wondered if he was trying to protect himself from having two mean people to deal with at once.

Vaylan slid into Wilder's seat at her side.

"This is supposed to be my break," said Rose stiffly. "I'm not sure why you feel the need to harass me during my few free moments."

He smiled, showing his dimple. "You are an extremely busy Priest. I have to take my opportunities when I can get them."

"Don't waste your time trying to convert me."

"I'm not trying to convert you, Rose. I'm just trying to get you to be honest with what you actually believe."

She turned to face him. "Why me? There is an entire City of people out there for you to convince. Can't you spend your time focusing on them?"

"I spend plenty of time focusing on the rest of the City. But this is my only chance to talk to you."

She sighed and rubbed her forehead. "Fine. What would you like to convince me of today?"

"Did you know that someone has gathered all the Sentinel armor?" he asked.

She narrowed her eyes. "Yes, I do. And how do you know that?"

"There are multiples factions at odds in this City. I make it my business to sort out who is plotting what."

"So, who is plotting to build their own army of Sentinels?" she asked.

He leaned back in his chair. "I think the question is, who has the most to gain by resurrecting an army that was dedicated to the High Priests?"

Her eyes widened. Mayra.

He studied her with knowing eyes. "You have some ideas. That's good. I haven't been able to get much information about their timeline, but perhaps you are closer to the source?"

She narrowed her eyes again. "Why should I tell you what I know? I don't trust you any more than I trust anyone else."

"I know you aren't willing to admit how much we have in common, but there is one belief we definitely share: Under no circumstances can we allow High Priests to take over the City again."

She pursed her lips. "I admit we share that belief. But I'm not promising you any information."

"I understand. But will you at least agree to seek out those who are planning on appointing themselves High Priests?"

Her voice was fierce. "Of course I will. But not because you asked."

He smiled warmly. "I should have expected nothing less." He pulled a sheet of paper from his tailored jacket. "In case you are interested, there is another gathering here in Harmony tonight. I'm not expecting them to convert you, but I think it would be good for you to know the kinds of messages being preached in the City." He looked at her black dress. "This faction isn't fond of Priests, so come dressed appropriately."

"I can handle my clothing choices on my own." She grumbled but snatched the paper from his hand.

He stood and bowed to her in one smooth movement. "Enjoy the rest of your day, Rose."

When Wilder finally returned, she was still scowling.

"Everything okay?" he asked.

"Fine."

He raised an eyebrow as he studied her. "Auditions seem to put you in a peculiar mood. Are you sure you're okay?"

She wanted to launch into a lecture about how she didn't need him to check on her mood, but when she looked into his eyes, she saw concern. And even deeper, she saw hesitation. Like he was preparing for her to attack.

She took a deep breath and reminded herself she wasn't angry with Wilder. She was angry with that know-it-all Vaylan.

She shoved that anger into the same pocket that held the flyer he handed her.

She turned back to Wilder with a mostly real smile. "I'm fine. How did your conversation with Kieran go? Was he as mean as usual?"

Wilder considered her face some more but answered. "Just as mean. He sure is a piece of work. But he can sing." He shrugged.

"The good news is that once we finish the auditions, we won't have to deal with any of them. We can let whoever they choose as Director deal with him."

He nodded, but his mind was somewhere else. He turned in his chair to face her with a serious expression. "Rose, did you plan for us to train tonight?"

"I considered it." She had actually spent a good portion of the morning considering Wilder pinning her again.

"Well, normally I would love to, and I know I agreed to it, but since this is our last night here and I'm so close to Rivalry, I thought about going to see a few people."

She tried to cover her disappointment. "Of course! I totally understand. It's fine."

He seemed embarrassed. "I'd like to go see the headmaster and a few more people from the school where I grew up. They are the closest thing to family I have."

She blinked as the implications of his family sank in. "I didn't realize how close you must be to them."

He chuckled softly. "I can't say I'm equally fond of them all, but they are a family of sorts. The headmaster shaped me into the man I am today. I owe a lot to him. My birth parents were terrible people, so I was extremely lucky to have someone like him in my life."

"He must be proud to have you as a son." She was surprised to find that the kind words sprang naturally to her lips.

Wilder blinked bright eyes, then cleared his throat. "You aren't always mean, Rose."

She ducked her head to hide her warming cheeks.

His voice was still a little rough with emotion when he spoke again. "I'm glad you had good people in your life, too. Mims, Kai ... even Caed."

"Yes," she said. "Kind people have surrounded me my whole life." Her eyes included him on that list.

He smiled, and they turned back to finish the auditions.

31

As Rose walked through the streets of Harmony, she tried to ignore her lingering sense of disappointment. She was a competent young woman who could go places by herself. She didn't need a guy beside her to enjoy a walk through the City. Nothing had changed. She smiled harder to prove that was true. Judging by the reactions of the people she passed, she wasn't sure she was succeeding.

She pulled her orange cloak tighter as she continued stomping through the streets. Disguising the fact that she was a Priest was distasteful to her. Wilder said that being quiet and unobtrusive was the best way to discover secrets. No one had ever described her as "quiet and unobtrusive." She didn't think she was cut out to be a spy, but she was curious enough about the various factions in the City that she wanted to give it another try.

She could hear sounds of a party as she approached the looping bridge leading to the Underneath. The event had a similar feel to what she had seen in Perfection; however, instead of animals and gymnasts, tonight they had fighting demonstrations. Small crowds surrounded a few informal matches on side streets, but she pushed forward until she arrived at the main match.

A massive ring stood at the head of the looping bridge, with a fight underway between a muscular young woman and a beefy older man. They appeared evenly matched, and Rose found the fight entertaining despite herself. The man was much heavier than the woman, but she landed several precise hits that left him staggering. Rose thought the woman might win, but she took too long to press her advantage, allowing the big man to catch her in a headlock, and she had to tap out. Cheers and groans came from the crowd, and Rose saw money being exchanged.

As the fighters left the ring, a gray-haired woman stepped through the ropes. The crowd stilled as she raised her hands.

"Our next match is a real treat. We have two of the treasures of Rivalry, the Sisters." The crowd cheered as two young girls in lacy nightgowns entered the ring. Their dark hair was pulled up in pigtails, and they each carried a staff much taller than they were.

The woman raised her hands, and the crowd stilled. "And on the other side, we have a truly evil foe for them to battle. Priests."

Rose's mouth fell open as four men dressed in black entered the ring. The crowd booed and yelled insults. Rose froze as she looked at the screaming crowd around her. A few moments ago, she believed she was in the middle of her fellow citizens. Now she realized they all hated her.

The woman calmed the crowd and turned to the girls. "Ladies, try to remember these aren't actual Priests. They are men paid to dress up like the enemy. This is just an exhibition match. So, please, try not to kill them, okay?"

The girls' eyes glittered as they stared at the black-clad men.

The woman's loud voice carried down the streets. "I know many of you have lost someone at the hands of Priests. Even now, the Sentinels continue to terrorize the people of the City. And on top of all that, they still believe they should control the flow of crystalline as they wish. Those of us that speak out against the Priests lose our access to crystalline everywhere we go. The Priests are trying to keep us in the dark, but we won't let them. You've heard Brother Owyn's words: we are free. And no one will tell us otherwise."

The crowd cheered as the woman nodded to the fighters and stepped out of the ring. The girls tapped their staffs, and the fight began.

Normally Rose would be intrigued by such an interesting combo of fighters, but she couldn't think beyond the fear churning in her gut. She pulled her cloak tighter and backed out of the crowd. She got a few strange looks from people wondering why she was heading away from such a good fight, but she ducked her head to avoid their eyes. Quiet and unobtrusive. That was her only way out of this.

She headed straight for the place where she had always felt safe—the bright light of the crystal spire she called her home. As she considered the size of the crowd gathered around the bridge, she wondered how long she would be safe in the temple. Even though the temples were fuller than usual with new Priest hopefuls from the Underneath, when would a faction decide they were large enough to take them on? Other than a few Priests like her in Temple Discipline, most Priests weren't fighters. When the Wardens attacked, they'd overrun the temples with barely a fight. The Priests were equally vulnerable now.

She ran up the steps of Temple Harmony and into the courtyard before she took a small breath of relief. No one had followed her, but she still felt eyes watching her. She circled the courtyard, careful to not disturb the animals that lived there. They weren't as tame as usual, so she didn't want to wake them suddenly. She made it to the dance studio and slid through the curtains with a sigh.

The room was dim, with only the barest breeze flowing through the curtains. She leaned against the archway as she caught her breath.

Rose's mind finally stilled enough to think through the woman's words. She'd implied the Priests were currently causing crystalline to stop flowing. Crystalline only flowed through stone pipes leading from the crystalline pool in the Heart of the Grottos. The Goddess had put the framework in place when she formed the City, and after that, Purpose Priests had shaped new stone pipes to allow the crystalline to flow to different areas.

Her knowledge about how the Underneath controlled their crystalline flow was limited. She knew the High Priests sent Purpose Priests down there to create lighting to suit their needs. And like the other Gifts, she assumed the Underneath had found an alternative to get by without the help of Priests.

But the curious thing was the idea that specific people were losing their access to crystalline. She had once seen a wagon back up onto one of the delicate stone lanterns that lit the streets. The wagon hit with enough force to crack the stone pipe leading up to the lantern. The crystalline slid down to the bottom of the stone pipe, never losing connection with itself. But other than breaking an occasional delicate stone pipe, it was impossible to stop the flow of crystalline through the City.

Impossible unless someone could reshape stone.

Rose paced the floor of the dark studio as she looked for any other explanation. Maybe the woman was lying and everyone's crystalline lamps still worked? Although, that seemed like a fairly simple statement to verify.

Maybe someone was breaking the flow of crystalline in conventional ways? If someone used massive hammers and chisels, they could dig their way down to the stone pipes to crack a few. Although the pipes usually ran through the stone streets and buildings themselves. Digging through that much stone would take a long time and be loud enough to alert the entire area.

Her mind reached for any other explanation, but she could find none. The only way to stop the crystalline flow strategically was if someone could reform the stone pipes and change the infrastructure.

A Purpose Priest still had their Gift.

Her body shook with fury as she paced faster. Someone still had their Gift and kept the knowledge quiet. This person was using their Gift in a strategic power play. Rose's blood burned at the abuse of the Goddess's Gift. It was heresy at the highest level.

A quieter, more dangerous question wiggled its way into her mind. She wanted to push it away as irrelevant, but it continued to dig at her. It was at the core of every sleepless night, every silent prayer, every rush of angry tears she had shed over the last few weeks.

Why would the Goddess return a Gift to this unknown Priest yet withhold it from Rose?

The question itself filled her with guilt. She clung to the belief that the Goddess would return Rose's Gift, yet the fact that someone else regained their Gift led her to doubt the Goddess anew.

Her mind was running wild, and her body shook in response. She moved to the center of the room, and her body fell into its natural rhythm of practicing katas. As she practiced the stylized kicks and jabs, her mind traveled down the paths she avoided when she was still.

Why would the Goddess return her Gift to a single Priest? She kicked harder. Were there more Priests out there with their Gifts returned but keeping it secret? She lunged deeper. Maybe they were all working together in a group with the belief that they were the Goddess's true chosen ones. She punched quicker.

Maybe they *were* the Goddess's true chosen ones.

Her leg sliced through the air, but she unbalanced and slipped. She caught herself before crashing face first, but her wrists and knees screamed at the impact, and her breath escaped in a rush. She closed her eyes, savoring the moment that the physical pain distracted her from her sacrilegious thoughts. But all too soon, the present moment returned, and she slid to the floor in defeat.

Maybe Rose wasn't chosen by the Goddess. The Goddess chose her at one point, but now she had abandoned Rose. The Goddess had moved on without her.

And Rose was fighting for someone who had already given up on her.

She crouched on the floor with her head in her hands. Tears slipped through her fingers. Rose felt each drop like a betrayal. The Goddess had led Rose to believe she was special, that she was the Goddess's chosen. But the Goddess had chosen someone else and left Rose playing the fool.

Rose would not be made the fool. She stood up and faced the mirror with unbowed back. Her tear-streaked face shamed her. She wiped off every tear until all that remained were anger and pain. She would no longer chase after the Goddess. If the Goddess wanted Rose, she could come and find her.

KNOWLEDGE

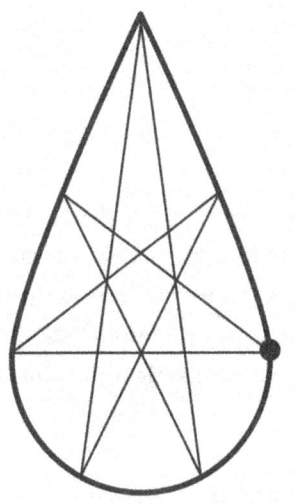

32

Rose was quieter than usual on the walk to Temple Knowledge. She tried to take the attention off herself by asking Wilder about his night visiting his family, and he shyly talked about his quiet dinner with the headmaster and a few of his nicer "siblings." He was happy and well-rested.

Rose was not.

She hadn't slept at all. Every time she closed her eyes, the cold void threatened to swallow her. The space used to be filled with her Gift, and when that was gone, hope lived in its place. But now even that hope was gone. She was empty.

Her body felt strange, as if the void inside affected her outside. She tried her best to wrap her vacant heart in the body she used to know, but nothing fit together properly anymore. Even her neatly tailored black clothes seemed ill-fitting compared to the day before.

The long walk to Temple Knowledge passed in a daze, and soon the three of them were walking up the stairs. The courtyard seemed different to Rose. She wondered if that was another effect of the emptiness she felt inside.

Mayra greeted them as they walked into the common room. Rose felt a flare of anger as she looked at Mayra, but quickly smothered it with the cold void.

Fitz left as Mayra ushered Wilder and Rose into the room with the next audition paperwork.

"Shall we begin?" Mayra asked Rose.

Wilder interrupted. "Priest Mayra, if I may ask a question? What happened to all the books in the courtyard?"

Rose realized with a start that was the difference she couldn't identify. The shelves in the courtyard used to be filled with books, but now, they were empty.

Mayra pursed her lips and seemed hesitant to respond. "All the books are now at the Library. It makes for an easier time distributing them."

A touch of heat flared inside Rose's icy heart. "You mean, it makes it easier to *charge* for them?"

Guilt flitted behind Mayra's shifting eyes. "I understand you might find it distasteful, but we must adapt."

Rose ground her teeth. "It's not 'adapting.' It's heresy."

Mayra's eyes flared at the accusation. "Priest Rose, I would appreciate it if you keep your inflammatory remarks to yourself."

"I'm sure you would appreciate that; however, I'm afraid I can't. Restricting access to Knowledge is anathema to the Goddess. I can't believe you would forsake your beliefs for a few coins." Rose's own lack of beliefs still lingered in the void, but yelling at Mayra for the same thing soothed the darkness.

"A few coins?" Mayra stepped closer to Rose, unwilling to be cowed. "In case you haven't noticed, this entire City switched to the Underneath's currency practically overnight. We have had to leverage every one of our assets to earn enough coins to survive in this new reality." Mayra was shorter than Rose, but she seemed to tower over her. "You have spent your last few weeks pouting about the way things used to be, but some of us have been clawing and fighting to hold our religion together. We can't provide food or water for the people like we used to, so we have to use the other things the Goddess has given us. So, unless you've picked up a marketable skill in the last few weeks, I'm going to continue selling Knowledge. And I suggest you thank the Goddess for those books the next time you sit down for dinner."

Rose was stunned by the onslaught of words, but one word stuck out. "Dinner?"

Priest Mayra shook her head in disgust. "How do you think you've been eating, Priest Rose?"

The flame inside Rose snuffed out.

Mayra straightened her back. "You should spend less time accusing me of heresy and more time thanking me you haven't starved."

Rose sat down, stunned. She had naively assumed the Priests had a cache of food they were living off of until they finally regained their Gifts. She had never considered their temple would need funds to continue. Mayra was right. Losing her Gift had distracted Rose too much to consider it.

Rose grabbed a stack of paperwork and began filling it out without another word. Mayra nodded primly and sat down with her own stack. Wilder tried to catch her eye, but she ignored him. At some point, he wandered off, because when she looked up again, he was gone.

After she finished looking over the stack of auditioners for the next day, she walked numbly to her room. It looked exactly like the rooms in every temple, but this one felt smaller than usual. She shoved her bag in the little closet and flopped onto the bed. It was still early afternoon, but she had no idea what to do with the rest of her day.

She always had something to do. Somewhere to go. Plans to accomplish. But now, all her plans meant nothing, and there was nowhere to go.

She assumed there was another party happening near the bridge to the Underneath tonight. Just another a crowd of people cheering for her death and the end of her religion. The thought of going to an event where everyone hated her wasn't very motivating. Although, the thought of wearing a color other than black wasn't as bad as it once seemed.

She hadn't moved when Fitz entered the room.

"I'm surprised to see you here. I thought you might be at the Library already, screaming at all the heretics." His smile turned to a frown when he saw her flinch. "Are you sure you're okay?"

"Do you believe it's heresy, Fitz?" She couldn't look at him but continued to lie on her back, staring at the ceiling. "Selling Knowledge to feed all the people living in the temples?"

Fitz sat down on his bed slowly. "Heresy is a pretty strong accusation. I usually reserve it for things I'm very sure about."

"I used to be sure about everything. But since I lost my Gift, nothing feels the same." She couldn't believe she had revealed something so personal to him.

"I can't imagine what it's like to have a Gift then lose it." His voice was quiet and thoughtful. "I don't know you well, Rose, but I can tell you are tough. I think you can make it through this with a stronger faith than before."

She scoffed. "Stronger? I used to call the wind and direct it to do my bidding. I was fast and unstoppable. Now I'm weak. I'm nothing."

"No, Rose." Fitz's voice was sharper than she had heard before. "You are just like everyone else."

She flinched uncomfortably.

"Is the thought of being like the rest of us so distasteful to you?"

She couldn't form an answer, but he must have seen one on her face.

His voice reminded her of Mims, loving but firm. "The Goddess's followers in the Underneath believed in her despite what we saw. The only Gifts we saw were from children we surrendered to a temple for their safety. We never saw the Pageant. Never received healing. We saw nothing that would hint that she was real at all. The only thing we had was our belief. So tell me, Priest Rose, who had the stronger faith?"

She closed her eyes, unable to answer.

He sighed, and his scolding tone softened. "I know it feels like you've lost everything, but you've gained the potential to have a faith as strong as the people you once overlooked. Sometimes, when everything else is stripped away, faith is all that we have left."

He gathered up a few books and left her alone with the words hanging in the air.

33

Fitz's words continued to sting long after he left. They stung bad enough that she pulled herself out of bed, out of the temple, and to the Library. She hoped that when she arrived, the warmth from her dream of storming the Library with Wilder would drive away the coldness inside.

As she approached the massive seven-story structure, she felt some of the loss subside. The Library always was a refuge for her. Books were less complicated than people. Books made sense. The author wrote the words once, and they remained unchanged in perfect black and white.

An old man stopped her at the door. "Good afternoon, Priest."

"Am I supposed to pay you so I can enter?" She tried to stir her anger, but the man's face was kind, and her heart wasn't in it.

"No, Priest," he said. "Other people must pay to go inside, but Priests can enter for free. But if you want to borrow a book, there will be a charge, like for everyone else."

She gave him a tight smile. "I'm just like everyone else, so I guess that makes sense."

His brow crinkled in confusion, but he let her go inside.

The late afternoon sunlight streamed through the tall windows in the central foyer. It surprised her to find even more people inside than before the Uprising. Since they were charging people to enter, she'd assumed the Library would be empty. She made a rough count of all the people and wondered exactly how much money Mayra and her cronies were bringing in.

As she wandered through the stacks, she found parents quietly reading books to children and friends reading together at a table, stacks of books between them. Every row she walked down had someone else browsing. She hunted for the most remote location so she could be alone with her dark thoughts.

She found Wilder among the narrow aisles of the east stacks. He was leaning against the shelves with a small book open in his hands, so engrossed in the pages that he didn't see her standing at the end of the row. She froze, unable to breathe. People were complicated, and in her heart, Wilder was perhaps the most complicated of all.

She took a quiet step backward, and his eyes popped up to catch her. He was perfectly still, reacting as if she were a scared animal. She didn't know if his reaction was based on her expression or if he could hear the way her pulse pounded in her veins. She briefly considered running away to find an empty row, but even though everything had changed, running away still wasn't in her nature.

At her first step toward him, he stood up from his leaning position. She didn't want the Priest librarians reprimanding her for speaking loudly, so she drew close enough to whisper.

"Hi," she said.

He smiled tentatively. "I haven't heard any screaming. Did you change your mind about burning all the heretics?"

She growled. "I don't change my mind."

His lips tightened into a line.

She rubbed her hands across her eyes. "I'm sorry. I don't feel like myself today."

He raised an eyebrow. "I think that's the most you've sounded like yourself all day. Do you want to talk about it?"

She thought about her conversation with Fitz and wasn't sure if she wanted to discuss that again. "Not really. I came here so I wouldn't have to talk at all."

"Me too."

Despite his words, there was something in his eyes that beckoned her to stay. It reminded her of the night of their sparring match. After he forgave her, he said the next move was hers. She wasn't sure what kind of game they were playing, so she had to guess what move to make.

"This aisle seems like a good place for not talking." She plucked a book from the shelf, then leaned against the shelves across from him.

His lips curled into a smile. He gave a little bow before reopening his own book and leaning against his shelves again.

Rose pretended to read for a few minutes before raising her eyes from her book to study him. He cradled the small book in his broad hands, turning the pages slowly, rereading each page multiple times. She couldn't see the title of the book without moving more than just her eyes. She was curious what kind of books Wilder liked to read, but she didn't want to be the first to speak.

Her eyes flicked down to the book she held. It was from the same shelf as his.

Lothaire's Anthology of First-Century Sonnets.

Rose coughed in shock.

Wilder looked up at her with a question in his eyes. He didn't speak, so she didn't either. She ducked her head back into her book until he started reading again.

Poetry? Wilder read poetry? Since his eyes were focused on his book again, she looked up to study him. She wasn't sure what she expected him to read, but she wouldn't have guessed poetry. She watched his expression shift as he read, and she tried to guess what the poem was about. Her book was full of love poems. Was that really what he was reading?

"Enjoying the book?" Wilder's eyes didn't shift from his book.

She fumbled the book in her hand slightly. "Um ... yes, of course."

He raised his eyes, and by his slight grin, Rose knew he had noticed her staring. "I appreciate how Lothaire organized the sonnets into chapters based on the Virtues."

"Oh ... yes, that's nice," she said lamely.

"A clever reminder of how the Goddess's Virtues are expressed through the love of her people for one another."

Rose blinked stupidly at him. "You've studied the theology of first-century love poetry?"

His eyes twinkled mysteriously, as if he enjoyed surprising her. "And you haven't?" he asked with a mischievous smile. "That seems like something you would study in Priest school."

His words brought her attention back to the cold void inside. "I don't want to discuss what I learned to become a Priest. Most of it is pointless now."

He looked taken aback. "I'm surprised to hear you say that. Is that what's been bothering you?"

She didn't want to discuss her own internal struggles, but she thought it was safe to discuss what she had learned. She stepped closer to him so she could drop her voice even quieter.

"The people speaking out against Priests have their crystalline shut off everywhere they go."

His face was not as shocked as she expected.

"You knew," she said flatly.

"I've heard the rumors, but they only recently became widespread enough for me to take it seriously."

A fire blazed to life in her. "You heard there was a rogue

Priest who still has their Gift and kept that information from me?"

He cleared his throat. "Honestly, I assumed you would react like you did to Mayra and ruin any chance I had of getting close to the truth."

If she weren't in the Library, she would scream. Instead, she dropped her voice to a deadly whisper. "You knew I had only one goal: to get my Gift back. There is someone out there who holds an answer, and I could make them tell me how they did it. And you hid it from me."

She could see an ember burning behind his eyes. "Yes, Rose. That's exactly why I hid it from you. I knew you would storm into the building on a rampage, and I would lose my chance at discovering what their motivation is."

She was struggling to keep her whisper below a hiss. "Their *motivation* is to rule this City as High Priests. I don't know what else you need to discover. Maybe in all your theological research, you believe we would be better off if the High Priests returned?"

Wilder shook with anger contained. "It's clear your Priest school training was severely lacking. You never learned how to keep your hateful accusations to yourself."

His words struck a little too close to the lessons Mims tried to teach her. They fanned the flames higher. "At least I'm ready to take action. I can't spend a lifetime sneaking around corners, pretending to be something I am not."

"Instead, you will run in and destroy those you care about. You'd risk everyone close to you if you thought you'd win."

She stepped right up to his chest and whispered, "Just because I'm close to someone does not mean I care for them."

He shook his head and slid his poetry book back onto the shelf before he walked away.

34

R ose was not looking forward to a day of auditions sitting next to an angry Wilder. Her walk back to Temple Knowledge that evening had only made her own anger at him feel even more righteous. He knew there was someone with the Gift in the City, and he hadn't told her. That was a piece of information that changed everything she believed about herself and the Goddess, and he thought he should keep it to himself. He liked to pretend they were on the same side, but that's all it was: pretending.

She scowled when she found him already seated at their table. She'd wanted to be seated calmly when he arrived, but now she was starting off at a disadvantage. It was no matter. She would not let him win.

"Good morning, Priest Rose." Wilder's voice was pleasant coolness.

"Goddess blessing upon you, Wilder." She tried to instill as much formality into the words as possible as she took her seat.

A sharp silence fell between them. Neither of them budged from their stiff-backed positions on the wooden chairs. The minutes stretched on as they waited for the auditions to begin, and they held their stubborn silence.

Fitz walked toward their table with a smile, but as he got closer, his face became wary.

"Um ... Good morning?" he asked.

"Good morning, Fitz." Wilder's greeting held actual warmth for Fitz.

"I thought you should know that only a few performers scheduled have showed up. And I'm not sure if there will be many more."

"Why would someone sign up to audition and then not show up?" she asked.

Fitz frowned. "According to the other auditioners, this Diocese has one of the largest anti-Priest factions in the City. The performers who did show up are afraid of the repercussions if they actually win a spot in the Pageant. It won't surprise me if we lose a couple of them before they finally take the stage."

Rose stared at him with wide eyes. People were scared to audition? Scared to win a role? How did this faction get so out of hand?

Wilder turned to her with serious eyes. "I think we need to start officially assigning roles to the performers we've already seen. We need to know if those performers are just as willing to back out. I'd hate to show up to the first rehearsal with only half a cast."

The thought of someone winning a role and then refusing it was ridiculous. She couldn't imagine such a thing. But the memory of the wild crowd cheering for the Sisters to kill the men dressed as Priests was enough to take the idea seriously.

She nodded. "Let's hear whoever showed up today, and then we will go through the past roster and start handing out roles."

Only six people auditioned. Previous Dioceses had dozens of performers auditioning. Rose felt a sick foreboding as Fitz signaled the last performer had taken the stage. She put the six performers' paperwork on top of the stack and sighed.

Wilder slouched back in his chair. "I didn't expect that faction to take over so quickly."

She raised an eyebrow at him. "But you expected it would take over eventually?"

"I thought it might. Considering the strange way this faction keeps losing their access to crystalline, it makes their propaganda easier to believe."

"Maybe they are right," she said.

He snorted. "You hate Priests, too?"

She glared. "No. But I hate whoever is doing this. And if they are planning to become High Priest using that Gift, I think the faction is right. They should be stopped."

"That's not all they believe, Rose. They want to dismantle all worship of the Goddess. No more Priests. No more temples. No more Virtues. Is that what you want?"

"Of course not! What do you think I've been fighting to protect? I want to find that rogue Priest and stop them."

"That's what this is all about, isn't it? That's why you've been so upset since you found out about the crystalline. You are jealous that someone else has a Gift and you don't."

His words had the ring of compassion, but all she felt was the cold sting of truth.

"It's not about jealousy," she hissed. "It's my job as a Priest to protect this City. I wouldn't expect you to understand."

His dark eyes glittered with daggers, and his voice was seductively low. "Oh, really? What if I found this rogue Priest and killed them for you? Would it make you happy that I protected the City? Or would you be angry that you didn't get to question them for yourself to find out exactly how they kept their Gift?"

His words cut her with a truth she hadn't recognized. She desperately wanted to look that rogue Priest in the eye and demand to know how they did it. She wanted to yank them forward by their collar and stare into their eyes until she understood. Even more than wanting to defeat a new High Priest, she wanted to steal the rogue Priest's secrets.

The guilt threatened to swallow her. Wilder's smile of vindication faded the longer he watched her. Neither of them noticed the woman walk up to the table until she scattered all their paperwork to the wind with a shout.

"All you Priests can go jump in the Abyss! We don't need your kind around here!"

Wilder stood, and the woman ran off. Rose leaped up to gather the papers before they blew away. Yet another reminder that she could have asked the breeze to gather the pages back to herself if she still had her Gift.

She and Wilder brought the collected pages back to their table and began smoothing them. They sorted them until they found the six who had auditioned and put them on top. And when they finished, they had one more page than before.

A flyer for an event at the bridge that night.

Rose realized that this was the only audition where she hadn't seen Vaylan. She had no doubt he was responsible for the flyer.

Celebrate equality and freedom at a casino at the bridge tonight!
Roulette, card games, and more!
Brother Owyn will be in attendance,
so don't miss it!

The woman at the last event had mentioned Brother Owyn

like everyone knew him. So, if everyone knew him, that meant …

"Wilder, do you know about Brother Owyn?"

He frowned. "I've heard of him, but I haven't seen him in person yet. He is a beloved figure in this faction. They speak about him as if they worship him instead of the Goddess. I don't think he tries to convince them otherwise."

She scowled. Vaylan. It had to be him. He was arrogant enough to allow others to worship him. He must have given Rose a fake name to throw her off track.

"I think I've met him," she said. "A strange man has been at every audition, trying to convert me to whatever it is he believes. He's the one who put this flyer in this stack."

Wilder tapped his lips in thought. "Interesting … I wonder why he's trying to convert a Priest to his side. Maybe he thinks it will be a sign of the Goddess's weakness if he can steal one of her Priests?"

"But why choose me? Does he think I'm that weak?" The idea made her angry and guilty that he might be right.

"Maybe it's your prominence in the auditions? Maybe it was just the ease of knowing where to find you each day? It's hard to know what motivates a true predator."

She shivered as she considered Vaylan stalking her. She only sensed smug arrogance and paternal condescension from him in person. But maybe that's what made him a better hunter.

"What are you planning?" asked Wilder.

"What do you mean?"

"Are you going tonight? Knowing that he is stalking you for unknown purposes?"

"I'm definitely going!" she said. "I have to find out what he wants from me."

Wilder rolled his eyes. "Of course you choose to run in without thinking this through."

"What's there to think through, Wilder? This strange guy has built up a faction of people who hate my kind, and he has some weird fascination with me. I have to find out why."

"Rose! That's exactly why you should *not* go! There is another reason he might have chosen you." He stared at her with hard eyes. "He might think you'll make a pretty sacrifice when his mob tears you limb from limb."

She caught her breath as she considered that. The Sisters fought paid actors dressed as Priests, but that might not always be the case. Could Vaylan be setting her up as an unwilling participant in his own sort of Pageant? That he saw her as easy prey made her furious. She wouldn't let him use her like that. Whatever script he had planned, she was prepared to destroy him.

Wilder saw her face and sank back in his chair with a sigh.

35

Rose strode through the City streets like she was the hunter, not the hunted. After a conversation with a woman from the temple laundry room, she'd traded one of her black outfits for a fitted vest and matching pants in rich plum and exchanged the orange cloak for one in dove gray. She didn't want to make it any easier for Vaylan to identify her; plus, she was happy to be rid of the orange.

Wilder had tried to talk her out of going. When that failed, he said he would go with her. She'd raged at him for quite a while about his lack of authority to do any such thing. He'd relented a little too easily, and when she walked out of the temple, she found out why.

"Hello, ladies," she said to the wolves. "I see you are following his orders again."

They bowed their heads in guilty submission, but when she headed down the stairs, they followed.

As Rose approached the bridge, she passed card games and people betting on fighting matches, but she walked by without a glance. All she cared about was confronting Vaylan.

On the stage near the bridge entrance, dancers and contortionists and jugglers performed in a chaotic version of a show. She found a place close to the front but at an angle where Vaylan couldn't see her when he took the stage. As she waited for him to arrive, she mentally counted and re-counted each blade she had hidden on her body.

A tall woman walked center stage, and the performers scattered.

"We have plenty more acts for you to enjoy tonight, but first, a word from the source of our inspiration, Brother Owyn."

Rose was shocked when an old man walked on stage, not Vaylan. Rose had never seen a man so old. Or at least not one that looked as old as he actually was.

Brother Owyn wore a simple linen tunic and pants that were so white they glowed from where he stood center stage. His thin, gray hair sprouted unevenly from his head. He walked slowly but with an unbowed back. The cheering crowd quieted when he raised his arms.

"'If the Goddess truly cared for her people, why didn't she stop the High Priests?' That's the question I asked that got my family executed."

Rose's breath caught in her throat. Of all the heresies she thought she'd hear, she didn't expect to hear the shameful question she asked herself on dark nights. His voice was stronger than she expected from a man so old, and his serene expression belied the fact that he had just punched her in the gut.

He clasped his hands before him in a sign of peaceful repose. "The High Priests should have killed me, too. Instead, they held me captive for fifty-six years—deep within stone and silence, lost to anyone who once knew my name.

"Yet still, my questions remained.

"If she cared, why did she allow the High Priests to reign unopposed?

"If she cared, why did generations of her children live and die in the Underneath?

"If she cared, why was she silent?

"If you've asked yourselves these questions ... stop.

"Just stop.

"There is no answer that will bring you comfort. No answer to ease your unsettled mind. I sought the answer for years, reached for it from within the darkness, from inside the fear and utter loneliness. I found no answer, but when I came to the end of myself, I found something else.

"I found a vision.

"They trapped my body, but they could not contain my soul. My soul was free to roam the streets of this City, and in those dreams, I saw the future that is to come.

"I saw a city without High Priests. A city with no division between above and below. I saw a city bigger than seven virtues —bigger than seven vices.

"I saw a city that was free."

Brother Owyn looked at everyone in the crowd, focusing on each person as if he were speaking to them alone. When his gaze landed on Rose, he stopped and blinked twice. His eyes unfocused, as if looking through her.

"The path ahead is dark and full of doubt, and though she battles earth and sky, her faithless tears will lead to betrayal."

His voice sounded the same, but the words caused the hair on the back of her neck to stand on end.

He blinked again, his eyes moving on to the rows of people behind her. "You are free. So eat, drink, and play, my children! And always seek the light." He nodded his head in a simple bow and walked offstage.

Music began to play, and gymnasts, contortionists, and dancers spilled out of the wings and into the crowd. The people chanted his name and danced wildly.

Rose backed out of the dancing crowd, the wolves close

behind. She moved slowly, but she couldn't catch her breath. The things Brother Owyn said ... so many ideas she disagreed with, and yet so many ideas she had secretly held inside her heart. She needed to sort through everything he'd said, but she couldn't think beyond escape.

She peered into the crowd, trying to find the shortest path, when a man stepped in front of her, blocking her view.

"I assumed your curiosity would bring you."

Her lingering confusion at Brother Owyn's words snapped into the clear focus of anger at Vaylan. "What do you want with me?"

"Nothing, Rose. I simply wanted to share the information I have with a like-minded soul."

"We are nothing alike," she spat, pushing past him and pressing her way through the crowd.

He caught up to her quickly. "So ... are you going to tell me what you think?"

She didn't stop walking. "About the heresy? Fascinating. The contortionists are a nice touch."

"It's easier to draw the people in with a show. I'm sure you can relate, considering the priority placed on your Pageants." He winked. "But I thought you might find his story interesting."

She stopped walking and stared at him. "I have devoted my life to serving the Goddess. What made you think I would find any of this interesting?"

"His family. The High Priests killed them, and he was powerless to stop them. I thought you might find that part familiar."

She took a step back. "I don't know why you think—"

"You told me they killed your sister and two brothers, and you couldn't stop them."

She couldn't believe she had let a part of her life slip out to this stranger who now believed he knew her. Her siblings died over five years ago, yet she still felt their loss like a gaping hole in her heart.

"It's a terrible story, Rose, and it's all too common. The High Priests killed so many people. So many family members we will never get back. I thought you would understand what he felt."

She hissed. "I can understand what he felt without spouting heresy. The High Priests were terrible people who ruled by using fear. I agree with him on that. I just disagree on where to go from there." She spun on her heel and began walking toward the temple again.

He called out but didn't follow her. "I was there, Rose. I was with Brother Owyn in the High Priests' prison."

She stopped and turned around.

He spoke in a low, hypnotizing voice. "I was in that same prison for over a decade. Brother Owyn is the only reason I stayed sane. His vision of a free City kept me alive. If I believed the City would always remain as it was, I would have died in that prison. But I knew that someday I would be free—free of prison, free of the Goddess, and free of her Priests."

She shook her head and whispered, "Why are you telling me this?"

"I've seen you fighting so hard to hold everything together, but you don't have to. It's not your responsibility. You can let go, Rose. You can be free."

She couldn't respond to his seemingly kind words. He sounded so sincere and paternal, and yet, everything inside her screamed out in warning.

"Good night, Vaylan." She spun and walked quicker this time, hoping he wouldn't call out again.

36

Rose practically ran the rest of the way back to Temple Knowledge. She had to get away from Brother Owyn and Vaylan and the confusing thoughts swirling around in her head. Her steps felt too slow with the wind fighting her every move.

She stumbled up the temple stairs and ran straight to the dance studio. The second she slid inside the dark studio, the tears began to fall. The wolves peeked in through the wispy curtains, then backed out to the courtyard.

Why did she go tonight? She should have known she wouldn't get the satisfaction of defeating Vaylan. Instead, she was defeated by an old man.

Brother Owyn's story represented all her dark nights of doubt, and yet he stood there so vibrant and alive. He seemed free in a way she would never be. She wasn't even sure she wanted that freedom. She liked the security of knowing the rules and doing the right thing. Without the structure of everything she believed, she would be unmoored, set adrift to float to places she didn't want to go.

She shed her restraints as she crossed the dance floor.

Cloak, boots, knives, fitted vest, and hairpins all clattered to the floor behind her.

Rose danced.

She couldn't count the number of nights she ended with tear-soaked dancing since the Uprising. Her katas and dance warm-ups blended together in a seamless loop. Every night, she ran through the same combinations, timed only to the sad rhythm of her heart. Her bare feet echoed as they pounded against the hardwood floors, and even the swish of her hair seemed loud in the silent room.

Until he began his song.

She stilled as Wilder's voice trickled in from the back of the studio. She didn't turn to face him, but in the mirror, she could see where he stood silhouetted in an archway. The tender sound of his voice wrapped around her, and she closed her eyes at the embrace.

The words of the song were unfamiliar, and the melody looped in a curious way that she found fascinating. The lyrics were about wind and storms and fire and ... love. He sang with a clear baritone that sank through her skin and into her bones. With each note, she found strength.

She slid back into her katas and dance combos, only to find them changed. No longer were they set to the lonely rhythm of her heartbeat, but instead, they flowed in time to his melody. Each sad step had been transformed into an expression of hope. Her movements never changed, but the tempo of her heart shifted.

His voice never faltered. He was Rivalry-trained and Pageant-tested. He could sing for hours and never miss a note. She had last heard him sing the night of the deadly Pageant. His voice was just as brilliant now as it had been that night.

Rose sank into the comfort of his steady song.

She moved with a simple grace unaided by the wind. Each movement was perfectly ordinary, and yet her soul floated on the gentle breeze of his melody. Her steps were just as slow, but instead of finding frustration, she found ease. The wind still offered the same stiff resistance, but now it also contained his song.

And his song was for her.

She let his melody wind its way into her heart. Her insides were still a mess of storms and void, but curling through it all was the smallest glimmer of light. Each note of his song nestled into a dark corner of her soul. And in the silence between each note, tendrils of hope sprouted around the broken pieces of her heart.

She danced until her body was made anew. Until she was reborn. She didn't know what she had become, only that she was different. Changed. Remade into another version of herself. She danced with the body of her new self and marveled at the beauty of the metamorphosis.

Despite her new strength, she began to tire. He sensed her exhaustion and slowed his tempo to the rhythm of her steps. She wanted to dance forever in this new body, but her intensity waned, and she wanted to finish well.

Wilder continued to sing as she strode to where he stood. She timed each footstep to his rhythm, and at the final note, she stood a single step away. His last note echoed through the dark room, and only warm silence surrounded them.

Her voice was rough with sobs and exertion. "Thank you."

"You looked so sad." His low voice was gentle, unaltered by his singing.

"How did you know I was here?"

He lifted his arm to reveal a sleeve ripped by a set of canine fangs. "I was summoned," he said with a wry grin.

"Thanks for sending them with me. I was an idiot to go on my own."

He closed the step between them. "Did he hurt you?" He studied her, looking for injuries.

"Not physically," she said. "And I honestly can't blame my broken soul on him, either. That was cracking long before I met him."

Wilder considered her with a tentative expression. "I should tell you something, but I'm unsure if you will be angry or not."

"I'm too exhausted to be angry."

"I followed you to the event. I lost you in the crowd, but I heard Brother Owyn speak." He looked at her hesitantly, waiting to see her reaction.

"That wasn't the man I expected. But I must admit, his story was ... disturbing."

Wilder looked at her with eyes as deep as the night. "I wish I had been with you."

She looked down, unable to meet his eyes. "Because I wasn't strong enough to handle it alone."

He lifted her chin with a soft hand. "Because I didn't want to handle it alone, either."

Her heartbeat slowed to a crawl. She looked into his eyes and lived in the space between one breath and the next.

"Rose."

His whisper was softer than a spring breeze, and her crawling heart skidded to a stop. He leaned close enough for her to count each of his long eyelashes. His breath stirred the air between them, but her lungs had forgotten how to function. She couldn't even blink because her eyes refused to stop watching his lips move closer.

He glanced at his fingertips resting on her tear-stained cheek, then blinked and appeared to mentally travel somewhere else. She saw a brief flash of pain behind his eyes before he returned to her.

The moment delicately shifted.

He pulled her closer and laid a gentle kiss of blessing upon her forehead. It wasn't what she expected, but she still sighed at the touch. His lips were soft and warm, and when he pulled away, she felt his kiss blazoned across her forehead like a glowing circlet.

He took a small step back and let his hand fall to his side. He stared at her as if studying every line of her transformed soul.

She felt exposed before his searching eyes. Could he see the doubt still threatening to break her? Could he see the warm hope his song spread through her heart? Could he see how badly she had wanted that kiss to be on her lips?

She inhaled sharply. "I should go." She bent down to gather her discarded clothing. She slid her dagger back into the sheath, then awkwardly grabbed her boots, vest, and cloak, unwilling to take the time to put them on before making her escape.

As she straightened, Wilder stood up behind her and held out a handful of her fallen hairpins. She reached for them, but his soft smile caused her thoughts to slow, and her hand stilled on his.

The same faraway look crossed his eyes, and he gently released her hand.

"It's late," he said softly.

His words snapped her out of her daze. "Yes, it's late." Her voice was too breathy, so she cleared her throat before saying, "Goodnight, Wilder."

He paused as if he might say more, but he bowed his head and said, "Goodnight, Rose," letting her slip out of the studio into the night.

PURITY

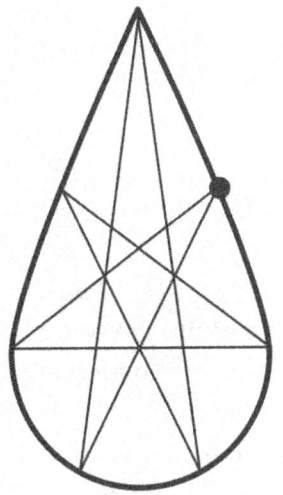

37

The next morning, Rose was a set of precariously balanced contradictions. The void still remained, but tendrils of hope from Wilder's song had taken root, and her forehead blazed like the sun. She was less like herself than ever, yet she felt more comfortable in her skin than she had the day before.

She planned to carry that comfort into their walk to the next temple. However, when she found Wilder talking to Fitz in the courtyard, she nearly stumbled as each of the seeds of hope inside her flared to life in his presence. They had wished each other good night in the dim dance studio, but under the bright light of day, everything between them felt laid bare. She was sure everyone could see Wilder's kiss burned clearly into her forehead.

From Fitz's expression, she wondered if he literally could. "Good morning, Rose. Ready to head to Temple Purity?"

A blush threatened to spring up at his words, but she wasn't sure why. She pulled herself together with a confident stride down the temple stairs. "Yes, of course."

Wilder and Fitz picked up their bags and followed her.

They walked in silence for a while. She couldn't think of a single topic that wouldn't break the fragile equilibrium she held inside.

Wilder's mischievous voice broke the silence. "One of my friends from the Pageant used to tease me that I must be from Purity Diocese." He whispered, "Goddess rest her soul," under his breath. Then louder, he said, "I told everyone I was from Perfection, but I think she was right. Purity would have been more believable." He smiled smugly.

Rose snorted. "The fact that you take it as a compliment is proof that she was right."

Fitz's eyes lit up with curiosity. "What are you talking about?"

Rose didn't trust Wilder to give anything other than a smug response, so she answered. "There are stereotypes around each Diocese, and Purity Diocese is known for a combination of two: those who are pure because they don't have a choice and those who believe purity is a game to be won."

Wilder made a pious face. "If you have any impure thoughts about me, that's your problem. Myself, I am completely pure." A roguish glint in his eye belied his words and made Rose's heart flutter oddly.

"Fascinating!" said Fitz. "I wonder if anyone has studied how these stereotypes tie into the Underneath's Vice of Desire. Usually, the dichotomy divides above and below, but perhaps Purity retained a balance on its own."

Wilder shook his head. "Fitz, don't get distracted by the theological. The most important thing to remember is that I'm going home to my people." He raised his arms toward the crystal spire in the distance, as if in embrace.

Rose rolled her eyes. "Meaning, we should be prepared for you to be even cockier than usual."

His swagger grew more pronounced, and a provocative smile graced his lips.

Her heart fluttered again, and she studied the ground carefully to make sure she didn't trip.

~

As they approached the temple steps, Rose turned to Wilder. "Aren't you going to warn me about not provoking Mayra today? This is usually the point when you try to talk me into being subtle."

Wilder's face was perfectly calm. "I trust you will be exactly as subtle as necessary."

She narrowed her eyes at him but couldn't decipher the statement. She took a deep breath and walked up the steps.

Temple Purity's courtyard used to be filled with the sound of waterfalls, but now the courtyard was silent. Gone were the flowing statues of water held in place by the Priests' magic. Now only a single symbolic pool of water remained.

"Glad to see you finally arrived, Priest Rose." Mayra sat next to the symbolic pool with only a small stack of papers before her. "I thought that since you only auditioned six people at the last Diocese, you might decide to arrive here early for once, but I guess you have other priorities." Her eyes flitted to Wilder before she turned back to her paperwork.

Rose's calm evaporated in flames, but she kept her voice wreathed in civility. "I don't think I can ever arrive earlier than you, Priest Mayra. You are very efficient with your time. I have no idea how you handle so many meetings with specific Priests in each Diocese. You really must tell me how you manage it."

Even though Rose hadn't caught her meeting with Priests other than the one time, she saw from Mayra's tight expression that she hit the mark.

"There is no need for you to concern yourself with what I do," said Mayra. "You and Wilder need to focus on the auditions. That's your task. Leave the bigger concerns to me."

Rose finally noticed Wilder was no longer in the room. He was probably disappointed in her for not keeping her temper in check.

"I know you chose me to handle the auditions so you could spend your time on 'bigger concerns' in each Diocese. But why did you drag Wilder into this? What are your plans for him?"

Mayra gave her a scornful look. "I didn't expect you to be one of those girls who gets weak at a pretty face, Rose. I always took you to be stronger than that."

Rose ground her teeth together. She wanted to shout a comeback but couldn't. She was ashamed that Mayra might be right.

Mayra smiled smugly, knowing she had struck true. "No need to worry. Despite what you believe about me, I don't have any nefarious plans for dear Wilder. Choosing him was purely fiscal. If we want to keep our temples functional, we need the support of not just the believers Upstairs, but those from the Underneath as well. Wilder is beloved by the Underneath. I wanted to tie him to us. Allowing him to take part in the auditions was a very low-risk way to get others on our side."

"Auditions for the Pageant are low risk?" asked Rose. "Making sure the Pageant goes well should be our number one priority! How can you say anything about this is low risk?"

Mayra gave her a condescending frown. "The auditions are a long shot, Rose. We need to make all our plans as if our Gifts never return."

Rose narrowed her eyes at Mayra. "That's an easier statement to make if you are someone who still has their Gift."

Mayra actually rolled her eyes. "Don't be ridiculous. If I had my Gift, I would use it every day to ensure our survival."

"Maybe you are using it every day. Someone is stopping the flow of crystalline to dissidents of the temples. It has to be the work of a Purpose Priest like yourself."

"You don't seriously believe those rumors, do you? Brother

Owyn's cult is spreading false information to turn people to his cause. I can't believe you would listen to heretics, Rose." She shook her head disapprovingly.

"It's easy to verify, Mayra." She actually hadn't verified it, but she didn't want to admit that. "Using our Gifts to punish dissidents is no better than what the High Priests did."

Mayra's eyes were steel. "Believe me, Rose, if I still had my Gift, you would know it. I will use everything in my power to protect our religion."

Rose studied her with hard eyes. "Would you kill to save it?"

Mayra's voice was deadly calm. "Maybe. But I would surely die for it."

She walked off, leaving Rose to finish the paperwork alone.

38

Rose shoved her clothes in her closet and slammed the door. She'd finished the audition paperwork alone, which made her even angrier at Mayra than when she'd started. Not that there were many pages to sort through. Purity Diocese would likely have as few auditoners as in Knowledge. She was still fuming when she heard a knock.

She opened her door to find Wilder leaning against her doorframe. He gave his usual sly grin, trapping her like a fly in a web. Wilder had never come to her room before. She had never even considered him knowing where her room was. He peeked around her into the small room with beds for her and Fitz. Even though it was a borrowed room, his gaze inside felt very personal.

She brought her breathing back under control. "Can I help you with something?"

His grin spread wider. "Grab a swimsuit, and let's go."

"Swimming?" she looked at him incredulously. "You think I packed something to swim in while we are conducting auditions?"

He laughed. "Okay, that's fair. We'll just pick up something on our way out."

She crossed her arms across her chest. "And what makes you think I want to go out with you this evening?"

He looked down at her with his dark, bottomless eyes. "Don't you?"

She grabbed her gray cloak and followed him.

Their first stop was a clothing shop that had a few pieces of swimwear in the back. Since Purity was home to the Priests who controlled water, there used to be a lot of swimming in the Diocese. However, since the Purity Priests could no longer purify the water or cause it to flow where they wished, the pools had fallen out of use for higher priorities.

Wilder hadn't answered any of her questions about their destination. He only gave an enigmatic smile and kept walking. They walked deep into the Diocese before he stopped at a nondescript stone warehouse. He knocked on a plain wood door in a strangely specific pattern. A wooly haired man peeked his head out, then ushered them inside. She heard the clinking sound of coins changing hands, and the man nodded his head to usher them down a hallway.

Wilder raised his eyebrows at her in anticipation and practically skipped down the hallway, pulling her along with him. She had to stifle a laugh at his playfulness. The hallway was quiet, and she still didn't know where they were. At the end of the hallway, he opened the door and pulled her inside.

Warm steam hit her in the face and immediately dampened her cloak. Blue and green glass tiles covered the floor and walls in swirling patterns, and the ceiling was painted in shimmering bubbles. A couple of lounge chairs were grouped on the right, and on the left was a delicate metal filagree table with two low-backed chairs. And lounging in the pool of water at the center of the room was the crew.

Rev called to her. "Rose! You are extremely overdressed! Take everything off and get in here!" She floated over to the edge of the pool and patted the tile to summon Rose to her side.

"Rev!" Wilder laughed. "Give her a moment to adjust before you try to get her undressed!"

Rose still stood frozen in the doorway, trying to understand where they were.

Quinn sat on the edge of the pool next to the machinery pumping water inside. "Isn't it fascinating, Rose? Some of the water workers from the Underneath devised a way to bring water in by conventional ways. It's brilliant how they turned something that was devised to be used only with a Gift into a pool anyone can use."

Wilder shook his head. "Rev wants to get her undressed. Quinn wants to teach her about machinery. What are you adding to the party, Tayeh?"

Tayeh sat lounging with her feet draped inside the pool. Her lilac bikini seemed surprisingly delicate, considering Rose had only ever seen her in stiff leather armor. "I'd challenge her to a match, but I honestly don't want to get up at the moment." She leaned back on her hands and closed her eyes in relaxation.

Wilder shrugged. "That's what you've got to choose from." He nodded to a fabric screen in the corner. "You can change into your swimsuit there if you choose Rev's option."

Rev smiled at her and winked.

Wilder kicked his boots off. "I'm definitely choosing your option, Rev." He stripped his shirt off over his head, and Rose nearly choked when he started unbuckling his pants in the middle of the room. He had on shorts underneath. Rose prayed that the blush on her cheeks would appear to be from the warm steam.

Wilder backed up to make a running jump, but Tayeh spoke without opening her eyes. "If you splash me, Wilder, I will slice your gut open with one of Quinn's gears."

Wilder skidded to a halt, then gently stepped into the pool. Tayeh leaned back further on her elbows.

Rose stepped behind the screen and changed into the bright red bikini. She had a variety of black swimsuits back in Discipline, but the red bikini was the only swimsuit in the shop that was her size. She normally wasn't self-conscious about her body, but tonight, her skin felt highly sensitized. Her skin tingled with the warm steam and was alive in a way she had never felt before. She piled her blades on top of her clothes and stepped out.

She walked deliberately to the edge of the pool. Wilder's smile was playful, but she didn't let that distract her as she lowered herself into the warm water. She stepped down to the ledge where Rev and Wilder relaxed and sank down to her shoulders. Her hair was piled in a knot on her head, and the fallen tendrils clung to her neck. The water flowed in a soothing pattern she couldn't believe was created by machinery alone. She rested her head back against the ledge and sighed in pleasure.

Rev chuckled. "I knew you'd love it."

Rose cracked open an eye. "What is this place?"

Wilder answered. "It used to be a secret meeting place for the High Priest of Purity."

Both of her eyes shot open.

He gestured at the machinery Quinn was still examining. "The High Priest obviously didn't need any of that since he could control everything with his Gift. After the Uprising, an enterprising fellow from the Underneath discovered the place and made it operational. Having a luxurious place to conduct secret meetings is apparently pretty lucrative."

Rose raised an eyebrow at him. "Secret meetings? Is that what this is?"

Rev scooted closer to her. "Of course it is, dear! Wilder has some news for us, don't you?"

Quinn moved away from the machinery to sit closer to the pool, and Tayeh opened her eyes.

Wilder leaned back against the ledge and spread his arms in his typical smug posture. His tattoo of the Goddess glistened on his broad chest. She hurriedly snapped her attention to his face. She didn't need to encourage him to be any cockier.

"I gathered some useful information today. I found out that not only is Mayra planning something, but it will happen immediately after the audition in Order."

Rose sat up sharply. "How did you find that out?"

"She was sloppy and believed her room was a safe place to store important documents."

Rose gaped. "You snuck into her bedroom?"

Tayeh chuckled. "He doesn't have to sneak in. He gets invited."

Wilder grinned. "Thanks for the vote of confidence, Tayeh. But this time, I actually did sneak in."

"But what if she found you?" asked Rose.

"I knew she would be distracted for a while," he said mysteriously.

Rose thought back to when they arrived. She turned a flat stare on him. "You said you expected me to be as subtle as necessary."

He gave her a secret smile. "And you definitely were."

She wanted to be upset, but she couldn't. What could she be mad at? That he knew her so well?

"Mayra had letters from the other Priests she spoke to in

each temple. They never said what exactly they are planning, but the fact that it is scheduled once we arrive in Order is significant. That's a lot sooner than any of us imagined. She must be confident in the level of support these Priests can leverage."

Tayeh frowned. "Or she's getting desperate."

Rev nodded. "And if she's desperate, there's no telling what risks she will take."

Rose whispered, "She said she'd die to protect our religion." The statement sent a chill through the warm room.

Rose shook it off. "Mayra has to be the Purpose Priest who is cutting dissidents off from crystalline. Do you think any of her cronies also still have their Gifts somehow?" It was bad enough thinking about a single rogue Priest, much less a group of them.

Wilder shook his head. "There aren't any signs of that. That is the only sign of a Gift we've seen."

Quinn chimed in. "Maybe it's not a Gift. Maybe it's a Spark."

Rose turned to him slowly, trying to understand his words.

Tayeh slapped him on the arm. "Quinn! What have I told you about sharing your heretical ideas with believers? It either makes them cranky or sad. It's rude."

Quinn ducked his head. "Sorry."

"It's okay, Quinn," said Rev. "You can tell us. We won't get cranky or sad." She directed a pointed look at Rose.

Quinn brightened and looked relieved to share the information. "The books from the time before the City's founding discussed a type of magic they called the Spark. Sparks were randomly given to people and were a lot different from our Gifts today." He looked at them hesitantly before continuing. "Ylena's Spark is that she can gain any Gift she sees someone use. That's why she had them all. And um ... Lady Erenne ... the Goddess ... her Spark was similar."

Rose stared at him in shock. "How do you know this?"

"I translated some of those ancient books. That's how I

helped Ylena figure out how the High Priests lived so long. They knew a man with the Spark of granting long life, and they kept him to themselves."

"So, this rogue Priest might not have a Gift at all? They might have a Spark that was given to them completely by chance?"

"Maybe," said Quinn. "Considering there have been strict protocols put into place to keep the Gifts regulated, it makes sense that this single magical occurrence results from a random Spark."

It wasn't that the Goddess gave out Gifts again and forgot Rose. The Goddess was still silent, but some random person had gained the ability to shape stone. She couldn't decide if the thought was better or worse.

39

The audition the next day was the most boring yet, but Rose's mind couldn't stop racing. Only two people had auditioned, but Wilder and Rose stayed longer just in case someone else showed up. As she sat next to Wilder, her mind ran from idea to idea and ended up considering him more often than she wanted to admit.

She replayed Quinn's words about the Spark over and over. Some people had magical abilities that weren't granted by the Goddess at all. They were just random. Chaos.

Chaos was the opposite of the Goddess.

She clung to the thought. The Goddess hadn't passed her over. She was still frustratingly silent, but hope remained that she would return.

And Quinn said the High Priests lived so long because they took advantage of someone with a Spark. They exploited the chaos of a Spark in order to remain in power. That's what made them so evil.

She didn't know what to think about his statement that the Goddess had a Spark. That didn't quite fit in, so she discarded it.

But he said Ylena had a Spark. That definitely made sense. That girl was pure chaos. Rose had no idea what her brother saw in her.

Or what Wilder saw in her.

That thought didn't fit either, so she discarded it as well.

Whoever was using their Spark to terrorize the City was clearly evil. It was more proof that this Spark was the problem. Not the Goddess. Not the Priests. Not the Gifts.

She felt the fragile structure of her faith rebuilding inside the void. Things made sense. The pieces fit together. She fit together. Everything would be okay.

Wilder shifted slightly, immediately drawing her attention to him. She grumbled to herself. How had she allowed herself to become so easily distracted? This was exactly what Mayra had chided her for when they first started the auditions, and now Rose was even worse than she imagined.

She pulled her thoughts back to considering how the Spark fit into her theology when Fitz walked up to their table.

"I think that's all we are going to get today. It's like people are purposely avoiding the entire park." Fitz nodded at the empty grass, which used to be filled with an audience in previous auditions.

Rose sighed. "I think you are right. I was hoping we could find at least one more performer."

Fitz cheered up. "I have some good news, though. We got invited to a party tonight!" He held up a flyer that looked suspiciously familiar.

Rose snatched it out of his hand. "Who handed this to you?"

Fitz was stunned at her quick reaction, but he answered. "It was the last girl who performed. She said some guy was handing them out in the park."

The flyer looked like the others, except this one was an invitation to a masquerade. She couldn't stop herself from sighing.

Wilder looked at her with confusion. "Why are you disappointed? I thought you would be excited to go murder everyone in sight."

"It's a masquerade," she explained.

"Umm ... and?" he asked.

"I don't have anything to wear!" She covered her face with her hands at the admission of her guilt.

He laughed. "I need to go tell the crew about this. I'll mention your dilemma to Rev, and I'm sure she will help."

Wilder ran off to find the crew, Fitz headed to find some new clothes of his own, and Rose headed back to the temple alone. She was glad to finally have some peaceful time to think without Wilder's distracting presence by her side.

"Rose!"

She groaned as Vaylan fell into step beside her. So much for a peaceful walk.

"Isn't it enough that I'm attending your masquerade tonight? Do you have to harass me now, too?"

He smiled. "I knew you wouldn't miss it. You must admit that Brother Owyn's people throw much better parties than yours."

She rolled her eyes. "What do you want, Vaylan?"

"Have you heard anything about their timeline?"

"Why should I tell you what I know? The only thing you've told me is heresy. I don't owe you anything."

"What do you want to know? I'll answer anything if you tell me how much time we have to prepare."

She stopped walking and considered him. Vaylan was arrogant and preachy, but at least he had always been up front about his motives: to destroy her religion so there was no more division between Priests and everyone else. How could he possibly think she would want to assist him with that? He said they both agreed on doing whatever it took to keep new High Priests from being chosen. Did she really want to stop Mayra bad enough to give Vaylan even a shred of information?

She crossed her arms over her chest. "Why do you care so much about these High Priests being chosen? Even if we stop this group, what's stopping another group from popping up behind them?"

"Time, Rose. I need more time. I'm not worried about all the Priests out there. Over time, Brother Owyn and I will convince everyone of the need for equality. We will convince everyone that there is no Upstairs and Underneath ... no divisions between Priests and everyone else. I believe we can unite everyone. With time. But if the High Priests reorganize, we won't have that time. They will put the structure back in place to rule over us for another hundred years." His dark eyes pleaded with her.

She didn't like the way his words stirred her. Her delicate framework inside the void trembled but didn't fall. She knew the High Priests were never part of the Goddess's plan. On this, she agreed with Vaylan. And she wasn't afraid of time. The Goddess's temples had stood for thousands of years, and even the evil High Priests weren't enough to destroy them. These two men wouldn't either.

"You don't have much time," she said. "They are planning to make their move once we arrive in Order for the audition."

He sighed. "I had hoped they would wait until after the Pageant. They must not have much hope of regaining their Gifts. Otherwise, they would wait."

The logic of his statement angered Rose even more. How could a group of Priests with so little faith in the Goddess think they were worthy enough to set themselves above all other Priests?

"Thank you, Rose. I will warn Brother Owyn and the other

outspoken leaders to be careful. I'm sure it won't stop them from speaking out, but they need to know those Priests are coming for them."

"We don't know that's what they are planning." A shiver of unease crawled up her back. "These Priests need to set themselves up as the authority above all other Priests. I don't know if they are considering your people at all."

Vaylan shook his head sadly. "Brother Owyn was a threat to the original High Priests' power. Now that people have heard his story, he's an even bigger threat. At least we know now when they will try to strike, and we will be ready."

Rose chewed on her lip. She couldn't imagine Mayra and her cronies trying to attack Brother Owyn. Mayra called his followers a cult. Surely she didn't see the old man as a threat?

"I'm going to give him the warning now," said Vaylan. "I might not make it to the masquerade tonight, but I hope you enjoy yourself." He patted her arm indulgently before he strode away.

She walked back to the temple with dread swirling in her stomach, wondering what Mayra had planned and if Brother Owyn would survive it.

40

Rose opened the door to her room to find Rev already inside.

"How did you get here before I did?"

"When Wilder told me the situation, I realized it was an emergency, so I came as fast as I could."

Rose examined the piles of sparkly clothes on her bed. "I appreciate your priorities."

"This is all I could come up with on such short notice," said Rev. "But hopefully we can find something here that works."

There were dozens of dresses on the bed. Rose wondered how many she could have found if it wasn't short notice.

Rev sat down on Fitz's bed and handed Rose a gold dress from the top of the pile. "Start stripping, honey. We need to hustle if you want time to fix your hair, too."

Rose set the dress on her chair and started unbuttoning her blouse. Rev seemed to enjoy it a bit too much.

"Do I need to change in the bathroom, or can you control yourself?"

Rev threw her head back and laughed. "If I was really looking for a show, I would pay for a quality professional in the

Underneath. But that doesn't mean I don't find an amateur entertaining now and then."

Amateur? Rose grumbled at being called amateur at anything.

Rev propped her back against the wall and curled her legs beneath her on the bed. "While you dress is a perfect time for girl talk."

Rose hesitated with the gold dress half up. "Do we have to? For most of our girl talks, I feel the need to be armed."

Rev grinned. "Exactly. And while you're changing, I can catch you while you are vulnerable. Or at least as vulnerable as you ever allow yourself to be."

Rose sighed and raised the zipper on the dress. "Fine. Girl talk at me."

"First off, the gold dress is a no. Take it off immediately." She handed Rose a sky blue dress after she unzipped. "Second, tell me what happened after Wilder walked you home last night."

Rose's hands stilled with the gold dress clutched to her chest. "What do you mean?"

"I mean, you both left the pools together, and he walked you back to the temple." She spoke as if explaining the situation to a child. "Did he walk you to your door?"

Rose pulled the sky blue dress over her head to hide her expression and gather her thoughts. Why should she share anything with Rev? Well, Rev was helping her out in a major clothing emergency. And even more pressing, she desperately wanted to talk about it.

"Yes, he walked me to the door." She zipped the dress up to hide her eyes from Rev. "He told me good night. Then he left."

"Hmm ... Interesting ..." She handed Rose a deep burgundy dress. "Next." She rubbed her glittery eyepatch in thought. "It's not like Wilder to get cold feet at the last moment. He's usually good at knowing what he wants and going after it."

"What makes you think he *wants* anything?" She tried to say the words casually, but she stumbled while pulling up the burgundy dress in an attempt to study Rev's expression.

Rev scowled. "Don't dissemble, Rose. You're horrible at it." She turned her sharp blue eye on Rose. "Unless you aren't just lying to me. Maybe you are also lying to yourself."

Rose couldn't get the burgundy dress zipped, so she tugged it off and grabbed a bright yellow one. "I don't know what you are talking about."

Rev snorted. "Classic. I assumed that since you were so blunt in everything else, you'd be just as blunt in admitting what you want. Honestly, I assumed you would grab Wilder by the scruff of the neck and claim him by now."

Rose nearly choked at the image.

"I guess I should have seen this would be how your stubbornness would play out," said Rev. "It's just curious that Wilder would lose his nerve when he has you in the palm of his hand."

Rose threw the yellow dress at Rev. "I'm in no one's hand, Goddess-dammit. I'm my own woman."

Rev's lips curled in an appreciative smile as Rose stomped furiously in only her underwear. Rose took a calming breath, then walked to the bed with the utmost dignity and picked up a pale green dress.

Rev tapped her lips thoughtfully. "The two of you are definitely a good match. It's just surprising he hasn't tried to kiss you yet. It's unlike him."

Rose stilled with the pale green dress half on. Her mind returned to the night when she thought he might kiss her.

Rev sat up straight. "What's that look about? Are you holding out on me?"

Rose clutched her dress while she told Rev what happened that night. And how, at the end, he'd only kissed her on the forehead.

Rev leaned her head back against the wall. "The tears. I should have seen it. Poor guy is spooked about Priests now."

Rose huffed. "He's known I was a Priest from the first moment we met. And he also knows I don't have my Gift anymore."

"It's not you, dear," said Rev. She frowned as if considering how much to tell her. "Let's just say he had an unpleasant experience kissing a girl with a Gift, and now he's a bit skittish."

Ylena.

Rose didn't realize she was growling until Rev interrupted. "It won't do you any good to say anything bad about her. It will only make the situation worse. He will feel the need to defend her, and that's the opposite reaction we need right now."

Rev stood and began draping Rose's backless dress. It had a high neckline in the front with fabric that draped in a curve at her low back. The pale green silk flowed along her body as if made for her. She ran her fingers along the clever darts and perfect seams.

Rev was never getting this dress back.

"Lovely," said Rev. "It makes your red hair shine." She took hold of Rose's hands and gave her a firm shake. "Listen to me. You are a strong woman. Nothing will change that. If you decide you want a strong man by your side, you won't find a stronger one than Wilder. Normally, you could sit back and let him take the lead, but if you want him, you must prove how strong you really are. Admit what you want. Be honest. Be vulnerable. If you can be that strong, then you will win."

Rev dug through her bag until she pulled out a dark green mask, then gathered all the dresses from the bed. "I've got to get back and find a dress for myself. I believe you can do this, Rose." Rev smacked her on the butt. "Go get him, girl."

41

Wilder knocked on her door again. Even though she expected him this time, she still found his presence in her space startling. His mouth dropped open when he saw her. She was proud of the effect. She had pulled her hair up into a loose twist, and wavy tendrils hung around her neck. The pale green silk shimmered in the light of the crystal outside her door. She wasn't sure she was ready to trade in all her black, but this dress could definitely stay.

Wilder was stunning as usual. He wore dark emerald pants that were as tight as always. His white shirt was unbuttoned enough that she could occasionally see a glimpse of his tattoo.

He held up a dark green mask that matched her own. "Rev was involved in my clothing choice this evening." He chuckled. "I'm only now realizing it's because she wanted us to match. I guess she didn't want me spoiling her masterpiece."

His eyes roved over her body as if she was exactly that. She turned to pick up her mask from her desk to hide her blush. They hadn't even left yet, and she was already blushing like an idiot.

"Shall we go?" he asked, offering her his arm.

She stared at it like it was a snake.

What was she doing? There was no reason to go to this masquerade. If Vaylan got to him in time, Brother Owyn might not even be there. They wouldn't learn any secrets tonight. It was just a party and an excuse to get dressed up.

An excuse to spend time with Wilder.

But she could spend time with him without it meaning anything special. They spent a lot of time together at auditions. This was just the same.

Just the same.

She gave him a haughty stare before putting on her mask. "I can walk unassisted, Wilder."

He chuckled as he put his mask on. "Of course you can, Rose. My mistake."

She walked down the hallway without his arm, trying to forget the sound of her name on his lips.

Once they made it outside, she gained back some of her composure. The night shone with the light of crystalline street-lamps and bright crystal spires, but her mask covered enough of her face to hide some of her more embarrassing expressions. She sighed in relief and savored the cool air against her back.

"Are you looking forward to dancing?" Wilder asked.

She shrugged. "It still feels strange to dance without the wind. It's like I can't remember how my body is supposed to move anymore."

"I've seen your body move just fine, Rose."

She narrowed her eyes at him behind her mask, but she couldn't detect a trace of his flirty grin on his lips.

"It's the same as sparring," he said in the same neutral tone. "It will feel more natural with practice."

She frowned. "I'm learning to spar without the wind in case I get drugged with that tea after my Gift returns. What reason do I have for practicing to dance without the wind?"

"Someone drugs you right before a dance battle?" His face was still neutral, but this time, she knew he was teasing.

A laughing man and woman hurried past them. They both wore elaborate headdresses made from feathers, ribbons, and draped beads. Their ornate masks stood in strict contrast to the rest of their mostly non-existent clothing.

"Wow," said Wilder. "I'm concerned we might be over-dressed for this masquerade."

Rose studied the couple's costumes and appreciated them for the marvel of engineering they were. "Rev didn't know this was the theme, or I'm sure she would have tried to get me into something like that."

"There's always next time," he said with a grin.

She rolled her eyes but didn't admit that she had been considering Wilder in the same tight little shorts.

They approached the blocked-off street near the bridge that was now a dance floor. There were a few people as clothed as Rose and Wilder, but there were many more who wore a lot less.

"The fashion from the Underneath has definitely come Upstairs," she said.

Wilder snorted. "You can't blame this all on the Underneath. I saw what some of these people wore before the Uprising. They weren't exactly pinnacles of modesty."

Rose straightened primly. "The Virtue is Purity. Not modesty."

He laughed. "Fair enough, Priest Rose."

They walked further into the dancing crowd. Rose found it strange to be in a crowd while not wearing black. And with the mask covering her eyes, she was completely anonymous here. She didn't know if she liked the feeling or not.

Wilder held out a hand. "Ready?"

It wasn't until that moment that she realized she was going to dance.

With Wilder.

He reacted to the surprise on her face. "You were planning to dance, right?"

"Um ... I usually dance by myself. I know how to dance with a partner, but ... it's been a while." What she couldn't bring herself to admit was that she was terrible at partnering. She always took over the lead and stepped on her partner's toes, so no one wanted to dance with her. She couldn't imagine that kind of humiliation here in the middle of a crowd.

"That's not a problem," said Wilder with a cocky grin. "I'm good enough to remind you how it's done." He took her by the hand and pulled her close. The fingertips of his other hand rested lightly against her bare back. He took three steps in a quick circle, and her feet reacted without thinking.

"See?" he said. "It's best if you don't think about it too hard. You'll just get in your own way."

As they spun in the opposite direction, she definitely wasn't thinking about the steps. How could she think about her feet? Wilder's hand was light against her bare back, but he used enough pressure to lead her in the right direction. His other hand lightly clasped her own, and she could feel where his rough calluses from training lined up with her own. And his muscular chest pressed so close to hers that she could feel his heartbeat through her thin silk. She could barely think about breathing. Her feet were way down on the list.

She'd forgotten how magnificent of a dancer he was. The last time she had seen him dance was at the final Pageant. Of course she remembered him. She was a Priest who took the Pageant seriously. And if she had seen him on stage and fallen for him a little in that moment? Well, he was playing the role of the Companion, the Goddess's beloved. Finding him magnificent was a sign of her devotion to the Goddess.

But tonight, he didn't dance for the Goddess. He danced for

her. Was the thought a slight sacrilege? Possibly. But hopefully just a slight one.

He spun her across the dance floor without the help of the wind. Normally, she would use the wind to help her spin faster, but with Wilder, the wind floated along at her side, in no rush to speed her along. Each step with him was breathless anticipation and luxurious ease wrapped into one. The wind curled along her neck and down her spine, directed only by how Wilder spun her.

She thought back to what Rev said about Wilder normally taking the lead. She understood in this moment what that would be like. To allow herself to relax in his arms, to not have to rely only on herself, sensing by instinct what the next right step was. It was incredibly freeing.

And yet so terrifying. Relying on another person, counting on them to have her back ... She wasn't sure she trusted anyone other than Kai or Caed like that. But if she could trust them, maybe she could learn to trust someone else.

But Rev said Wilder was skittish of Priests right now. Obviously because of Ylena, though she didn't say why. Rose would have to prove herself by taking the lead. She wasn't sure if she was that strong.

"Are you taking lead now?" Wilder asked.

Rose snapped out of the thoughts in her head and wondered how he had read her mind. Then she realized her footsteps were no longer so confident.

"I don't mind if you lead," said Wilder. "But I'm going to need you to focus on the steps a little more. And I expect you to dip me! If you are going to lead, I expect at least one good dip."

She stopped dancing. "Sorry."

He raised his eyebrows. At the apology or her expression, she wasn't sure.

"Are you okay?" he asked. "You were doing so well."

She let go of his hand, but his other hand still rested

warmly against her back. They stood pressed close to one another in the middle of the dance floor, having a conversation like it was a normal thing.

It wasn't a normal thing. None of this was normal. Masked faces swirled past her, and she swayed with a sense of disorientation. Wilder pulled her tighter to keep her from falling.

"Are you dizzy?" His concerned eyes tried to study her beneath the mask. He was kind in a way that she would never be. She was born cranky and mean, and his kindness made her feel guilty. The guilt piled on top of the disorientation, and she closed her eyes to block it out.

"Ladies and gentlemen!" The musicians paused their song as a woman's voice cut through the night.

Wilder's hand on her back never faltered as he turned them both to face the speaker.

"Brother Owyn will not be speaking tonight." A sound of disapproval rose from the dance floor, but the woman continued. "He received word today that he's been targeted by the Priests." The crowd yelled their disbelief. "He's in hiding while he prepares for their attack, but he won't hide long. He will meet them on their turf soon enough." The crowd cheered in wild abandon.

"We need to get out of here," said Wilder. "Now."

42

"Whoa. I did not see that coming." said Wilder as he led them both through the crowd. He led them to a side street where they could still see the dancing, but they were far enough away to have the street to themselves. "Brother Owyn thinks they are preparing to attack him. I wonder who let that information slip."

She couldn't meet his eyes. "I did."

"You did what? Rose, we don't know what Mayra is planning. All we know is the time, not their plan!"

"It makes sense though, Wilder. They could use his defeat as their first act of power."

He rubbed his forehead. "It might make sense, but that doesn't mean that's what they were planning. Now look at that crowd. Because you revealed that information, his followers will be even angrier at the Priests. Did you catch the line about 'on their turf'? Are you ready for this crowd to attack the temple?"

"Of course not!" Her anger was a welcome relief from the storm of other feelings. "I want to stop the High Priests. It's the best way to keep the rest of the Priests safe."

"Rose! There are no High Priests! You jumped into bed with the enemy to prevent something that we don't even know is happening!"

All the confusion she felt earlier burned away in the pure clarity of fury. "We know enough. I don't know how much more information you need before you can actually make a decision, but to me, the situation is clear, and I'm willing to act. And I did not 'jump into bed' with anyone. I'm not as casual about that sort of thing as you are."

Wilder seethed. "I knew I shouldn't have told you what I learned. I mistakenly believed that you would be a little more thoughtful with who you shared that sensitive information with, but like usual, you just went in with swords bared, ready to fight. If this crowd attacks the temple and hurts innocent people like Fitz, that's going to be on you."

"On me? Just what are you doing to prevent any of this from happening? All you do is 'gather information' but do nothing about it. If I don't stop Mayra, no one will."

Wilder crossed her arms. "Because you're the only person around here who actually cares, right? You're the only one who loves the Goddess, the only one strong enough to do anything. The rest of us are just rejects from the Underneath. The Goddess's forgotten and useless children."

"I never said that!"

"You never had to, Rose. Your opinion about all of us has been clear from the beginning. You and the Priests are her chosen. The rest of us are the poor souls you must care for. Without your Gifts, how will we survive?" He gave a shocked gasp. "Guess what? We will survive exactly the same way as we have before. Relying on one another and trusting the Goddess in ways you never had to."

"Oh, you are so much more devout than me!" she said sarcastically. "You waste your time sneaking into bedrooms and seducing silly girls and then get mad at me for taking action."

His voice slid into a deadly calm. "Is that what you think I do, Rose? Seduce girls? Is that what you think I've been doing with you?"

She arched an eyebrow imperiously. "Isn't it?"

He stepped close enough that a deep breath would force them together and leaned down to whisper against her ear. "If I merely wanted you in my bed, Rose, you would have been there long ago."

A tickle of cool air shivered down her back, but she refused to back down before him.

His voice kept its icy calm. "I'm not ashamed of the women that have crawled willingly into my bed. But you continue to slander me by insinuating that I seduce girls against their will, and it's disgusting. I have never seduced a woman who wasn't fully in on the game."

She had no place for weapons in her silk dress, but she found one anyway. "What about Ylena?"

The blade slid home even deeper than expected. A sharp flash of pain seared behind his eyes. He staggered back a step before his expression hardened again.

"What do you want to hear, Rose?" Wilder's voice was rough with fury and shame. "I was weak and fell in love when I didn't expect it, and as a result, my heart got broken. I'm guessing that's never happened to you. There's no way you would ever let your guard down enough to experience that kind of love."

He rubbed his hands over his face, but it didn't wipe away the pained expression. "I felt a connection to you the first moment we met. Yes, you had a knife to my throat, but I felt a strength in you that was strong enough to match my own. But I've had to fight against that desire. Ylena hurt me out of her innocence, but you? You know exactly how bad you can hurt me. And I think that's exactly what you want to do. Hurting me is easier than facing what scares you."

Rose stood frozen by his words, her invisible blade still clutched in her hand. His face was so raw, so wounded.

She wanted to reach for him.

She wanted to lash out.

Instead, she did something she had never done before.

She ran away.

ORDER

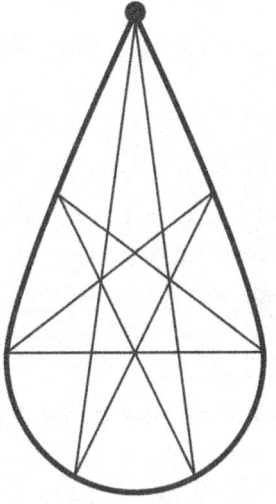

43

R ose heard Fitz pack up his things the next morning for their final trip to Order but kept her face turned to the wall and pretended to sleep. She didn't want to talk to him.

She was still running.

She stayed in bed long after he was gone, longer than she had ever stayed in bed before. She knew Mayra would be furious when she finally arrived, but she didn't care. They would probably only have a few auditions anyway. What was even the point?

The thought of seeing Wilder again caused her to break out in a sweat. She tried to imagine how he would react, but she couldn't picture his face in her vision. Would he be angry? Disgusted? Disappointed? Or would it be the terrible face he made when her verbal blade pierced his heart?

She felt sick to her stomach. She didn't know how she would make it through the last audition with him at her side. But then an even more awful thought crowded into her mind.

What if Wilder skipped the final audition? What if last night was the last time she saw him?

She felt an imaginary blade like her own slice her to the core. Those words could be the last words she ever spoke to him. He was here as a courtesy to Mayra, because he believed it was a good way to tie Upstairs to the Underneath. He could simply walk down any bridge, and she would never see him again.

Her hands flew to her mouth as she sucked in a heaving sob. What had she done? She'd injured him. And like her physical matches, she knew exactly where to strike. But this time, there was no Priest to heal the damage she did. He had to carry around the pain she had caused. And she had to carry the guilt for the rest of her life.

She'd wounded the man she ... cared for.

And she might not ever see him again.

She couldn't think about it. Throwing aside her blankets, she stumbled to her feet, still wearing the pale green gown from the night before. She pulled it off and shoved it deep into her bag. She considered throwing it out, except that it was Rev's, and she couldn't handle any more guilt.

She hurriedly wiped off all her sweat and tears and dressed in the first black clothing she grabbed. She wanted to run to Temple Order to find him, and she wanted to run to the opposite side of the City and hide. Her guts were a storm of chaos, but she kept moving, because the alternative was to fall back into bed and never get out.

It was well past noon by the time she headed to Order. The walk took a full morning on a good day, and it was not a good day. She alternated between running and stumbling the entire way. She could have probably made better time if she kept to her usual steady pace, but after running for long stretches, she spent the next hour gasping for breath, each breath sounding more like a sob than the last.

No one bothered her as she walked. She assumed they thought she was crazy, and maybe she was. If someone would have told her last week that she would have been stumbling through the City, crying about a boy like a fool, she would have punched them in the throat. But the Rose from a week ago was an idiot. It was that prideful thinking that got her into this situation, and yet she still had no idea how to get out.

It was late afternoon by the time she arrived at Temple Order. She tried to pull herself together before she saw Mayra by wiping her face on the sleeve of her black dress, but she thought it possibly just made her look more pathetic. She stumbled up the stairs and found Mayra calmly waiting at a bistro table formed out of curving branches.

"Priest Rose." Mayra's voice was clipped. She looked at Rose's wrecked face, then immediately put her head back down to her notes.

Rose lowered her bag to the ground and slid into her usual place across from Mayra. She had expected a lecture, but Mayra didn't look up again. Rose started on the small stack of papers without another word.

After a few minutes, Mayra stood and stretched her shoulders. She put her papers into a neat little stack and walked inside the temple.

Rose watched her go in shock. This was not what she'd expected at all. Why wouldn't Mayra scream at her for failing her duties with the Pageant?

Maybe she was fine with dropping the illusion that she cared about the auditions at all. They were now in Order, and whatever Mayra was planning, even if it didn't involve Brother Owyn, would take place here. Maybe Mayra finally had bigger things on her mind beyond getting into Rose's business.

The thought brought her no comfort.

Rose found Fitz's clothes neatly hung in the closet in their room but no sign of where he went. She wondered if he was avoiding her by hanging out with Wilder in his room. She realized that Wilder always knew where her room was, but she had never learned where his room was. Not that it would have been an appropriate question, but now she wished she had bucked propriety for once and found out. She had to know if he was still here.

She roamed around the temple blindly for a while and stopped by the kitchens, looking for something that would settle her stomach, but nothing looked good. It had been a struggle to eat at all since she found out money raised from the Library paid for all her meals, but the food tasted even worse to her than usual.

She walked around the courtyard that was still teaming with plants despite the lack of the Gift the Order Priests previously had. She saw a Priest with a watering can tend to a tomato vine. It was so different here now, yet the plant survived. Rose had to learn the same.

Rose walked to the laundry. It had been a while since she spoke to anyone about the Sentinel armor since it all appeared to be gone, but she didn't want to leave the temple, and she was running out of places to visit.

"Priest Rose! It's good to see you!" Daida stopped folding clothes and gave Rose a hug. "Are you okay, sweetie? You look sad." Daida was only in her early thirties, so she wasn't near old enough to be Rose's mom, but in her embrace, Rose burst into tears like a child.

Daida didn't speak other than cooing sounds as she stroked Rose's disheveled hair. After Rose felt like she had no more tears left, she pulled back from Daida and wiped her face with her sleeve.

"I'm sorry, Daida. I'm not feeling quite like myself."

At Daida's surprised expression, she realized that was probably the first time Daida received an apology from a Priest.

"Of course, Priest Rose. You are more than welcome to cry on my shoulder whenever necessary." She found a handkerchief in the clean laundry and passed it to Rose.

Rose wiped her face and blew her nose. "Thanks for your kindness. I've been an awful person, so I don't deserve it, but I appreciate it."

"That's sweet of you to say, Rose, but I'm sure it's not as bad as you think. You know better than me how much the Goddess loves her Priests. She wouldn't want you to call one of them awful, even if it is yourself."

Rose sighed. "I guess I'm not very good at remembering that."

"Are you here to ask another question about the Sentinel armor?" Daida asked.

"Another question? Who else was asking about it?"

She looked at her in confusion. "Wilder was here. I assumed you knew since you are doing the auditions together."

"Oh ... We didn't discuss it today. But yes, I guess you told him the armor has been missing for some time."

She nodded. "I can't say I was sorry to see it go, although I don't like the idea of it roaming around out there." She shivered. "And it's sad to hear about Clayr. She was a sweet lady."

"Clayr?" That was the woman Wilder and the crew had been searching for in Purpose. "You knew her?"

"Yeah, she was originally from Chaos, so she came up here to Order first looking for a job. She told me she saw someone she knew a long time ago from Chaos. Just seeing him from a distance was enough to send her off to another temple. Wilder said they still hadn't found her. He's really so sweet for remembering to stop by and let me know." A tender smile lit up her heart-shaped face. She leaned over the table with a sigh, and Rose realized just how low-cut Daida's blouse was.

Wilder had been here comforting Daida. Why was she not surprised?

"He's just such a sweetheart, don't you agree?" Daida's voice was wistful, and Rose grunted in response. "Something about him reminds me of my father."

Rose leaned back with a start. "Your father? Wilder's got to be at least ten years younger than you."

Daida laughed. "It's not about his age. It's just his presence, you know. My father could walk into the room and make you feel like you were the most special person in the world. When he looked at me, I felt like he really saw me. The real me, not the me I pretend to be around others. My dad knew the core of me, and when he spoke, that's who he spoke to. He's been gone for several years now, but when Wilder stops by, I feel like there's at least one person in the world who still sees me that way."

Rose couldn't move. She had once again accused Wilder of being something he wasn't, even if the accusation remained unspoken. And that accusation was met with the truest statement she had heard about Wilder, spoken by a woman who barely knew him.

Daida had seen the core of Wilder that Rose had missed. Rose had surely felt it and soaked it in, but she had refused to acknowledge it. The apologies she owed him stacked up around her.

"Thank you, Daida. You are truly Goddess-blessed with eyes to see what others do not."

Daida's eyes widened in surprise at the blessing. She nodded numbly in thanks.

Rose set off to figure out how to make amends.

44

Rose fell asleep early that night, and when she woke, Fitz was already gone. His neatly made bed was the only sign he had ever been home. She wondered if he was avoiding her, too. She left earlier than usual, just in case Wilder decided to leave her to run the audition on her own.

When she arrived, she realized this audition would be much different from the last two. There was already a line of auditioners circling the park, and the audience was full of people seated on the grass. She had assumed it would be as slow as the others, and when she realized the difference, her blood boiled.

Young girls wearing white dresses in the traditional style of the Goddess chatted with each other while they waited. These girls must have been waiting until this final audition to win the role of Goddess in the last moment.

She headed to her usual table with her paperwork in her arms. Multiple new performers stopped her with their last-minute sign up. She finally made it through the crowd and to her seat.

Wilder's chair was empty.

She couldn't say she was surprised. He had no reason to attend. Not only because she had been terrible to him, but also because they had already assigned all the roles. That morning, she had seen a few of the acolytes who had already arrived. If they had known there would be so many auditioning today, they might have held out on some parts.

She stared at his empty seat and the long line of performers. She didn't want to be here.

She didn't want to be here without him.

Rose stormed toward the stage and raised her voice so all the girls could hear. "If you plan to walk onto this stage like some wide-eyed child who just wandered into this City and sing the Goddess's Aria, you can go home right now. You better have come prepared with another song. Any other song. Because if I hear *one note* of the Goddess-damn Aria today, I will send all of you home. Do you understand me?"

The girls stared at her in shock. She sighed. So much for staying calm and collected. She stalked back to her seat and plopped down, resting her head in her hands and settling in for the long day.

After Rose's declaration, a few girls left immediately. Only a few of them were in tears, which she took as a good sign. The other girls got on stage with focused attention on keeping their eyes *not* starry-eyed. There were a lot of songs she didn't recognize, and she wondered if those were from the Underneath. Thinking about the Underneath brought her back to thinking about Wilder. Had he headed back to Rivalry? Would he ever come back? Then her heart would hurt until she distracted herself with the next singer.

They had only made it through six performances when the next girl in white stepped on stage. And directly on her heels followed a man in all white.

Brother Owyn.

The girl turned to see him following her. She yelped and then ran quickly offstage.

Brother Owyn walked to the front of the stage. His voice rang out to the people seated on the grass. "There is no need to sit through elaborate Pageants to win the love of your deity. You are already loved."

Rose narrowed her eyes at the old man invading her audition. She strode across the lawn to the front of the stage so she could speak to him personally without screaming.

"You need to leave now. I know you are just trying to spread your own religion, but you can't do that here." She spoke as calmly as possible to an elderly heretic.

"This City does not belong to the Goddess." Despite his age, his strong voice still carried through the park. "The City belongs to those who love one another and seek the light."

"This is not the time for theology." Rose's "calm" voice sounded a bit more strained. "I don't want to hurt you, but I will escort you off stage if necessary."

"Hurt me?" He chuckled. "I am not ruled by pain. The High Priests relied on pain to control this City, but there is another way forward for those willing to take it."

The crowd stirred uneasily. The man was still on the stage with Rose below on the grass. She did not look intimidating at all, but the crowd murmured in a way that caused the hair on the back of her neck to raise. This was getting out of control. She needed to do something.

She hopped up onto the stage and slowly came to standing. Brother Owyn slid away from her with arms raised, even though she hadn't made an aggressive move at all.

"You can't stop what's coming by using your power against me. The harder you grasp for control, the more it will slip away."

Rose raised her hands to show she was unarmed. "I'm not using any power against you. I'm simply asking you to leave."

Brother Owyn's voice lowered to a hypnotizing whisper. "I know your servants will kill me, Priest. I have seen it. Your servants will kill me, and the people will blame you." He shook his head at her sadly.

Rose took a step back in shock. Her servants?

An entire troop of Sentinels streamed from backstage. Rose's body froze in instinctive fear. It had been so long since she had seen a Sentinel in person, yet they still caused her mind to go blank with terror. It took several heartbeats before she finally realized they weren't there for her.

They were there for Brother Owyn.

The audience began screaming. Some screamed as they ran away. A brave few screamed as they ran for the stage. The majority froze in fear, like Rose. The same way they froze when the High Priests ruled the City.

This is exactly what Rose wanted to stop. She refused to let the High Priests win again.

"Stop!" she yelled at the Sentinels. "Leave him alone! I won't let you hurt him."

Two of the Sentinels held Brother Owyn, one arm each. The entire troop turned to look at her through their uncanny masks. The black masks completely covered their face and fell around their necks like a hood. Light sank into their matte black armor like they drained the sunlight out of the sky. Her breath froze in her lungs, but she pulled two blades out of the sheaths at her waist and prepared to stand her ground.

The Sentinels said nothing, only staring at her with unnerving silence. A few of the brave crowd members arrived at the front of the stage and tried to decide if they should jump up awkwardly or run to the side stairs.

While they hesitated, one Sentinel opened his fist in front of Brother Owyn's face. A fine dust flew from his hands. Brother Owyn immediately began to choke. The crowd around the stage backed up hesitantly.

The Sentinels dropped Brother Owyn unceremoniously onto the stage, then turned as a unit and filed out of the park at a fast march. The crowd shrank away in fear as they passed.

Rose slid to her knees in front of Brother Owyn. He was suffocating, and there was nothing she could do. Tears poured down her face as she clutched the front of his white robes.

Brother Owyn struggled to speak while gasping for air. "You can't stop what I've already seen."

Rose looked around, hoping someone would rush forward with the antidote, but it was already too late.

His lips were turning blue, but they curved into a smile. "I knew they would kill me. I saw you weep."

"Then why did you come here?" She knew she shouldn't yell at a dying man, but she couldn't stop. "If you knew, why didn't you bring the cure with you? You didn't have to die! You could have stopped this!"

"I ... saw ... you ... weep." His eyes unfocused as his mouth formed the words with no air. "Seek the light."

Fury ripped through her, and she screamed at the sky. Everything she had been working toward to stop the High Priests, and yet they managed to not only form their troop of Sentinels again, but to send them here. To her stage. She would not let this stand.

"Which way did they go?" she screamed. Only then did she notice the crowd was looking at her with a mixture of revulsion and fear. She didn't have time to deal with that now. She screamed again, "I said, which way did they go?"

Several people raised shaking hands in the same direction. She leaped off the stage, pulling her blades back out as she ran. It wasn't hard to follow them. She only had to follow the trail of terrified people they left in their wake.

45

This must have been the High Priests' plan all along. Wait until everyone gathered for the audition, kill Brother Owyn, then run the Sentinels through the City, spreading fear wherever they went. Rose followed their trail past hundreds of people working in fields growing the same amount of food that used to be created by just a single Order Priest in a day. The people turned to watch her go as she chased the Sentinels.

She wouldn't let them get away.

The Sentinels ran through double doors in a stone barn. They slammed the heavy doors shut, and Rose couldn't open them. She growled, then ran around the side of a building. A guard wearing simple brown leather armor turned to face her. She slid to a stop, kicked him on the side of his knee, then cracked him over the head with the pommel of her blade.

She shoved him out of the way and slid the door open. There was no sign of the Sentinels in the hallway, but voices came from the large room ahead.

"I promise to honor the Goddess, with her Gifts or without, for the rest of my life."

"Goddess bless you, my child."

"I promise to honor the Goddess, with her Gifts or without—"

"What in the Abyss is happening here?" yelled Rose.

Priest Mayra's hands hovered over the head of a Priest with a tall crown. Three other Priests were already kneeling with crowns on their head. They turned to Rose with fear bright in their eyes.

"How could you do this?" Rose growled. "This is an abomination against the Goddess and her Virtues. You send your Sentinels out to kill while you hide in here for your secret ceremony. You are evil. Truly evil."

Mayra walked toward her with raised hands. "Rose, please listen—"

"I will not listen to you." Her voice was a deadly whisper. "You will each set your crown onto the ground and come with me calmly back to the temple. There you will cast yourself onto the mercy of the City for the death of Brother Owyn. I don't know if they will forgive you, but I won't let you take all of us down with you."

Mayra took another step forward, but Rose lifted her blade to fend her off.

The sound of shouting echoed through the hallway.

"What have you done, Rose?" asked Mayra.

"What have I done? I'll tell you what I didn't do. I didn't murder an old man in cold blood. That's on your hands."

Mayra looked at her in confusion as a group of men stormed into the room. They had rakes and shovels and wielded them like weapons.

Rose looked at them sideways as she kept her eyes on Mayra. "Don't worry, guys. It's all under control now. They are going to surrender."

The man with the shovel laughed. "Surrender? You didn't

give Brother Owyn that chance. And I don't know what you mean by 'they.'"

Rose was still focused on Mayra, so she didn't see the shovel until it cracked into her ribs. She dropped to her knees, and the man moved on to the kneeling Priest by her side. The shovel cracked him in the forehead. He was dead before he hit the floor.

Rose tried to scream at them to stop, but her lungs hurt so much she couldn't breathe. She tried to get to her feet as more people crowded into the barn. They were all dressed in their farm clothes. And Rose was wearing black, just like the rest of the Priests.

The Priests fell quickly. They were not trained warriors, and most of Mayra's cronies were her same age. They fell to shovels and daggers and fists until only Rose was standing.

She couldn't straighten fully without a stabbing pain in her chest, but the mob avoided her because she was the only Priest who was armed. She backed up until she stood over Mayra's bleeding body.

"Get out!" she gasped. "You've killed them all. Just go."

The man with the shovel stared at her with narrowed eyes. "Not all of them."

She adjusted the grip on her blades as she studied the angry faces surrounding her. She was going to end up dead on the floor with all the rest of the High Priests.

Two white wolves shot down the hallway and through the crowd. They came to a skidding halt at Rose's feet. She formed up a circle with them at her sides.

She hissed down at them. "I appreciate the help, ladies, but I'm not sure you should be here. This won't end well."

The next one to step out of the hallway was Wilder.

Rose's knees nearly buckled at the sight of him. She thought she was going to die without seeing him again, that she would never get to apologize to him. If she died, he would never know show she truly felt about him.

"Wilder!" she gasped, then flinched in pain.

The crowd parted and let him pass. He was clearly not a Priest, and he still held at least a portion of his celebrity status. The mob appeared unsure what role Wilder played. Was he on her side? Or was he on theirs?

Rose could see from his eyes that his answer was still unknown.

He stopped within reach of her blades, either believing her too weak to hurt him or believing himself strong enough to stop her.

"Wilder." Her voice was a ragged whisper. "I'm so sorry." The crowd murmured in surprise at the sound of a Priest apologizing. She didn't spare them a glance. "You were right. I slandered you over and over when you had done nothing wrong. My accusations were based on jealousy. I was purposefully hurtful. I wanted to wound you because I am scared ... of us ... I'm a coward."

He studied her face for several moments. Whatever he saw written there must have been enough, because he turned to the crowd and said, "Okay, that's enough. It's time to leave."

The man with the shovel stepped forward and bared his teeth. "Why should we leave before the job is done?"

Wilder's lips curled into a hint of his usual smirk, except with a dark current below the surface. "I don't think finishing the job will work out in your favor."

He cocked a thumb at Rose. "She's in rough shape, so that means she can probably only kill a few of you today." He pointed at three guys on Rose's left. "The wolves will tear out several throats before you can stop them." He pointed solemnly at four more. "So then the question is, how many of you can I take out?"

Wilder rose to his full height, looking into the faces of the dozens of people surrounding them. "I haven't been working in a field all day or slaughtering unarmed Priests, so I'm feeling pretty good right now. Let's say that means I kill you, you, you, you, and you." As he pointed to each person, they shrank back a step. "It's true, there would still be a lot of you left, and we will eventually fall." He looked around to stare each of them in the eyes. "Although maybe I miscounted. Maybe I'll be able to take out just one more of you ..."

Rose could feel the crowd checking his math and considering how they would fare. Wilder continued to stare them down, slowly moving until he stood back-to-back with her. The wolves squared up at their sides, then growled low in their throats, and the tide appeared to turn.

A familiar voice from the back said, "Let's get outta here. It's not worth it."

The group shuffled down the hallway, never taking their eyes off Wilder. When they had all left, only the crew remained.

Tayeh stood with her back leaning against the wall. "I like your math, Wilder. But if you would have added me to the equation, they would have left a lot sooner."

Rev looked around at all the fallen Priests. "Wow. This is not what I expected to see when I heard we were following Sentinels." Hers was the voice that suggested the mob leave.

Quinn picked up a fallen crown. "They reforged them." He shook his head. "Why would they do that?"

Rose dropped to her knees beside Mayra. Someone had punched Mayra repeatedly, but it was the knife wound that was killing her. Her eyes fluttered open, and she briefly focused on Rose.

"I told you I would die for this religion." Mayra's voice was almost smug.

Despite her conflict with Mayra, tears filled her eyes. "I didn't want you to die for it, Goddess-dammit!"

Mayra's voice was getting weaker. "You shouldn't curse, dear."

"Why did you kill Brother Owyn? He was just an old man. You didn't need to send your Sentinels after him." She wanted to scream at Mayra like she had at Owyn, but she took hold of her hand instead.

Mayra blinked at her slowly. Rose wasn't sure she would answer. "We don't have Sentinels, Rose."

"I saw them kill him, Mayra! An entire troop of them led me here!"

Mayra clutched her hand weakly. "If we had Sentinels, we would all still be alive."

Rose sat up and looked around. There were no Sentinels dead in the room. She hadn't seen one since they ran inside the large barn door. When she came to the side door, she had only found one guard.

He wasn't a Sentinel.

Rose shook her head, as if to dislodge all the conflicting thoughts from her mind.

Mayra pulled her closer with the slightest touch. "I forgive you, Priest Rose. I forgive you for leading them to us." She closed her eyes, and they didn't reopen.

46

The crew walked back to Temple Order in silence. Rose's run toward the barn had been quick, but the trip back out to the edge of the City was long. She stumbled a few times but refused to let any of the crew help her. She ran her fingers carefully along her ribs. They didn't seem broken, but she couldn't be sure. The last time someone hit her that hard had been in a training accident, and a Priest had been onsite to heal her. She had no idea how long it would take for her to heal on her own.

She replayed Mayra's final words over and over. Rose led the mob to Mayra's door. Of course she wanted to stop Mayra, but that's not the way she had planned.

To be honest, she didn't have a plan. She did what she always did. She ran in with blades bared, just like Wilder said. And this time, it got a lot of people killed.

It was hard to breathe, but she couldn't tell if the problem was her ribs or more tears threatening to fall. She stumbled up the stairs at the temple and went to her room without a word to anyone.

Rose sat on the edge of her bed, staring blindly ahead. She

wasn't sure how long she sat like that before Fitz arrived. He carried a cup of tea in one hand and some bandages in the other.

He handed her the tea. "Drink this."

She drank the bitter tea without complaint.

He studied the blood on her shirt. "Will you take this off so I can see how much of this blood belongs to you?"

She unbuttoned her shirt but couldn't remove it without help. Fitz examined her critically for wounds, finding only a few minor cuts, which he wrapped. He gingerly touched her ribs, and she grimaced.

"I think you might have cracked a few ribs. Wrapping them can cause more trouble than it's worth, so I'm going to trust you will remember to take it easy the next few weeks until they heal?"

She gave him a flat look. "I don't think I can forget the pain if I tried."

He smiled. "Well, hopefully the tea will help with that." He grabbed a fresh black shirt from her closet and helped her pull it on.

"Thank you," she said. She breathed a little deeper than she had before. "I think whatever you put in the tea is helping."

He gave her a serious look. "It's not a cure. It just blocks some of the pain. But it can be dangerous. Pain is usually the only thing that convinces a person to stop doing something they shouldn't be doing."

"Believe me, I can relate to that better than you know." She thought her tears had run dry, but she blinked and found a few more tears that were still lurking inside. "I thought I understood, Fitz. I thought I knew how the world worked. Then the Uprising happened. Everything changed, but I grasped hold of another idea, and I thought that was surely it. Over and over, I've been reaching out for something to explain how this all makes sense. But every time I think I finally understand, everything falls apart again. I'm trying, Fitz, but I just can't make the pieces fit."

Fitz took hold of her hand. "The pieces never fit together, Rose. No matter how much you learn, you will always find one more piece that won't snap into place. Faith is believing there is something bigger than you that can hold the broken pieces together, even if you don't see how."

She sighed, then winced. "It seems like all I am is broken pieces."

He squeezed her hand. "We all are, Rose. Some days more than others."

She studied his sweet, concerned face. "Are all the acolytes here?"

Fitz nodded. "The last one arrived right before you did. We settled them in on the second floor."

"I don't know what your plans are after the auditions, but would you help me look after them? Now that Mayra is gone, I'm not sure what that means for these acolytes. I believe we still should put on the Pageant, but I'm not sure how safe these kids will be with the feelings against Priests out there."

"Of course I will help. But you should remember, these 'kids' are our age or a couple of years younger."

She frowned at him. "I know they aren't kids, but I feel responsible for them. I chose each of them, and I don't want them to get hurt because of my choice. There are plenty of other people in that category."

He nodded. "I understand. I'll help you look out for them."

"The tea is making me sleepy. I might rest before I have to explain to the acolytes what happened to Mayra."

"Of course," said Fitz. He gathered the teacup and extra bandages. "I'll help you explain it to them when you wake up. You aren't alone in this, Rose."

She choked down a small sob. "Thanks, Fitz. For everything."

He gave her a comforting smile as he closed the door.

As soon as the door clicked shut, she stood with a groan and went to her closet. She sheathed the extra blades she hadn't been wearing for the audition, pulled her disheveled hair into a tighter knot, and added sharp hairpins for good measure.

Once she was fully armed with steel and anger, she snuck quietly out of the temple. She didn't expect to find all the answers. In fact, she probably never would. But there was one answer she was determined to discover before the night was over.

Who controlled the Sentinels?

Someone charismatic enough to convince skilled fighters to put on the armor of the feared Sentinels.

Someone clever enough to play Brother Owyn and the Priests off one another.

Someone conniving enough to set Rose up so she was stuck in the middle when it all went down.

She didn't know where he was hiding, but she would find Vaylan.

And then kill him.

THE AMPHITHEATER

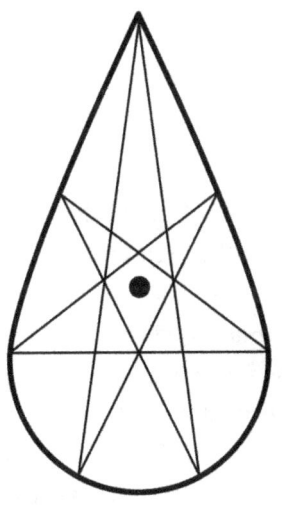

47

The sun's last rays filtered down from the mountains as Rose walked through Order Diocese. The further she walked, the easier it became to draw in a breath. She wanted to pretend that walking was helping her injured ribs, but she knew it was just Fitz's tea kicking in. It was one more way that the people in the Underneath had survived so long without Priests to heal them. They found ways to adapt.

Now it was her turn to adapt. She usually ran straight into the middle of a fight, which is exactly what killed Mayra and the other Priests today. Tonight, she would sneak around quietly, gather some clues, and formulate the best plan to kill Vaylan. She could be sneaky. Wilder had taught her how.

Wilder.

The thought of him caused a completely different pain in her chest. Once again, she'd stood before him, apologizing, waiting to see if he would forgive her. By some miracle, he had. Why did he bother? He had no reason to believe she would change. In fact, it was likely she would make the same stupid mistake again. Why would he choose to forgive her? And not only forgive her, but to fight a mob for her sake?

The memory of him standing at her back sent a chill down her spine. Her back remembered the warmth of him and now felt the lack of his presence. The moment he'd stepped into place, she knew they would fight the crowd together. And they would win. They could take on the world. The two of them back-to-back would be unstoppable.

But first, she had to convince him of that.

He had forgiven her enough to save her life, but she wasn't sure how much further his forgiveness ran. Other than her apology, they hadn't spoken at all. After Mayra's death, she didn't have the words to speak, and he walked quietly by her side on their way back to the temple. She still owed him another apology, but she wasn't sure if he would give her the chance to make it.

As she made her way to the barn, she slowed, wondering if someone had collected the bodies. She remembered the last sight of them before she left. Seven bodies in a rough circle, lying in puddles of their own blood. She was furious with them for attempting to put themselves into power above her and the rest of the City, but she never wanted it to come to that.

She avoided the side door that led into that room and instead went to the barn door she had seen the Sentinels enter. She had assumed they'd entered that door to head straight to the Priests, but they must have left as soon as she ran around the building.

The doors stood open, so she walked inside to see if she could find any clues to where they had gone. She inspected the wagon first, looking for anything that seemed out of place. Several woven baskets lined the bottom of the wagon. Most of the lids were off, proving they were empty. She lifted the lid off the single covered basket and found a pile of Sentinel armor shoved inside.

She stepped back with a gasp. The Sentinels had run in here, taken off their uniforms, and then what? They must have had other clothes stashed here so they could blend into the crowd and escape.

Some of them might have been part of the mob.

She was trying to decide what to do with this clue when she heard footsteps outside. She backed further around the wagon and hid behind a giant clay cask. There were two rules, he'd said. Don't be seen. Don't be heard. She could do that.

Two stocky men shuffled into the barn. They glanced around before heading toward the wagon. They lifted the large basket out of the wagon, but the man on the right stumbled, almost dumping out the armor.

The man on the left hissed, "Be careful, Remy!"

Rose's eyes widened at the sound of the missing laundry worker's name. Her first reaction was to pummel them both until they told her where they were going. However, her first reaction hadn't worked well today, so she obeyed her second thought instead.

Follow them.

They were dressed as farm workers, so they looked completely normal carrying the basket through the streets. They didn't need to hide, so Rose didn't have to be very skilled to keep sight of them. All she had to do was stay far enough away that they didn't notice her.

They adjusted the load between them several times on the long walk. The black armor was lightweight, but they carried enough for the entire troop in the large basket. She had no sympathy for them, and it was all she could do to keep from running at them with a blade in her hand. Her blood pounded at the thought, but she kept it in check. She had to.

She had larger prey in her sights.

Each step brought her closer to Vaylan. A small part of her wondered if she could be wrong about him. After all, she'd thought the Sentinels were under Mayra's command, and that assumption got seven Priests killed. But this time, she knew she was right. And she would stop him.

As they approached the center of the City, she realized where he must be hiding. She ground her teeth at his presumption of hiding in the very amphitheater where they held their most sacred ceremony.

She was going to kill him for that. And for the death of Brother Owyn. For the deaths of the Priests. And most of all, for causing her to doubt herself.

From the very beginning, he had wormed his way into her thoughts, causing her to doubt what she believed. True, she had experienced her own doubts since the Uprising, but he'd taken those doubts and used them against her. He wanted to make her weak and use her for his purposes. He'd pretended to be benevolent and enlightened, but he'd used her.

And he'd used Brother Owyn.

She wondered how much the old man had known about Vaylan, or if he knew he existed at all. Brother Owyn died believing it was Priests who murdered him. She recalled his strange words about "seeing" his death. Did Vaylan put that idea into his head, or did Vaylan just exploit what he already believed? Vaylan had said they'd met in the High Priests' prison.

She finally asked herself the question, what did they imprison Vaylan for?

Of all the stories he'd told her, that one felt the truest. He had been an enemy of the High Priests as surely as Brother Owyn, but for some reason, they'd kept him alive in prison rather than kill him.

She watched the men carry the basket around to the side entrance of the amphitheater that led backstage. Rose knew her way around the amphitheater like any good Priest, so she headed them off by going to the other side entrance, which led into the orchestra pit. She cracked the door open and peeked inside.

The amphitheater was as dark as it had been since the night the Priests lost their Gifts. The only light came from the glowing crystal basin at front center stage. She crept forward, hiding behind the stone rail around the orchestra pit. The men pushed open a panel that led under the stage, then lifted a trapdoor. Glowing light streamed from below. The men called out to someone who helped them maneuver the basket inside. The men followed the basket, closing the stage panel on their way.

Rose stood from her hiding spot in shock. Vaylan was hiding in the Underneath? In the Heart of the Grottos? He could have an entire army hidden down in the giant cavern, and no one would be the wiser. She needed to find out how many people he had with him.

She stepped forward.

"You honestly cannot be considering going down there," said Wilder from the shadows.

48

He stepped out of a shadow and shook his head. "Just this morning, you ran after a troop of Sentinels *on your own*. You tried to battle a mob *on your own*. And despite how horrendous that turned out, you still snuck out of the temple to follow this lead *on your own*." His voice rose with each statement until the amphitheater echoed his words in a loop.

On your own ... on your own ... on your own.

"And now here you are, actually considering following those Sentinels down into their lair. And then what? Fight your way down that staircase? Battle through Goddess knows how many Sentinels lurking down there? Do you think you can defeat an army of them on your own?"

He was several steps away, but she could feel the anger boiling off him like an inferno. His breathing was ragged, and his hands were clenched at his sides. He was furious at her for coming here alone.

Rose didn't flinch at his anger, because she saw the truth written in his stormy eyes. She whispered gently, "You followed me."

"Of course I followed you. I knew you would try something like this." His nostrils flared as he took a deep breath in, and a muscle in his jaw tensed.

She felt light-headed, but not from the pain in her ribs. "You found me before the mob could get me."

His furrowed brow twitched in confusion. "The wolves helped. You ran off before I could see which way you went."

"You were watching me," she breathed.

His fists unclenched at her gentle accusation, and he sighed, "Yes."

She swallowed down a lump in her throat. "Despite the terrible things I said. Despite the way I hurt you. Despite the fact that I keep doing the same idiotic things over and over. You were watching me."

His whisper was an awful mix of shame and sadness. "Yes."

She closed her eyes and tipped her head back with a sigh. "Goddess, Wilder. You make me furious."

He leaned back, unsure how to react to the gentle words that sounded nothing like her usual fury.

"Do you realize what you've done to me?" she asked. "How you've broken me? When you walk into a room, my heart literally skips a beat. Do you realize how much of a cliché that is? When you stand close to me, I can't breathe. I end up out of breath, panting like some common animal. When you talk to me, I can't think straight. I've become one of those silly girls I have always ridiculed!"

She gasped out the words, ribs in pain and heart aching. "I had plans for my future. Goals laid out for the rest of my life. Now those dreams have all fallen to dust because I can't imagine a future without you in it. I am a strong, independent woman. But look at me! I'm falling apart." Her words were the quiet sob of a whisper. "You've ruined me, Wilder. And I don't want to change back."

He stood completely still, undisguised longing on his face.

Her name crossed his lips, the stirring wind as gentle as from a butterfly's wing. The pieces of her heart shattered from the force.

Within the space of a heartbeat, they were in each other's arms.

They came together like a storm. Two whirlwinds crashing into each other until they swirled into a tempest. Wilder held her face in his hands, gentle as a soft rain yet stronger than steel. She clutched hold of him as if she would drown in the storm, as if he were her way to stay afloat.

His lips on hers seared like a flame. Their kiss was tender and furious, a fire that could both warm and consume her. Her conscious thought floated away until there was nothing but Wilder. Nothing but every place their bodies connected.

Lightning zipped through her until her hair seemed to stand on end with it. She clutched him tighter and melded herself into him. He dropped his hands from her face and grabbed her in a fierce embrace.

She straightened with a gasp as pain shot through her ribs.

"What is it?" Wilder pulled back and examined her, looking for injuries. "What's wrong?"

She rubbed her ribs tenderly. "I may have a cracked rib or two."

She saw guilt cross his face at causing her pain. Then she watched that guilt transform into something more pointed.

"You were considering storming their lair *with cracked ribs*?"

She gave him an innocent look.

He groaned.

"I agree I am not storming their lair tonight," she sighed. "So then, what's the plan?"

"You're willing to make a plan?" he asked. "And stick with it?"

She looked at him with serious eyes. "Probably."

He laughed. "Sounds about right."

His eyes held hers, and she couldn't look away. She didn't care about her ribs. She wanted to collide with him again.

Wilder must have read her mind, because he rested his hands lightly on her arms, stopping her forward momentum toward him. "I've always appreciated your enthusiasm, Rose. But perhaps you should heal more before you throw yourself into any strenuous activity."

Rose bit her lip, considering just how long it would take her ribs to heal before she could kiss Wilder as enthusiastically as she would like. She sighed as deep as her ribs would allow and took a grudging step away from him.

She walked forward to study the glowing basin at the front of the stage. It glowed with the same white light as the crystal spires since the Goddess's appearance the night of the Uprising.

"This was where the whole trajectory of my life changed," she said. "I guess it's when all of our lives changed."

Wilder walked to her side. "I poured in the children's tears and walked away."

"I was sad to see Caed take your place," she said, lost in the memory. "You were exceptionally good."

His lips curled in a smug smile. "You enjoyed watching me? Did you have any impure thoughts about me as the Goddess's Companion?"

His words hit a little too close to the mark. Even though she had just laid her soul bare to him, she still had a little pride left. "Of course not! Just the Goddess's own appreciation for the arts."

"Of course," he said knowingly. "You are very pious."

She snorted and continued to stare at the glowing basin. The white light shone brightly against her skin, but with no warmth. Her voice shook as she asked the question that burned in her mind.

"Do you think she's still here?"

Wilder moved to stand next to her. He wrapped a careful hand around her back and surrounded her with his warmth.

"I think she is," he said. "I believe it."

"If she's still here, why isn't she saying anything?" The first question Vaylan asked her returned to haunt her. "If the Goddess truly cares for her people, why is it so difficult to receive her blessing?" Rose's voice broke on a sob. "Why can't she be clearer about what she wants? If she told me what she wanted me to do, I would do it. I swear it." She smacked her hand against the basin. "Answer me, Goddess-dammit! What do you want from me?"

She would find no answers here. The Goddess was silent. Rose was alone.

Except she wasn't. Wilder hadn't left her side. He held her gently as she tried to calm her breathing for the sake of her ribs. Back at Temple Order was the rest of the crew who had followed her into the heart of a mob. Fitz, who had patched her up physically and spiritually, was there. On the other side of the City were Kai and Mims and the rest of her siblings. And somewhere across the mountains was Caed.

She wasn't alone. Not even close.

She took one last breath and nodded. Both to herself and to the Goddess. She was not alone.

Her voice was stronger when she turned to speak to Wilder. "Thanks for being here. Tonight. And all the other times. I have felt the Goddess's blessing through you. I should have admitted it that night in Perfection after we escaped those men who attacked us. You spoke a blessing over me that healed a piece of my soul, but I was too scared to admit it. I should have confessed my feelings for you long ago."

His eyes twinkled with the light of the basin as he reached a gentle hand to her chin. Time slid to a stop as he leaned down to her with tender slowness. Her lips parted, and she closed her eyes on a sigh.

His lips were soft as velvet and his fingertips as light as a cloud brushing against her cheek. Her body longed to crash into him again, but he pinned her in place with his delicate touch.

Their first kiss had been a whirlwind of energy and passion like their fights, but this kiss was as gentle as his love song on her dark night of doubt. His right hand rested lightly against her spine, carefully avoiding her ribs, while the fingers of his left hand traced a leisurely path from her cheek to the back of her neck. She melted into him, trusting in his strength.

He pulled away, and his eyes opened lazily. He studied the rapturous look on her face and smiled smugly. "I enjoy putting that look on your face."

She didn't move from her position in his arms, but she raised an eyebrow. "Feeling pretty good about your skills?"

"We all have to be good at something. I happen to be good at quite a few things." He gave her a cocky grin.

She swatted his arm playfully. "You can prove it to me some more later. We should get going."

His face turned serious again. "Before we go, will you offer a prayer to the Goddess with me?" He seemed embarrassed by the question, as if it were more personal than anything they had shared that evening.

She took careful hold of his request. "Of course. I'm honored you would ask me."

He smiled shyly, then paused for a moment with closed eyes; and when he opened them, he wiped away a tear. She saw it glittering in the crystal light on the tip of his finger.

She had a variety of memories that she could use to stir the tears to honor the Goddess. But she chose a happy memory. The thought of dancing with Wilder.

She took the tear on her finger and offered it before the basin. She turned to Wilder, willing to let him lead in this moment, too.

His soft whisper set her skin to tingling again. "Goddess, we offer you what we have, little though it may be. Use us as you will."

Rose held her breath at the beautiful words. He looked at her, and she nodded in agreement.

They touched their hands to the basin as one.

The City exploded in light.

49

The white light of the crystal basin expanded until it bled into the light pouring out of the crystal spires. It forced Rose's eyes shut, and when she blinked her eyes open, all she could see was white.

Wilder at her side.

And the Goddess before her.

She looked the same as she had on the night of the Uprising. Beautiful in her flowing white dress, with her dark hair falling in loose curls down her back. Her warm brown skin glowed as if she were part of the crystal. Rose had known her before as Lady Erenne, and though she looked similar, she was aflame with power. She was every part a Goddess.

Rose swayed, unable to speak. Wilder gripped her hand, and she saw the same look of awe on his face.

The Goddess smiled as she looked at their clasped hands. "Ah ... Yes, I see. That must be what did it." Rose realized the Goddess was speaking to someone else. As soon as the thought entered her head, she saw the Companion at the Goddess's side.

"I won't make you say it in front of our guests," said the

Companion. "But later, I will require you to confess to me in detail that I was correct."

The Goddess rolled her eyes. "Yes, Nelson, you were correct. I admit that you occasionally have better eyesight than me. Is that sufficient?"

The Companion gave her a wicked smile. "Not nearly enough, dear one."

She swatted him on the arm. "Quiet now. We don't have long with them."

Rose finally found her voice. "Where are we?"

The Goddess looked around at the completely blank space. "That answer would be quite a lot for me to explain to you, Rose. Metaphysics, space-time, quantum particles, and the like ... Being a Goddess can be very tedious."

Rose blinked in confusion.

"Exactly," said the Goddess. "Let's just say that you conjured up enough power between the two of you to make a link between us possible. That's terrific. I'm thrilled for you both!"

Rose tried to find more words, but her brain was having trouble processing a Goddess congratulating her for liking a boy.

"Like I said, we have little time. I don't think mortal brains handle this realm well, so let's get on with it." She clapped her hands together. "You're planning a Pageant, correct?"

Rose shook herself. Those were words she could understand. "You need a Pageant? Of course. We can do that."

"I do like a good musical, right, Nelson?" He smiled warmly as she continued. "However, I don't particularly need it to be *the Pageant* per se. That's just a helpful mechanism for moving the power along. Understand?"

Rose and Wilder clearly did not.

The Goddess sighed. "We'll keep it simple. Yes. Please put on a Pageant. It doesn't need to be perfect, but it needs to stir the emotions of the people. That will create enough energy to allow me to do some spectacular things."

Rose nodded in partial understanding. "A Pageant, yes. Then you can return our Gifts."

The Goddess chewed on her bottom lip, a surprisingly sheepish look for a Goddess. "I tried to return the Gifts immediately after the Uprising, but I underestimated the amount of power I would need to do it." She took hold of the Companion's hand and studied his face with troubled eyes. "Plus, Nelson has been suffering from bouts of a strange illness, and I've been ... distracted." The Companion squeezed her hand with a comforting smile.

Rose's mouth dropped open that the Goddess admitted to being distracted ... by a boy.

The Goddess looked back at Rose and Wilder, her glowing smile returned. "Can you do that for me? Put on an inspiring Pageant?"

"Whatever you want!" breathed Rose. "I swear it will be the best Goddess-damn Pageant ..." Rose slapped a hand over her mouth, and her eyes widened in fear.

The Goddess laughed. "I'm sure you will, dear. Hear that, Nelson? Rose wants to compete with you for the best director out there!"

Nelson gave her a chiding look. "Now, dear, you shouldn't tease the girl for her devotion. We can't help it that all we want to do is please you."

She smiled as if she were a cat pleased that he stroked her fur.

Rose looked between the two of them and wondered if she and Wilder should leave them alone.

The Goddess pried her eyes away from the Companion and turned back to Rose and Wilder. "Thanks to the power you added to the basin, I have a little energy to spare before the

Pageant. It's not as much as I would like, but I will do what I can."

She stepped forward and cupped each of their cheeks with a hand. She stared into their eyes, and Rose felt a jolt of energy flow from the Goddess, into her and Wilder, and then through their still clasped hands.

Her voice rang out through the empty white void and whispered directly in their ears.

"You are my children, from above and below. Go forth and unite my City with my blessing."

A gong shook through Rose's bones, and she crumpled to the ground.

50

As Rose drifted back to consciousness, the first thing she felt was Wilder's hand in hers. Then she realized that the relief the tea brought her ribs had worn off. She grimaced in pain and opened her eyes.

Vaylan stood over her.

Rose scrambled backward but hit the edge of the stage, jarring her ribs. Her gasp of pain woke Wilder, who came alert quickly, then froze.

"Vaylan?" Wilder whispered, eyes widening.

"Hello, son. It's been a while." He had that same condescending paternal voice Rose remembered, but she could tell from Wilder's shaking hands that it didn't soothe him.

"Vaylan is your father?" Her head swung back and forth between the two of them. If she didn't let herself get distracted by Vaylan's irritating dimple, she could see hints of Wilder in his grin. But Wilder definitely wasn't smiling now. She tried to get his attention, but his eyes never left his father's face.

Vaylan stared at his son with joy, clearly pleased to see him. It was obvious from Wilder's face he didn't share the sentiment.

"It's so good to see you! We should catch up." He sat down in one of the High Priests' thrones in the front row, his grin widening. "It's good to see you, too, Rose. I'm glad to see you made it away from the mob unscathed."

"You're glad?" Her rage flooded back in an instant, smothering her fear. "I was only there because of you and your schemes!"

He leaned back on the throne and steepled his hands before him. "I know it is hard to understand my motives from the outside, but believe me, everything I have done has been for the good of the City."

Rose remembered what drew her to the amphitheater in the first place. She planned to kill Vaylan. She pushed herself to her feet despite the shooting pain. Wilder followed her up, standing protectively at her side.

Despite her anger, she realized she wasn't strong enough to take on Vaylan by herself. She trusted Wilder to have her back against the mob, but could she really ask him to attack his own father for her? If she couldn't kill Vaylan yet, she would at least get some answers.

She leveled him with a hard stare. "You had Brother Owyn killed and blamed it on me."

Despite her accusation, his voice never lost his warm, patronizing tone. "I didn't blame his death on you, Rose. Brother Owyn did. Everyone watched your religion kill him."

"My religion?" She took a deep breath with nostrils flaring wide. "You convinced people like Remy to steal the Sentinel uniforms for you. How many Sentinels have you recruited now?"

Vaylan waved his hand as if it was no concern. "There are many people devoted to me and my cause."

"Clayr ... the missing woman," Wilder whispered, staring at Vaylan. "She was from Chaos ... like us."

Vaylan's grin fell flat. "Chaos was never my home. Anyone who says otherwise must be mistaken."

Wilder flinched.

The movement was so out of character for Wilder that even though Rose was never one to run away from a fight, at that moment, all she wanted to do was to take his hand and run.

Her lips pulled into a hard line. "What do you want with us?"

"What do I want?" he asked. "You were the ones who came seeking me."

"So, we are free to go?" asked Wilder in a tentative voice.

Vaylan studied them both with his piercing dark eyes. Vaylan's skin wasn't as deep brown as Wilder's, and his hair was cropped so close she wasn't sure if it curled the same as Wilder's, but their eyes were the same. Dark as the night sky and equally able to crinkle in laughter or narrow to hide secrets in their depths.

"It's a little dark in here, don't you agree?" Vaylan raised an authoritative hand, as if summoning troops. Then he flicked his fingers open, and the crystalline roared to life.

Rose blinked as light flooded the stage. "You're the Purpose Priest who shut off the crystalline! Why would you do that to your own people?"

"I'm not a Priest of any sort, Rose. Not even close." He flexed his hand, and the thin stream of crystalline running along the front of the stage reshaped into the form of his hand.

Rose had never seen anything like it. Crystalline reacted in very specific ways, flowing up and around the stone pipes that formed the infrastructure of the City. She looked closer at the crystalline hand at her side and realized there was no stone.

He was controlling the crystalline itself.

"Controlling crystalline is your Spark!" she breathed.

He tilted his head and frowned. He clearly didn't know the word.

"You have a Spark," she repeated. "Like Ylena. And the Goddess."

"I am nothing like the Goddess." His dimple faded, and his face was grim. "She abandoned this City and left it to be split in two. I have come to make everyone whole. No more division between Upstairs and Underneath. No more Priests ruling over the rest of us. I will unite the City under one hand." He clenched his hand into a fist, and the crystalline balled into a fist in response. "Mine."

Rose groaned in disgust. "After all your words about equality and freedom, your plan was always to rule? How disappointing."

He tilted his head and looked at her as if she was a child. "I am bringing equality, Rose. I believe in what Brother Owyn preached. Everyone will be equal. I will make sure of it."

"Everyone except you."

"Well, of course not me," he said matter-of-factly. "I am the Founder."

"The Founder? Of what?" She studied his face, trying to find any sign of illness, but she could detect nothing.

He chuckled. "I'm the Founder of the way forward, Rose. Soon, you will believe it, too. By the way, I never got to thank you for your assistance. Your warning about the Priests planning something in Order was just what I needed."

Only Wilder's hand kept her on her feet.

"I'm benevolent, so I will grant you time to come to me willingly. But until then, I want to make sure the others recognize you for who you are." He pointed at her chest, and the crystalline hand at her side mimicked the movement. "You are no longer a Priest, Rose." Vaylan's voice rang with finality. "You are mine." The crystalline finger moved quickly, and before she knew what was happening, it pressed against her skin, directly in the center of her collarbone.

She screamed as the crystalline burned her skin. The touch

lasted just a moment, but the pain didn't lessen as the crystalline finger withdrew. The shining liquid seared her skin red and black, with a detailed fingerprint burned into the space directly beneath the hollow of her throat.

Wilder had pulled out a blade and looked between Vaylan and the crystalline hand, trying to decide who or what to strike first, but one look at Vaylan's perfectly calm face told Rose Wilder would never succeed. She pulled his hand firmly to her side and squeezed until his bones ground together. He finally caught her eyes and lowered his blade to his side.

Vaylan walked closer and studied the mark. "Now everyone will know I have marked you. That will stop any more mobs from trying to attack." He winked, then stepped back to look at the two of them. "I think it's time for you to be on your way, Rose. Wilder and I have a lot of catching up to do."

Wilder growled a denial, but Rose's voice was louder. "You are a Goddess-damn fool if you think I am leaving here without him, Vaylan!"

Vaylan's voice dropped low. "I have marked you as my own, Rose. But I can just as easily destroy my chosen as save them."

She opened her mouth to curse him again, but Wilder pulled her to his side. "Rose, it's okay. I'll be fine. You should go."

He was trying to protect her by offering himself to Vaylan. She would kill him for even considering it.

She studied his eyes, full of love, with tears pooling at the edges. How had she been blind for so long? She wouldn't lose him. Not for any reason.

She blinked, and her own tears fell. "I don't care what you do to me, Vaylan. I'm not leaving him."

Vaylan frowned, then raised his hand and prepared to strike, but suddenly, his eyes opened wide. A whirlwind gathered overhead and launched itself at him. Rose and Wilder ducked below the edge of the stage and watched it sail past them.

They both stared at the wind, invisible except for gathered leaves and petals, their mouths hanging open. The powerful storm knocked Vaylan backward and pressed him tightly against the stone throne. Rose tilted her head, trying to understand, but Wilder pulled her hand, waking her out of her daze.

Wilder hopped neatly onto the stage, but Rose rolled up awkwardly, gasping as he helped her stand. They took each other's hand and ran toward the wings. Rose was in so much physical pain, with thoughts swirling like a hurricane in her mind, she couldn't formulate a plan to fight. Escape was their only option.

Vaylan slowly raised his hand, struggling against the windstorm, to signal the crystalline, sending it flowing down from above the stage.

Crystalline flowing down? Rose shook her head at how unnatural it was.

A glowing crystalline fence blocked their path backstage. Rose turned back to Vaylan and tried to direct a gust of air toward his hand, but the wind wouldn't cooperate. As Wilder grabbed her hand to pull her forward, a narrow blast of air slammed Vaylan's hand down onto his throne. Vaylan bared his teeth as he struggled against his restraint, and the crystalline flowed back up into its natural position.

Wilder didn't release her hand as he pulled her backstage and out the side door. They ran without stopping until they stepped into the grove of trees ringing the amphitheater.

They both bent over, trying to catch their breath. Her ribs screamed in pain, and she dropped to her hands and knees.

She wanted to cry.

She wanted to scream.

She wanted to die.

Wilder kneeled at her side and pulled her gently to a seated position, careful of her ribs. He smoothed her sweaty hair away from her forehead and studied her for wounds other than the one blazing on her collarbone.

He purposefully avoided looking at that one.

"Breathe, Rose. We made it. It's going to be okay. We need to get back to Temple Order to get the others and regroup. We will figure this out together, you and me. Do you hear me?"

His voice was gentle and wise and everything she needed to hear, but his logical words slipped through the shattered pieces of her heart.

"It wasn't enough," she whispered. "I wasn't enough." Her head dropped into her hands, and she twisted her fingers into her windblown hair despite the pain it caused her ribs.

Wilder caught hold of her hands to stop her frantic movements. "Shh ..." he whispered, as if soothing a crying child. "It will be okay. We will figure it out."

Her confession fell from her lips. "When the storm came, I thought I did it. I thought I could call the wind again." She swallowed a sob. "But I couldn't."

He stilled, and a shadow of guilt flashed across his face.

"I know it was you," she whispered. "I'm happy for you. I really am. I just thought ... I thought the Goddess ..." Her stupid tears kept falling, but the wind didn't answer.

Wilder sighed. "Oh, Rose. I'm so sorry." He continued smoothing back her hair, trying to comfort her. "It might still come. Maybe it will take a little time?"

She nodded numbly, but she knew it was false comfort.

He tucked a loose tendril behind her ear and studied her with solemn eyes as dark as Vaylan's. "Are you able to walk?" She nodded, and he pulled her carefully to her feet. "I'm here, okay? We will find a way through this." He gave her a gentle kiss on the forehead. "You aren't alone, Rose."

She leaned into him, letting the kiss on her forehead sink deep into her soul. Her heart and ribs were broken, but Wilder held her hand, and for today, that was enough.

∽

*To Be Continued in *Fight with the Dark - City of Virtue and Vice Book 5**

∽

ACKNOWLEDGMENTS

When writing love triangles, there is a big question an author must answer: What do you do with your odd man out? (In some stories, it's an odd girl out, but in my case, it was a dude.)

Some authors decide to make The Leftover a bad guy. The rejection stings less if we decide he doesn't deserve to be the love interest.

Some authors kill off The Leftover. A tidy solution, but one I rarely find satisfying.

At the end of the first trilogy, Wilder was a Leftover, but I loved him too much to turn him bad or kill him. So what other options did I have?

Some authors in my writer group suggested I let Ylena keep them both. (Ylena jokingly suggested the same thing in Book 2, but Rev warned her it wouldn't work.) While I understand the appeal of those stories, that's a different genre entirely!

My only other option was to write a new trilogy, and give him the love interest he deserved. I hope you enjoyed reading the first book in their love story as much as I enjoyed writing it.

Thank you to my family and friends for continuing to support my writing obsession.

And all my love to Kent—my Caed, my Wilder, and all my princes.

∽

Subscribe to my newsletter for a free prequel novella and more at www.susannahwelch.com/newsletter

ABOUT THE AUTHOR

Susannah Welch lives in sunny South Florida with her brilliant husband and a magically hypoallergenic cat. She enjoys singing and dancing and showing off. She likes her stories with a little bit of drama, and a whole lot of sparkle.

 facebook.com/susannah.welch.author

 instagram.com/susannahwelchauthor

CPSIA information can be obtained
at www.ICGtesting.com
Printed in the USA
LVHW110630220722
724100LV00017B/193/J

9 781958 568019